# JOAN DENEVE

# FREEING ELLIE

Book Two in the Redeemed Side of Broken Series

*Freeing Ellie*

© 2016 Joan Deneve

ISBN-13: 978-1-944120-04-7
ISBN-10: 1-944120-04-1
e-ISBN-13: 978-1-944120-05-4

Scriptures are from *The Holy Bible*, the Authorized (King James) Version.

This book is a work of fiction. Names, characters, places, and incidents are either products of the author's imagination or used fictitiously. Any similarity to actual people and/or events is purely coincidental.

Published by Write Integrity Press, 2631 Holly Springs Parkway, Box 35, Holly Springs, GA 30142

www.WriteIntegrity.com

Printed in the United States of America.

## *Dedication*

*For Phoenix*
*Who knows what it feels like to be free indeed.*
*"If the Son, therefore, shall make you free, ye shall be*
*free indeed."*
John 8:36

## *Acknowledgements*

Special thanks to Tracy Ruckman for her amazing leadership with Write Integrity Press. I am so blessed to be part of such a faith-driven, God-honoring company. The help and encouragement I receive from Tracy and all my sisters at Write Integrity mean more than I can convey in this small space. "I thank my God upon every remembrance of you" (Philippians 1:3).

Thanks to my dear friend Fay Lamb who inspires me with her quirky life stories and unshakable faith in God. Thank you, Fay, for the hours you put into helping me fine-tune my manuscript to make it the best it could be.

Special acknowledgment to the authors of two superb books about medical missions in Africa: *Mine Eyes Have Seen the Glory* by Lowell A. Gess and *The Hand on my Scalpel* by David C. Thompson. Their real-life stories were the inspiration behind many of Brock's patients.

My deepest gratitude to Deb Raney for the excellent help she gave to help me shape this novel. Deb's expertise is outdone only by her kindness and patience.

For additional technical support, I must thank and acknowledge my OB-GYN nurse practitioner Martha. I also want to thank my son who not only lends his expertise but also his love and support. Couldn't do this without you, Jig.

Special Thanks

I am so blessed to have a host of people in my corner to love me through each step of this glorious process. The list will read like the genealogies in the Old Testament, but like those long lists, each name is inspired with its own unique reason for being included.

My husband and best friend, Rene' Deneve.

My mother: who loves me unconditionally and boasts with total confidence that her daughter's books are the best books you'll ever read. Thanks, Mom, for taking my hand and praying out loud on that day when I really needed some divine inspiration.

My sweet sisters: Phalia and Sheila. No greater love and

no truer friends.

My daughter Jessie: the light of my life and a far better author than I can ever hope to be.

For all my dear family: Harvie Smith, who has to put up with long hours of "book talk." Sarah Deneve, Michael Bush, Auston Deneve, Ethan Deneve, Lacey Jane Deneve, Cloe Deneve, Hannah Bush, Haley Bush, Christian Bush. My people. My heart.

Shane Smith and Shonna Smith: The extended family who painstakingly troubleshoot my computer issues with kindness and grace.

Michele Bradley: My friend and the most Christ-like person I know. She inspires me daily with her generosity, quiet spirit and gentle love.

Nancy Kimball: My friend who delights my heart with her dynamic faith in Jesus Christ. This talented author has done so much to help me "plus" my manuscripts. I'm so blessed to have her in my corner and in my life.

Jericha Kingston, Carolyn Hill, and Diane Dean White: dear author friends who go the extra mile to encourage me.

Thank you to all my dear friends from church and school who have read Saving Eric and have encouraged me as I was writing this sequel.

Always my students who infuse life and love into my heart. Special thanks to Brooke, my sweet beta reader, who blessed me so much when she did a book report on Freeing Ellie (before it was published!) and said, "I'm quite positive Ellie Templeton is my best friend." Brooke loves my characters and gave good advice on the way the plot should go.

Thank you, Jesus, for saving me and giving me this wonderfully abundant life.

# CHAPTER ONE

The third victim in as many weeks. Ellie Templeton worked quietly beside her dad, keeping pace with his swift, precise movements. Sweat darkening his green surgical cap, Brock Whitfield leaned in, not a man to give up without a fight. The Angolan national lay unconscious on the gurney with lacerations so deep, parts of the abdominal cavity gaped open and exposed.

In the two years she'd worked at the mission hospital with her dad, Ellie had seen worse. Worked on worse. But today, the smell of sweat and warm blood got to her. She whirled from the table. Dad would have to handle the rest. She stripped off the bloody gloves and mask and flung them on the concrete floor before blasting through the screen doors. Hot liquid gurgled from deep inside and spewed with projectile force, spraying the bushes beside the steps. Her rubbery knees almost buckled.

Strong arms caught her from behind. "I've got you, baby."

She sagged against her husband, limp as a ragdoll but too grateful to be embarrassed. The nausea ended almost as suddenly as it had come. She straightened and wiped her mouth. "I hoped no one would see me ... Especially not you."

Eric grinned and loosened the hair plastered to her face. He put his arm around her and sat on the first step, pulling her onto his lap.

Ellie relaxed against him, loving his strength. He shifted slightly, and she squirmed to lighten her weight. "I'm hurting you."

"No. You're not." His voice was soft but determined.

She let her full weight rest again on him, now more concerned with protecting his ego than the leg connected to his prosthesis.

"Tell me what's going on."

"I'm not sure." She had suspicions but no positive proof yet. "It was so hot in that curtained off cubicle. Usually blood doesn't faze me." She raised her head and met his eyes, hoping to deflect his attention. "Good thing I didn't react that way when Toby flew you here last April." An involuntary shudder shook her. She would never forget that first glimpse of Eric, covered in his own blood and still bleeding out faster than they could pump more into him.

He kissed the top of her head then tightened his grip as he leaned over to retrieve the packages scattered on the steps. "I tossed these when I saw you were going down. I hope nothing broke."

"Is that the order from Luanda?" She reached for the box by his foot.

He nodded and scanned her face. "Sure you're okay?"

"I'm sure. The heat got to me. That's all." She grinned.

The dimple must have worked its magic because his brown eyes softened, wielding an enchantment of their own. "How's Yafatu?"

"Lucky to be alive." She leaned on his shoulder, resting her hand against his chest. "Two tribes with territorial issues."

The thud of his heart quickened beneath her fingertips, and his muscles stiffened like a predator getting ready to spring. "Someone needs to step in and avert a full-scale confrontation."

This time she tensed. "Not you."

The door behind them swung open. In one fluid move, Eric swooped them both to a standing position.

Dad grabbed Eric's arm as if to steady him. "I'm sorry. I meant to check on Ellie, not knock you off the steps." He let the door close and turned back to her. "Good to see some color back in your cheeks. How are you feeling, honey?"

"Fine now. Sorry I bailed. I'll go back in and help clean up."

Dad shook his head. "Miriam's there already. You're off-duty. Go back home until the afternoon rush."

"I was thinking maybe the dining hall. I'm starving."

Eric lowered his chin and gave her a disbelieving look. "Starving?"

"Uh-huh." Ellie picked up the last box from the steps and handed it to Eric.

One side of his mouth curled into a quirky grin. He took the remaining boxes from her and stacked them all in his arms. "Dining hall it is."

Ceiling fans placed at strategic intervals in the hallway created a cooling vortex, and Ellie lifted her head to enjoy the rush of air.

She paused outside the dining hall doorway and took the smaller package from the top of the stack Eric carried, hoping he wouldn't ask why. "Get some coffee. I'll duck into my room and wash up a little."

Her old bedroom, just a few feet down the hall on the left, still held a bed and a closet full of scrubs for a quick change if necessary. She entered the bathroom, and her hands shook as she ripped open the package. A blood test would've worked, but she had a crazy sentimental need to experience it again like she had the first time. Regret seared through her as it always did whenever she let herself remember that dark time in her life. What a fool she'd been.

She removed the meter and followed the directions to the letter. The waiting interval seemed to take forever. She stared, holding her breath and willing the plus sign to magically appear.

Finally, the prize she'd been longing for. The most

beautiful plus sign she'd ever seen blurred immediately by tears. One hand flew to her mouth, and the other one, still clutching the meter, slid down and caressed her belly.

Her breaths came in heaving hiccups as she gave vent to the years of grief and loss. "Thank you, God. Thank you so much."

In the dining hall, Eric waited as long as he could and then went looking for Ellie. With a soft knock, he pushed open the door. Her wracking sobs hit him in the gut as he eased toward the bathroom. He lingered outside the closed door. Should he knock? Call her name? Right now, he could use a manual for new husbands. His hands curled into a fist to keep from opening the door. He didn't want to ruin her surprise even though he'd suspected for a few days.

Why was she crying? Maybe she wasn't pregnant after all. But all the signs were there. At least, all the ones he'd read about. Even the not-so physical signs like when he'd caught her looking sideways in the mirror with her hand on her stomach.

What went wrong? And how could he fix it if she didn't want to tell him?

Years of specialized CIA training, yet he had no clue how to take care of this complex woman who was now his wife. Eric stood rooted to the spot. Maybe he could text Rocco for a little advice. He pulled out his phone but stopped. Ten in the morning here would be 4:00 a.m. in Minnesota.

*Jesus, help me out here.*

Water splashed into the sink. He dashed back to the now empty dining hall with just enough time to grab the creamer and sit.

Despite her puffy eyes and red nose, Ellie seemed happy when she came into the room. She positioned herself at the end of the table beside his chair, her hands clasped. "Guess what today is."

"Hmm." He took a wild stab. "Our two month anniversary?"

Her entire face lit up. "You remembered!"

More like lucked out. Apparently, month anniversaries carried some weight. He hit save on the new piece of information and scooted his chair back. "Come here, pixie."

She moved closer but hesitated, giving him a worried look.

"Sit. My leg can handle it. You hardly weigh anything."

She eased onto his lap and slid her hands around his neck. "That's about to change real soon."

Which could only mean one thing. He shifted to get a good look at her face.

She nodded, her eyes wide and glistening with a new batch of tears that made them seem even bluer than usual. Eric swallowed hard as Ellie burrowed her face in the crook of his neck.

So why the meltdown only minutes before?

No matter. He quit analyzing it. He was holding his world on his lap, and she was carrying his child. Their child. A fierce protectiveness swept over him, and he tightened his hold. Could he keep them both safe in this vast and savage land?

# FREEING ELLIE

# CHAPTER TWO

In the dark bedroom, Eric slid his arm from underneath Ellie. She shifted and scooted closer to the middle of the bed. He waited for her breathing to become long and steady then swung his leg over the side of the mattress. Choosing from two prosthetic legs that stood ready for duty beside the dresser, he reached for the one he liked best, the leg he used for running. He clicked it into place and then stood like a statue. Ellie didn't stir. With one hand on the side of the mattress to guide him through the dark room, he maneuvered toward the door.

Inching down the hallway in stealth mode, he tried to sneak past the dog, asleep on the kitchen floor. The score was Eric-0/Lady-2. A game he'd happened upon by chance. A night like this one when he couldn't sleep. He chuckled to himself, remembering. Lady's cold nose on the back of his leg had spooked him so much, he'd almost toppled over. The golden retriever, still a pup in a grown body, seemed convinced he'd gotten up to play. From that night, it was game on.

Moonlight streamed through the large slats of the blinds and lit up the great room like a nightlight. He made it to the door and gripped the knob, turning in slow motion. Lady seemed to come from nowhere. She body-slammed him, skidded past as he cracked open the front door, and then whirled back around, propping her sharp paws on his leg. "Aha! I almost beat you this time." He held his hand flat. "Down."

Lady sat on her haunches, every muscle straining for permission to move. "Good girl." He bent and nuzzled her head, and she came to life again, wagging her tail and prancing around his feet. She raced past him out the door and wandered to the mahogany tree beside the house.

Eric moved to the swing at the end of the porch and sat, stretching his arms across the back. The moon shone almost as bright as the sun. White nights, Stu, his former mentor, used to call them. Not good for agents who did their best field work in the dark. Not good for sleeping either, especially when he had things to work out. Like what to do with his life now that he'd walked away from the agency. Thirty-six was a little old to be starting a new career.

Ellie pushed open the screen door, carrying a bottle of water and flashing him the sleepy smile that told him with more than words that she loved him. The kind of smile that motivated him every morning to get out of bed before her and bring her coffee just to see it.

His lips quirked up in welcome as she wandered toward him. Her hair tumbled about her shoulders, and her T-shirt and pajama pants made her look more like a teenager than a woman who was carrying their child.

With a yap of greeting, Lady leapt onto the porch and knocked the water out of Ellie's hand.

"Whoa, girl." Ellie bent to retrieve the bottle. Lady nudged again, sending Ellie sprawling backward. Lady tried to lick every inch of Ellie's face. "Ooh, Lady! No! Get back." Ellie laughed but then clamped her mouth shut against Lady's ever present tongue.

The show was almost too entertaining to interrupt, but Eric pushed off the swing anyway. He offered Ellie his hand and wedged himself between her and the dog.

"Whew. Thanks." She walked with him back to the swing. "If our baby is that energetic, I'll be in trouble." Lady jumped onto the seat as Ellie turned. "See what I mean?"

He chuckled, giving the dog a shove to the backside. "Go lie down." Lady gave a little whine but obeyed, lying close with her eyes on him.

"Poor thing. She gets excited when Mommy and Daddy

are together."

Eric sat and draped his arm across Ellie's shoulder. "Did we wake you?"

"Had to pee." She nestled against him. "What about you?"

He grinned. "No. I didn't have to pee."

She nudged him playfully. "That's not what I meant, you goof." Her smile faded. "Another nightmare?"

"Not this time. Still trying to wrap my head around becoming a father."

"You knew, didn't you?" Ellie shifted and looked him square in the face. "Tell the truth. You *Sherlocked* it."

"*Sherlocked*? Is that even a word?"

"Don't change the subject. I was really careful not to tip you off. How'd you figure it out?"

"Law of probability. We don't use birth control." He waited for that to sink in.

"That was it? You just assumed?"

"And hoped. Seeing you puke your guts out today confirmed it."

"By the way, as embarrassing as that episode was, I'm really glad you happened along when you did. I was going down when you swooped in and held me up."

He played along even though there was no happenstance involved. He went out of his way to keep an eye on her. Especially now. He reached up and twirled a lock of her hair. "Why were you crying?"

Her eyes widened. "You heard? From the dining hall?"

"Not exactly. You were gone a long time, so I went looking for you."

She dropped her gaze. "I was so happy to be pregnant."

Okay. He'd give her that. She did cry when she was happy. But this hadn't sounded like a happy cry. More like a gut-wrenching sob. Eric bit back anything he might have said and waited for the thing she wasn't telling him.

"I was afraid God wouldn't give me another chance. I mean, why would He after I—" She kept her focus on her hands that fidgeted on her lap. "I don't deserve to be so happy."

His gut tightened. Crazy or not, it was pretty clear Ellie still carried a load of guilt over her abortion. If anyone didn't deserve this happiness, it was him.

"Ellie, I …"

She swatted at her arm. "Let's go in. The mosquitoes are bad tonight."

Truth or diversion? He wasn't sure. They weren't biting him, but then they rarely did. "Okay." He held the swing steady while she stood then followed her into the house, Lady at his heels. He went to the kitchen and retrieved a water bottle from the fridge. Lady seemed to have the same idea. Her chain jangled against the water bowl as she slurped, spraying water onto the floor.

"Can I have a sip of yours? Mine's covered with doggie saliva."

Eric handed her the half empty bottle. She drank most of what was left and handed it back with an apologetic smile. "Sorry. The baby was thirsty."

He wiped away the drops of water around her lips then caressed her cheek. "You deserve to be happy. You'll be the world's best mother."

She held his gaze without flinching. "Thank you. That really means a lot to me. But I'm so scared."

"Me, too."

"You? Scared?"

"Terrified."

Ellie placed her hands on his shoulders and tilted her chin. "Somehow that makes me feel better." She smiled a brave little smile.

He wanted to kiss her, and love her. And hold her for the

rest of the night. But it was late. She was probably worn out.

She stood on her tiptoes and with her hands behind his neck, pulled him down for a kiss. Eric set the bottle on the counter and wrapped his arms around her, so full of love he could hardly breathe.

Lady rooted her nose between them. Ellie giggled at his futile attempts to push her away with the side of his leg.

He gave up with a sigh. "Let's take this someplace else."

# FREEING ELLIE

# CHAPTER THREE

Brock sat on the stool beside Yufatu's bed and pored over the stats one more time, hoping he was wrong. Tachycardia, low blood count, decreased blood pressure, and increased heart rate: The patient was losing blood and would continue to do so until the problem was fixed. A problem he should've caught the first time. Yufatu might be too weak to survive the surgery, but Brock had to try.

They needed blood—more blood than they had on hand. Moses was a match. So was Eric. He pulled out his phone to check the time and then shot a text to Ellie. *GOING BACK IN. BRING ERIC.*

Less than fifteen minutes later, Ellie showed up, dressed in scrubs with Eric not far behind.

"Great. Ellie, I need your hands." Brock put his hand on Eric's shoulder. "And, Eric, I need your blood."

"Yes, sir."

No hesitation or questions except for where.

"Observation Room One. Mac's already there with Moses."

Ellie began scrubbing. "He's losing more blood?"

Brock stuck his hands into the stream of water and nodded. "Truth is, I need your eyes to help me find what I missed the first time."

Two African medical residents already had the patient prepped and sedated. Brock moved into position and prayed, as he always did, for God to guide his hands. Fifteen minutes later, Mac brought in two units of blood and hung them on the IV pole beside the patient. Brock made the incision, and Ellie irrigated. They both searched for the bleeder much like looking for an air leak in a tire, only this involved blood. Lots of it. And a man's life.

Ellie manipulated the folds of the intestines. "It looks like all your sutures held."

The words meant to encourage only made him feel worse. He'd left a bleeder. But where? His fingers ran the length of the small intestine, examining every inch.

"There?" Ellie pointed to a suspicious area.

"Okay. Worth a try." He reinforced three places with inverted sutures. The best he could do but maybe not good enough.

Brock finished closing and lowered his mask. "Iyegha, stay with him. Bolus fluid. Give two more units of blood. Send me word if his pressure drops." He turned to Ellie. "Good work, honey."

She smiled and stripped off her surgical gloves. "I was about to say the same to you, Dad."

"Go check on Eric. Make sure he's drinking plenty of fluids. Mac and I will help the new team get acquainted with the clinic."

"Good idea. I'll catch up with you later."

Ellie collected the scalpel and other instruments. Then she rolled up the soiled linens and masks and stuffed them into the hamper by the door. Quick damage control before Miriam and the cleaning crew took over. She washed her hands again and pulled her ponytail loose, fluffing her hair as she left the room in search of Eric. She didn't have to go far. He sat on the cushioned bench across from the OR double doors. His forearms rested on his thighs with his hands folded in front. A swath of gauze encircled his left elbow, and an empty bucket sat by his feet. Poor guy looked a little green.

She tilted the bucket to look inside. Empty. "Feeling sick?"

Eric stood, a little slower than usual. "The bucket's for you. No bushes by these doors."

She gave him a grateful look. He'd just given two pints of blood and still showed up with an empty bucket for her, just in case. She slid her hand under his arm and wrapped it around his waist for extra support.

Eric reached for her hand and pulled her even closer. "Just like last summer when you were my human crutch."

She was thinking the same thing. "Only a lot easier now with your super spy leg attached."

"Agreed."

They started down the hall together. "Do you miss it?" she asked.

"My leg?"

"Your spy days." His former profession. The one that almost got him killed. She'd asked before but had to hear the answer again. Especially now. "Do you miss the life you used to live?"

Two men rounded the corner and interrupted his reply. The doctors visiting from the States. "Hello, again." Their names? Her mind blanked, but she plastered on her best smile. "This is my husband, Eric."

Bless him. Eric took it from there, extending his right hand. "Eric Templeton."

"Ned Tanner."

"Steve Newcomb."

"I see you've discovered Nicci's famous coffee."

Steve, the tall one on the left, swirled what was left in his cup. "This stuff's amazing. You ought to market it. You'd make a killing."

"Not a bad idea." Eric returned their grin. "But it's our way of getting you to come back."

"Are you a doctor, too?" Steve asked.

Eric shook his head and diverted the question like a pro.

"How long will you be helping out?"

"Four weeks," Steve answered. "Great time to get away from Boston. We left right before the blizzard hit."

"No kidding. No danger of that here. Before you leave, I'll drive you around and show you some of the country."

"Sounds great." Steve seemed to be the talker of the two. The conversation lagged, and he looked at Ned. "We'd better get back to the clinic."

Eric shook their hands again. "Good to meet you."

"You, too." They nodded to Ellie and left.

*Steve and Ned. Steve, the tall one. Ned never talks.*

The two men exited through the side doors.

Eric turned and braced his hand on the wall behind her. "Now. Where were we?"

"Never mind. You just gave two pints of blood. Let's get you home." Ellie slid her hand through the crook of his arm. "The bucket was a great idea."

"Did you get sick during surgery?"

"Amazingly, no. Probably need to keep a bucket outside the door, just in case, so I won't contaminate the workspace."

They moved down the hallway, and Eric paused outside his former bedroom. "I learned something today."

"Oh, yeah? What?"

"That most of the blood pumped into me last April came from the team."

She turned to him and poked his chest with her forefinger. "Okay, Sherlock. Did you figure it out, or did someone tell you?"

He laughed and grabbed her finger. "Both. I had time to think while Moses and I were hooked up to the tubes. So I asked."

He opened the double doors leading to the terrace. Their cat, sunning herself on one of the patio chairs, looked up as they approached and rolled over onto her back. "Bits." Eric slid his fingers over the white, furry belly.

Ellie grinned. He had them all—Bitsy, Lady, and her … especially her—wrapped around his little finger. Heaven help them if they had a little girl.

As soon as he stopped, Bitsy rose and arched her back, not ready to give up the attention.

Eric straightened and gave Ellie a serious look. "I had no idea. Why didn't you tell me about the team's transfusion?"

"Not exactly the kind of thing that comes up. We were too concerned with keeping you alive." She leaned down to stroke Bitsy. "Toby begged to give blood, too. Dad wouldn't let him since Toby'd already lost too much himself." She kept her focus on Bitsy but added, almost as an afterthought, "Dad gave more than any of us."

Eric went silent. They moved off the terrace, and Lady raced across the field toward them. For once, Eric didn't push her down when she jumped up to greet him. He bent to pet her, his jaw working.

Ellie bit her lower lip. Eric was retreating again, going all radio-silent on her. It might be nothing. And maybe it was the wrong time. But she didn't want to be shut out. Not of any part of his life.

"Eric, I'm not good at reading people like you are. So help me out here. Tell me. What is it that keeps you awake at night?"

Eric tousled the fur between Lady's ears. The golden retriever, in turn, angled around to nibble his fingers. He muzzled her mouth with his hand, which only made her more determined to play.

An evasion tactic if ever Ellie saw one.

He raised and shrugged but met her gaze full on. "I've never slept well." His hand gripped the underside of her elbow and nudged her forward. "Anyway, I love to watch you sleep. I'm even jealous. I wish I could curl up and sleep as soundly as you."

She slid her hand down and laced her fingers through his. "Pregnant sleep is the best."

He swung her hand up and kissed it. "Guess I'm out of luck then."

They reached the porch, and Eric opened the door. Ellie stepped aside as Lady blasted past, determined to be the first through the doorway.

"One of these days, I need to teach that dog that I'm the alpha female around here."

Eric went straight for the fridge. Ellie washed her hands again and grabbed the saltines.

He poured orange juice into a glass. "Before I married you, I skipped this step. Want some?"

She laughed. "Yes, but don't think I don't see you drinking out of the bottle when you think I'm not looking, buster." She leaned back against the counter and watched him fill her glass.

The almost imperceptible tremor of his hand as he poured meant he was feeling the effects of the loss of blood. He handed her the juice and then downed his own in almost one long gulp.

Ellie pulled him over to the table. "Come sit. We need to talk."

He put his empty cup on the counter and let her tug him over to the chairs without resistance. He pulled a chair out for her then sat across from her, his hands folded on the table and his eyebrows raised.

She finished off the orange juice and placed the empty cup in front of her. She traced the moisture seeping down the side of the cup and tried to put her jumbled thoughts into words. "I'm scared."

The eyes that had the power to see into her soul, softened. "About the baby?"

She shook her head. "I'm afraid you're not happy."

He slid his fingers across the table and connected with hers. "Why would you think that?"

"Because." The universal female answer. He'd make her be more specific. "You don't sleep. And when you do, you toss and turn. And you're quiet. Like there's a wall around you—a wall I can't break through." She blurted it all out knowing full well it was probably just hormonal hysteria. "I just love you so much. I don't want you to be unhappy."

Without breaking his hold on her hand, Eric stood and pulled her up with him.

She babbled on. "I couldn't stand it if you went back to the agency, but I'm afraid that's what—"

His kiss cut her off. Made her forget whatever it was she'd been going to say. He raised his head, and his voice was as soft as the fingers caressing her cheek. "Ellie, we've been through this before."

"I know, but—"

His finger on her lips stilled her. "I love you. There's nothing for me back there. My life's with you." His arms engulfed her, and he held her head close to his chest. The steady beat of his heart soothed her, calmed her.

After a long moment, she looked up at him. "I think I need a nap."

"Come on. I'll tuck you in." He walked her to the bedroom and closed the blinds while she went to the bathroom.

She returned to the darkened bedroom. Eric stood at the foot of the bed, holding the afghan up like a curtain. She kicked off her shoes and curled up on her side. Eric placed the afghan over her and tucked in the sides under her legs.

She gave an appreciative sigh. "Thank you, honey."

The mattress dipped as Eric crawled in beside her. He wrapped his arm around her, splaying his hand across her stomach. "I couldn't resist."

She placed her hand on top of his and pulled him even

tighter against her. "This feels so good. I love you, Eric Templeton."

No matter how Eric repositioned his head, he could not escape Ellie's mass of golden hair. He waited until her breathing slowed to a deep and regular cadence before sliding out from under the arm that held him captive. He pushed the hair away and scratched his nose. Then he snuggled close again, this time pinning her arm under his. "I love you, too."

She was already too far gone to hear, but he said it anyway. He'd have to say it more often. How could she ever doubt it?

She was right. This bed felt good. Real good. What a wimp. Only two pints of blood. Felt more like he'd been sucked dry. Thank God for Lady. Stooping over to pet her kept him from passing out until he could get to the OJ.

Ellie was right about something eating him, too. But how could he tell her what he hadn't figured out for himself?

Maybe he needed to see a shrink next time he went back to Washington. The agency provided mental health services. Or maybe it was time to have another session with Ellie's dad. The kind he'd had last summer when everything in his life got turned upside down.

# CHAPTER FOUR

Ellie knelt, one hand capturing her hair and the other gripping the side of the toilet.

She felt Eric behind her and was grateful for the wet washcloth he wielded.

He sponged her forehead. "So, this is how you felt when you were taking care of me?"

"No." She flushed away the remains of her breakfast and swiped her mouth with a tissue. "You didn't want me around when you were puking. Remember? Just Rocco."

He sat beside her on the tiled bathroom floor and pulled her back to rest against his shoulder. "You want me to call Rocco, baby? He's pretty good at cleaning up puke."

"No way." She coughed to clear the gravel from her voice. "You're the only one with clearance for this job."

He hugged her close and patted her stomach. "Our baby feels like a walnut."

She placed her hand over his. "I know. A walnut that will morph into a watermelon."

He chuckled and kissed her cheek. "Feel better?"

"Uh-huh. Help me up, big guy."

He shifted and seemed to rise with little effort, then with a heave, pulled her up.

Ellie squeezed toothpaste onto her toothbrush and tried not to gag as she brushed her teeth. She rinsed and took the towel he handed her. "Thanks."

"Will you be all right now? I need to run some things by your dad before Toby gets here."

Ellie followed him through the bedroom. "I'm fine now. I'll walk with you as far as the dining hall."

"Baby hungry again?"

"Maybe." She punched his shoulder. "But I'm going to see Nicci."

"Who is probably stationed somewhere by a window watching the sky for a certain helicopter."

She followed Eric down the hall and into the great room. Lady bounded over and for once didn't jump up on them. "Good girl. You're getting some manners."

"Walk?" Eric barely got out the word.

Lady raced to the door and then back, skidding on the wood floor. Then she reared up and left a red welt down Ellie's leg. Eric held his hand out flat and changed his tone. "Down." His hand put pressure on the dog's neck. "Sorry. She's a work in progress."

Ellie skipped ahead, brushing past Lady. "I'm going to beat you this time."

Lady scampered after her and managed to squeeze out the door first. Eric trailed behind. "You must be feeling better."

"I am. I'm so happy, I think I could fly."

Eric's eyes crinkled with a hint of amusement and something very close to worship. He let the door slam behind him, and with one long step, took a flying leap off the porch. Then he backed up with his arms spread. "Climb on. I'll give you a ride."

"Oh, fun." She wrapped her arms around his neck and swung her legs around his waist.

He tucked his hands under her thighs. "Hold on." He took off down the field, dodging clumps of scraggly weeds as if they were mud puddles.

Ellie squealed and clung to his neck, trying not to choke his air supply. "Feels just like I'm flying!"

"If Lady doesn't stay out of my way, we might crash and burn."

"She's jealous."

"Hang on. I'll race her." He tightened his grip, jumped

over a scrubby bush and sprinted toward the terrace. Lady barked and hit the concrete seconds after they did.

Eric's chest heaved as he released his hold and bent backward to let Ellie down. "There you go."

"Whew."

His hand shot out to steady her.

"Thanks."

"Did I shake you up too much?"

"Uh-uh. I loved it." Bitsy jumped down from the terrace bench where she'd been sunning. The cat ambled over and rubbed against Ellie's leg.

"Good morning, Miss Priss."

Lady intercepted and nudged her nose under Ellie's hand.

"Good thing I have two hands."

Eric tweaked her arm. "Okay, baby. I'm outta here. See you later."

"Okay."

Lady followed him around the corner. Ellie opened the double doors to the hallway of the staff dormitory. The cinder block walls and concrete floors gave it a unique, musty smell that she loved. The door to her dad's bedroom on the right was open. She took a quick peek into the dimly lit room. Not one thing out of place. His Bible lay open on the table by his recliner.

Her fingers slid across her abdomen. Thank God, their child wouldn't have to grow up without a father like she had.

But at least Dad came for her when she needed him most. Loved her back to health. Helped her find the Savior.

Now, if only she could trust God the way her dad did. She had so much to learn.

A quick glance at her watch got her moving. When Toby arrived, Nicci would have time for no one else.

A few minutes later, the cold, greasy smell of cooked bacon hit her as she entered the dining hall, despite the fact that all the breakfast trays had been removed. She swallowed hard and tried to fight the inevitable but had to whip around and run to the closest bathroom. She made it. Barely. Mostly bile and dry heaves. Cold water from the faucet revived her, but her hands shook as she cupped them to sip water and rinse.

She returned to the dining hall, intentionally breathing through her mouth. The sound of clanking aluminum pans came through the closed swinging doors at the corner of the room. Ellie pushed through them and entered the kitchen. No trouble locating Nicci who stood at the industrial-sized sink. She was dressed in a floral orange and red sarong. Flamboyant even for Nicci. "Good morning."

"There you are." Nicci's smile brightened her dark face. "I had hoped to see you at breakfast."

"Couldn't quite stomach it. But I could use some toast now."

Ellie reached for the bread, but Nicci took it from her hands. "Sit here, missy. I'll take care of you."

"I can do it."

Nicci shook her head. "You sit there."

Ellie sat on the stool, finding it easier to let Nicci win than to argue. "You look very pretty. Like a tropical flower."

Nicci responded with a smile then looked out the window for what seemed the tenth time. Each time, Ellie looked, too. Nicci's antsy anticipation must be contagious. Toby should've been here by now. The clouds were low and threatening but not a problem for a seasoned pilot like Toby. So where was he?

Nicci handed her the crusty chunk of homemade toast with butter oozing over the side.

"Hmm. Thank you."

"Would you like pear preserves or honey?"

She shook her head and wiped her mouth. "It would spoil this wonderful taste. Nobody makes bread like you."

Nicci's hands flew to her cheeks, an unconscious gesture

Ellie had witnessed many times. Precious Nicci. Would she never realize the ridges from those scars, tribal markings from a lifetime ago, only seemed to accentuate her beauty?

Nicci smiled. "I'm glad it pleases you."

Ellie finished chewing her last bite. "Everything you do pleases me."

The swinging doors burst open. Eric stood, his chest heaving as if he'd been on one of his long runs. Ellie searched his face and braced, fully aware she would not like what he had come to say.

He closed the distance and stood between them. "Toby's been kidnapped."

"No." Nicci swayed and almost went down.

Ellie lunged to help, but Eric was quicker. He gripped both of Nicci's arms and used his good foot to slide a stool closer.

He stayed beside Nicci but glanced back to Ellie. "Your dad's alerting the rest of the team. He's called a meeting. I wanted to let you know first."

Nicci raised anguished eyes to Eric. "What will happen?"

The question Ellie had wanted to ask too but knew he couldn't answer. She went to the cooler and grabbed a water bottle for Nicci and Eric.

"Toby can handle himself in tight situations."

"But who took him?" Nicci clutched Eric's arm. "How will we get him back?"

"We're working on it." His voice was soft but determined.

Nicci's large frightened eyes held Eric's gaze for a long moment. Then she took a deep breath and said, "I'll make fresh coffee in the conference room."

Ellie waited until Nicci left and then faced Eric, trying to hide the panic rising within her. "Do you know details?"

"A few. That's what this meeting is about."

Her Rambo husband already had a plan. She would put

money on it. She scanned his face, searching for some hint of what the plan might be.

Chairs scraped the concrete floor in the adjacent dining room. Eric's armor dropped enough for him to give her a reassuring smile. "We'd better get out there."

He took her hand and led into the room. Mac, Al, and Leroy, who made up the tech and maintenance crew, were already seated. Eric nodded to the men as he pulled out Ellie's chair. He bent and whispered, his breath warm on her ear. "Be right back."

The rich scent of Nicci's special ground coffee filled the room with warmth and a measure of comfort.

Eric went to Nicci, who looked as if she were barely keeping it together. She stood with her head low and her back to the group, stacking cups, rearranging napkins, and wiping down a counter that was already spotless.

Instead of pouring himself a cup, Eric put his arm around Nicci. His sympathy seemed to shatter the last shred of the young woman's control. She turned and crumbled into Eric's arms. He held onto her, his eyes closed and his jaw working with the emotion he seemed determined to hold in check.

The sight was too much for Ellie, and the ever-present tears she had managed to repress all morning now coursed down her face and dripped onto her lap.

Nicci released her hold on Eric, stepped back, and wiped her wet cheeks as if she was embarrassed. He said something that at least made her smile and then guided her to a chair beside Ellie.

Eric returned to pour his coffee just as Dad entered the room with a purposeful gait. He set his clipboard on the table then walked behind Ellie and Nicci. With one arm on each, he managed to hug them both at the same time. "Hello, girls."

Nicci rose and again let herself be bolstered, this time by Dad's embrace. He held onto her, and the room fell silent, respectful, not staring but tuned in to what her dad had to say. "There now. It's all right. Don't you worry. God will be with Toby." His gentle words, meant to comfort Nicci, seemed to comfort all of them. "Moses and Miriam are on the way, and then we'll get started." He released his hold and smiled at her. "All right?"

Nicci nodded and took her seat. Ellie slid her hand over to clasp the dark, cold fingers.

Ellie's father moved to the maintenance crew and stooped to ask Mac something. Mac nodded, and Dad responded with a pat on the shoulder.

Eric stood, his back propped against the counter. Ellie knew his predator mode wouldn't let him sit. Dad walked over and Eric bent to hear what he had to say. Private talk. Serious. Eric nodded to whatever Dad had said before leaning over to reply.

Ellie put her face in her hands. Could this really be happening?

She looked up.

Miriam enter the room, followed by Moses. The national couple had been with her dad almost from the beginning. They approached the table with purpose and grace, as if they were African royalty. Miriam, her sable eyes full of sympathy, sat across from them, and extended her long, slender arm across the table. Nicci gripped the hand offered to her and held on tight.

Moses took his place beside his wife. His leathery face crinkled with genuine affection as he gave Ellie a deferential nod. "Hello, missy."

She returned his smile with equal warmth as her dad took his place at the head of the table. "Let's get right to business. Eric, tell us what you know."

Eric spoke from where he stood. Moses, Miriam, and Al shifted to see him better. "I got the call sometime around 0900 from Toby's hangar. A group we think connected to LRA stormed into the hangar with plans to take the airplane and a pilot for indefinite use. We have a lead on where they might be going, but it hasn't been confirmed. The good news is that as ruthless as this group can be, they won't hurt Toby as long as they can use him." Eric glanced at Dad. "That's all I've got for now, but I'm waiting on a call from the agency."

Ellie heard LRA and little else. The most ruthless militant group in Africa. No fear. No conscience. A chill ran through her. If this was true, what hope did Toby have?

Her dad took over. "I've called you here to inform you so that you can pray. This group is evil and powerful, but our God is greater. Moses, I'd like for you to lead us, and then I'll close."

*God is greater.* She believed that. Didn't she?

Moses stood and raised his long arms with palms facing upward. He pronounced each word with perfect precision in his rich African accent. "Our most gracious Father, we come before Your presence to ask for Your help and Your wisdom. We ask for You to protect our brother and deliver him from these evil men...."

Ellie's tears continued to flow. She tried to space out her sniffs to keep from interrupting the beautiful prayer. Eric touched her shoulder, and then placed some tissues in her lap. A thoughtful gesture that opened up more tears. Eric stayed behind her during the prayer, with his hand resting on her shoulder.

Eric's phone vibrated as her dad began his prayer. He was out the door in seconds. His "Yes, sir. Thank you for returning my call..." was all she caught as he moved down the hallway.

Her dad ended the prayer and glanced toward the empty doorway. "Not back yet. Iyegha, I'm going to let you and the visiting doctors handle the clinic for the rest of the day."

The man nodded and rose to leave.

Eric returned before the rest of them left. He turned a chair around and straddled it, by now needing to give his leg a rest, Ellie knew. He huffed out a deep breath. "The director listened, took some notes, and wants me to keep him briefed, but said his hands are tied. No official military intervention can be sanctioned."

No official intervention? But what about unofficial? Didn't they do that all the time? Ellie waited for Eric to continue, but he just sat there, his fingers steepled in front of his mouth.

"I'll be in my office the rest of the day. I'll make some calls. See what I can find out."

Eric stood and gave her father a brief hug. "Thank you."

Dad turned to her. "Don't you worry, honey. We'll trust God to give us direction and the best way to help Toby."

She nodded and embraced him. Easy for him to say. Did he really not worry? Ever?

No surprise. Nicci chose to stay busy in the kitchen. Everyone else left to carry on with the duties of the day.

Eric wrapped an arm around Ellie as they left the room. "How are you feeling?"

"My stomach is tied up in knots. I need to eat some crackers and drink some ginger ale before I get sick again." Had it only been one hour since her life was good and carefree and Eric had whisked her across the field piggyback? Now a heavier weight rested on those strong shoulders. "Did you tell them everything?"

"Mostly. Here's what I got from Terrance. You remember? Toby's spare pilot and mechanic."

She nodded and reached for Eric's hand as they started across the field.

"Like I said, four armed men stormed the hangar demanding a plane and a pilot. Terrance had the forethought to hit the intercom button. Toby came out with his hands up and basically sacrificed himself. Told them Terrance couldn't fly that kind of airplane. So he'd go. His condition—they let Terrance live."

She stopped and looked at him. "But what if they'd killed him anyway?"

"Then they'd have had to kill Toby, too."

Her eyes widened, and she placed her free hand against her throat.

Eric gave her a little nudge to keep walking. "Look, these guys play hardball. Toby took a gamble that they needed a pilot. The one thing that might keep him alive. For a while, at least."

They walked in silence the rest of the way, neither willing to address the obvious.

Cool air revived her sinking spell as she entered the house. She tore into a sleeve of saltines with shaking hands. Eric grabbed a water bottle and handed her the ginger ale.

"Thanks." She shoved an entire cracker into her mouth desperately trying to stop her jitters. Unable to wait any longer, she asked with her mouth still full, "What are you going to do?"

He held her gaze but said nothing. He was torn, no doubt about it. The truth was written all over his face, even with his mask up. And he knew what he had to do. He just couldn't say it.

So she said it for him. "You have to go."

# CHAPTER FIVE

Eric held his breath.

*You have to go.*

Had he heard right? "I made you a promise—"

Ellie grimaced and shook her head. "This isn't the agency you're going back to. And it isn't the world you're saving. It's Toby." She took a step toward him. "I know you. If something happened to him, and you did nothing to stop it, you wouldn't be able to live with yourself." All the anguish crushing his chest seemed to be in her eyes. "And I couldn't live with myself watching you go through it." She cupped his face with both her hands. "I love you. You're my life. But I know in my heart you've got to go."

He knew it, too. Had known it from the first phone call. And he knew what it cost her to release him from his promise. He reached for her left hand. "Ellie—I—"

"Go. Make a plan before I panic and take it all back." The tear that spilled over and slid down her cheek almost undid him. She swiped it away and raised her chin. "But I need another promise. One you have to keep."

"Anything."

"Promise you'll come back. Alive and in one piece."

The one thing he couldn't guarantee. He opened his mouth, but her finger on his lips stopped his response.

"Promise me." She was more insistent this time. Her baby blue eyes pleading with him left him no choice.

"I promise." From out of nowhere, he added, "And I need something from you."

She widened her eyes. "No." She backed away and wagged her finger at him. "Don't ask me to be brave and strong if you go missing. I'll fall apart. And don't tell me to go on and raise our child without you. I can't. So don't ask it." Her backside bumped against the counter. She inched sideways apparently with no clue how adorable she was.

He laughed in spite of the serious situation and closed the distance between them before she could scoot away. "Stay still. I'm more worried about how I could go on without you. I can't worry about you while I'm on this mission. So promise me you'll take care of yourself. And be here when I get back."

"If you promise to come back, I promise to be here." She snuggled up against his chest.

For her sake, he held her a moment longer then stepped back, his hands gripping her shoulders. "I have to take care of some things, but I'll be back later and tell you the plan." Part of another promise he'd made to never keep secrets from her. Ever.

The predator took over the moment he stepped through the door. With no time to lose, he reached for his phone, praying it wouldn't go to voice mail. At the resolute "Hello" with the pronounced southern drawl, Eric released the breath he'd held.

"Skeet. This is Eric."

Eric grazed his knuckles against the open door of Ellie's dad's office.

The man he now called Dad, too, turned and held up one finger. "Yes," he said into his phone. "I'd appreciate that." He left the window to grab a pen and scribbled something on a notepad in a scrawl as undecipherable as Ellie's. "Got it." He nodded. "Will do. Thank you." He sat and gestured for Eric to do the same.

Eric sank into the leather chair. "Any luck?"

"Not much. I have a friend who runs a mission hospital in the Congo. A real hotbed for terrorists. He'll call if he gets wind of anything new." He folded his hands on the desk.

"What about you?"

"Scaled the first hurdle. Ellie told me to go. I didn't have to say one word."

Dad gave him a knowing smile and nodded. "And the second hurdle?"

"I've called for backup. A guy who served with Toby in Afghanistan. Good man. Good soldier. He's all in. May even bring some of his buddies. We could use your help getting them here."

"Of course. Where are they? I'll make the call."

"Texas. Johnson City. Not too far from Austin."

"We have a hangar in Louisiana. I'll make the call. Maybe by the time they get here, we'll know where the rebels are keeping Toby."

"Thank you." He wanted to say more, but Dad waved it off as he usually did. Eric rose, but instead of leaving, he walked to the window. A lizard on the other side of the window pane skidded away and jumped onto the butterfly-shaped leaf of the mopane tree, creating a fresh shower of droplets to the ground. The rain from early morning had stopped, but heavy clouds hung over the compound much like the dark thoughts pressing down on Eric's soul. He took a deep breath and, with a quick glance toward the door, decided to return to his chair.

Dad had remained seated and seemed lost in his own thoughts. Or maybe he was praying.

Eric raked a hand through his hair. "I'd like to talk something out with you, if you don't mind."

Dad raised his head and gave him a look of encouragement. "Of course."

Eric leaned forward and tapped his fingertips together. "One year ago, this mission would've been a no-brainer. I'd have stormed their compound. Secured my target and gotten out, leaving any survivors to deal with the carnage." Eric straightened and risked a glance.

Dad nodded for him to continue.

"I've changed." His heart raced, and his mouth went dry. He had to spill it: The thing he found hard to admit, even to himself. "I've lost my stomach for killing." He could almost feel Bob Templeton, his merciless adopted father, turning over in his grave.

Eric stood, too pent up to stay in one spot. "And if I hesitate, for even a millisecond—"

"I see." Dad crooked his finger against his lips.

Eric stopped, relieved he didn't have to go on. Dad got it. Eric relaxed back into his seat. The man was a gold mine of wisdom. Eric waited for the nugget that would make sense of his dilemma.

The wait was a long one. Dad's folded hands tapped his mouth as he stared at Eric. So typical. To take the time to answer well. Eric gripped the armrest to keep from fidgeting. Finally, Dad's soft voice broke the tense silence. "Not long ago, you faced another impossible situation. You remember that day I found you in the chapel? Not three days after your amputation, was it?"

Eric nodded, every detail of that day etched in his memory.

"I found you there, praying. The entire CIA was after you with trumped up charges of treason. Do you remember what God told you?"

Perfectly. As if it were yesterday. "Surrender."

"That's right, son. And it made no sense, did it?'

Eric shook his head and met Dad's gaze. "But the only thing that would've worked."

Dad picked up the frayed black book from his desk and let it fall open to the middle. His finger traced down a well-worn page as if he had programmed it to open to that very spot. "Trust in the Lord, with all thine heart; and lean not unto thine own understanding. In all thy ways, acknowledge Him, and He shall direct thy path." He tilted the book to show Eric. "Son, I'm too close to the situation. I can't tell you what to do." Dad took off his glasses and gave Eric a direct look. "Let God call the shots."

No nugget. Just a pick-axe and the place he needed to mine.

Eric leaned forward and stared at the floor, his thoughts churning. It was what his former CIA mentor would've done, too. Stu never handed him answers. Always told him to trust his gut.

Right now, his gut had nothing. Either he was a ruthless killer, willing to do anything to get the job done, or he was a follower of God, wholeheartedly committed to his new faith. How could he be both?

Dad's hand on his shoulder startled him out of his dark thoughts. He shifted and started to raise his head until he realized Dad was praying over him. He stilled.

"Father, help Eric know what to do, how to proceed, how to help our dear brother Toby. We trust you to make it clear. Give Eric your wisdom. And your peace."

Short and to the point and said with much more faith than Eric felt. He rose, and they embraced.

"I'm praying for you, son."

Eric nodded but didn't try to answer. He left the room and the building with one agenda: To find out what God wanted him to do.

He almost tripped on Lady, who was lying on the concrete outside the double doors. That could only mean one thing: Ellie had left the house and was either with Nicci or at the clinic. He jogged back to the house with Lady keeping pace. He reached the door and held his hand out flat toward the golden retriever. "Stay."

Within seconds, he switched to his running shoe and strapped on his gun, something he'd learned never to run without.

Eric paused on the porch for a quick stretch then tore off down the steps. "Let's go, girl."

His breath quickened as he eased into his stride. Felt good. The last time he'd needed a definite answer from God, running wasn't an option, but he'd adjusted well to his prosthesis, and it had become like a part of him. Especially when he ran. He raced past the chapel down the red gravel road leading away from the mission compound and sprinted over the deep ruts frequent rains had left. The road ahead forked, and he angled toward the left, leaving the red mud for the grassy path winding through a more wooded region.

His thoughts became silent prayers as he dodged limbs and underbrush. *When I gave You my life, I vowed I'd never kill another person again.*

The path narrowed, and Lady took the lead.

*Why, God? Are You testing my commitment? If I go after these men, I'll have to take them out. Is that what You want? God, I have to know. I can't afford to hesitate. What do You want me to do?*

Sudden movement ahead on the left sent terror down his spine and sent his instincts into overdrive. A snake, poised to strike, blocked the path. "Lady. Stay." Eric ripped the gun from its holster and blasted every bullet he had into the reptile. God help him if there were two.

The ordeal was over in less than five seconds. His hands shook as he returned the gun to its holster. He took a deep breath and wiped at the sweat that stung his eyes. He scanned the area, still on red alert, and only then realized, Lady hadn't moved. He held out his hand to her. "Come."

She rushed over to him and fell at his feet, clearly shaken by his earlier gruff tone and the multiple gunshots.

He squatted beside her and hugged her. "Good girl. Good girl."

His praise brought her to life. She licked the sweat off his face and almost toppled him backward. "Okay, girl. Let's go home."

She took off down the trail. He gave one last glance at the mutilated snake, its tail still quivering. His gut was still shaking, too, but in that moment, he knew.

When the time came, he wouldn't hesitate.

# FREEING ELLIE

# CHAPTER SIX

Ellie left the chapel without the peace she had gone there seeking. The heavy weight squeezing her chest seemed to have moved to her lower back and made her legs feel heavy. Crazy. She reached behind her and tried to massage away the dull throbbing pain. She left the muddy red road and trudged through damp leaves to the clinic.

Relatives of patients had staked their claim on previous campfires and had set up lean-to tents to wait, sometimes for days, for their loved ones to be treated and released. Smoke from their ever-present fires hung heavy in the humid air. A greasy fetid smell hit her and seemed to come from the big black pot to her left. An old woman with a turban wrapped around her head stood over the pot. Perspiration dripped down the woman's face and into the frothy liquid she stirred. Ellie returned the woman's smile but quickened her pace to avoid being offered something to eat.

She kneaded the muscles of her lower back again before climbing the steps to the clinic. Maybe she'd slept wrong. For the next couple of hours, sounds of wailing children, clattering instruments, and jangling IVs on poles all seemed to bring a sense of normalcy and comfort.

She was examining a young boy who'd cut himself with a knife when moans from the far corner of the room drew her attention. Ned, one of the visiting doctors, worked on a man who looked to be in his late forties, old by African standards. The man thrashed and gripped his stomach. Ned put pressure on the man's shoulders and looked around the room until his eyes met hers. She responded to his silent plea for help by holding up one finger then finished wrapping gauze around her young patient's arm. "*Ta' fiche.*" She gestured to the boy's mother that he could leave with her. Then she ripped off her disposable gloves and joined Ned.

Ned maintained pressure on the man's shoulders but sent her a look of relief. "Thanks for coming to my rescue. I thought I was going to have to sedate him."

"I see what you mean." She walked to the other side of the cot and took the man's hand. "*Wakolapo*." She said hello over his moans and leaned closer. She pointed to her chest and smiled. "*Onduko yanze ame* Ellie."

The man quieted and visibly relaxed, which confirmed her suspicion that he was terrified as well as in pain. He mimicked her by placing his hand on his chest. "Sowa."

"Sowa." She repeated. "*Ove ovangula inglese*?"

Sowa shook his head and pointed to his stomach. "*Imo*."

Ellie nodded and glanced at Ned. "His name is Sowa. He doesn't speak English. And he has severe pain in his abdomen. I'm sure you already figured that out."

The corner of Ned's mouth almost lifted in a grin, the first she'd seen since he'd come to the compound. "At least you calmed him down." Ned took Sowa's hand and held it close to his own chest, a gesture she'd seen her dad do many times. He spoke more to her than to the patient. "I'll draw some blood and check his white count levels. Surgery looks inevitable."

"I'll get Iyegha to help. He speaks flawless Umbundo."

"Is that what you were speaking?"

"Attempting to speak. I only know a few phrases. Iyegha can inform Sowa's relatives when you make your decision."

Ned's eyes widened. "They're still here?"

Ellie nodded. "As long as he is here, they will stay and even cook for him. And if you're lucky, they might even offer you some."

Ellie hid her grin at Ned's grimace. "But I recommend you find a very polite way to decline," she added. "Point to your stomach and shake your head so they'll think you are sick and not being rude."

"Thanks for the heads-up." He tried to still the patient who had begun thrashing again.

"I'll get you some help." Ellie passed three cubicles until she found Iyegha holding the leg of a young boy while his assistant, Constance, sutured a gaping cut.

Ellie moved in closer. "I'll take your place here," she whispered. "Dr. Ned needs your translating skills."

"Yes, missy." Iyegha backed away from the patient, and Ellie slid into his place.

The boy looked to be around eight, but size among the nationals could be deceiving. He could be as old as fifteen. His big round eyes held pain as well as fear, but his mouth remained tightly clenched with not even a whimper coming from him. "

"Tell him he has been brave."

Constance nodded and spoke the words. The boy sat straighter and confirmed that he was older than he appeared. Ellie slipped some peppermint candy into the attendant's hand. Better that the candy came from the one who had given him the most pain.

The nagging pain in Ellie's back wasn't letting up. Time for a break. She reached into her pocket for her phone then glanced out the window. The clouds that had threatened rain all morning now unleashed a downpour of biblical proportions. Itinerant family members huddled under their makeshift tents seemingly unfazed.

Compassion flooded the hollow spaces in her heart like the rain filling the ruts in the road. These dear, humble people worked hard to survive in this savage land and showed a degree of gratitude she had never seen back in the States. They needed healing. And hope.

It's why her dad had come to this desolate place.

And why she had stayed.

If she could feel such love for these people, surely God must feel more. So why? Why did He allow suffering to go on? Why didn't He stop those wicked men from taking Toby? Why did Eric have to go—?

A soft touch broke through the cycle of her dead-end thoughts. Miriam placed her arm across Ellie's shoulders. The faint scent of ammonia and something like lemons clung to the flowered sarong she wore. "You look as though you could use a hug."

Ellie's throat got the tight, prickly feeling it always got before she had a meltdown. She swallowed hard and tried to hold it off. Then she shifted and leaned into the embrace, her head fitting naturally in the hollow between the older woman's breasts. A bosom hug, Miriam called them. The very best kind. The kind that made you feel like everything was going to be all right. She took a deep breath and slowly let it out. Even her back felt better.

With one more squeeze, Miriam released her and took a step back. "Come. Dr. Brock and your husband are in the dining hall with more news."

Ellie's heart skipped a beat. *Good news? Please let it be good news.* Maybe Eric wouldn't have to go after all. Ellie started to push through the double doors of the clinic, but Miriam's long, leathery fingers grabbed her and pulled her back. "This way, child."

Of course. No use walking through the deluge even if it was quicker. Ellie let herself be tugged through the maze of cots and cabinets to the long hallway connecting the clinic to the staff quarters and dining hall. Ellie's short legs seemed to be working double time, but she managed to scoot ahead of Miriam.

They entered the dining hall that could as easily be called the conference room or prayer chamber, depending on the need. Today it was both.

Eric left his seat and met her almost as soon as she cleared the door. He still wore his flex-fit leg which meant he'd gone for a run. No surprise. He ran whenever he needed to clear his mind or work out a problem. His hair was still damp, from a shower and not from the rain, judging by how good he smelled.

Eric returned to the table. An open laptop at his place revealed a satellite image of a compound similar in size to theirs. Ellie took the seat beside him but remained on the edge, not letting herself relax until she heard the news. Good. Or bad.

Nicci came through the double doors in the back right corner of the room, her usual cheerful countenance now serious and pinched. She took the place next to Miriam. Ellie smiled and stretched her hand across the table to connect with Nicci's.

Eric clicked an image on his laptop that sent a shiver down her spine. "The director located the plane. Sources tell us it's in this hangar." He turned the screen around and pointed to the area with a pen. "Next to their compound." He clicked another button, and the photo enlarged to reveal stucco buildings in a barren and remote area. "My guess is they're holding Toby here, but we won't know for sure until we get there and do some recon work." He closed the laptop and addressed the group. "Some guys from Texas are en route as we speak and should arrive at 0400."

The man beside her spoke in a no-nonsense manner she'd never heard before. This was the CIA agent Eric Templeton, who could take charge of a situation. The Eric she'd hoped never to have to see.

"I'll board the plane when they get here and brief them in flight. We'll land at the airport in Mbandaka." He held up a printed copy of a map of the region and pointed. "The agency arranged for some under-the-table transport from there to a drop-off point. Then we'll hike the rest of the way." He lowered the page and fingered the edge, his jaw working. After a long pause, he cleared his throat and spoke, his voice soft and no longer commanding. "This is my first—um— mission since I've become a believer." He stopped again and looked at her, meeting and holding her gaze, as if the words were meant for her alone. "But I won't be doing this on my own."

Clearly, he wasn't talking about the guys who were coming to help.

"And what I've seen of God in the past six months makes me think that's going to give me an edge. But I have to tell you—I'm going into this blind, without a clear plan. We won't know until we get there and scout out the area." This time Eric looked directly at Dad. "So I need you to pray."

Dad nodded before Eric finished speaking.

"And I know you have been but specifically for this: that God would make it plain how to get Toby out of there with the least amount of bloodshed possible."

*Bloodshed.*

The lump she swallowed became a full-fledged knot in her stomach.

They prayed, Dad once again leading their corporate prayer. She prayed, too. Silently, her heart begging God to protect them all—especially Eric.

There were no dry eyes when Dad said, "Amen." The group rose, and Ellie went straight for Nicci.

Along with the worry and fear in Nicci's large brown eyes, there seemed to be a hint of guilt, too. "I'm so sorry, missy, that your man must put himself in danger."

Ellie squeezed Nicci's cold fingers. "And I'm sorry your man is already in danger."

Eric came and stood beside them. The confident CIA Eric, all pumped up and almost too antsy to stand still. He hugged Nicci. "I'll bring him back to you."

She nodded, and tears ran down the scarred ridges in her cheeks. "Thank you." She took his hand and squeezed with both of hers. "*Bravo, amigo.*"

Eric turned to Ellie. "Ready to go home?"

She looped her hand through the crook in his arm and fell into step with him. "Yes," she said with emphasis. "It's been a long, hard day."

He leaned over and kissed her on the temple. "You know what I haven't seen all day?"

She looked up and gave him a questioning glance.

"Your dimple."

She grinned but not enough to produce it. "And you're not going to see it again. Not 'til you make it back home."

"Good incentive."

They stepped out onto the terrace. The rain had stopped, and a misty fog rose above the drenched field between the staff dormitory and their house. The sun, now close to setting, backlit purple clouds and shot out shafts of light, as if God was reaching down to them.

At the house, Lady greeted them with her typical excited frenzy. Eric took more time than usual to love on the dog. "You were such a good girl today."

Ellie stepped aside as Lady barreled into the house first. "She was?"

"She was. She went running with me. I gave her a command, and she actually obeyed."

"I guess that means you'll have to be the disciplinarian to our children. Lady walks all over me."

He grinned as he opened the large plastic container and scooped out a cup of dry dog food into Lady's bowl. Then he opened a can and spread meaty chunks on top. The warm water he added created a rich gravy.

Lady sat on her haunches, drool oozing from her mouth.

Ellie paid special attention, not knowing how long she'd have to take over this chore until he returned.

Tonight of all nights, she didn't want to share him. "Do you mind if we eat dinner here tonight?" Her unusually high-pitched voice shook.

Eric placed the bowl on the floor. Lady, a mass of pent-up tension, moved only when he nodded and said, "Ta' fiche."

Ellie scratched the fur between Lady's ears as she gobbled down her food. "Impressive. I bet ours is the only dog who understands *Okay* in English and Portuguese."

Eric washed his hands and came to her, smoothing back her hair. "Now. To answer your question. Yes, I was hoping you'd want to stay in tonight. I just want something light, and then we both need to rest for a little while."

"What time do you have to go?" She asked, but part of her really didn't want to know.

Mac's going to drive me out to the airfield. I need to leave no later than 0200.

She looked down so he wouldn't see the tears already forming. Again. She didn't want to be *that* woman. The kind who collapsed into hysteria whenever anything went wrong. Like her mother, who had her therapist on speed dial. No. She wanted to be strong. Like Miriam, who had a quiet grace no matter what life threw at her. Ellie wasn't there yet. Definitely a work in progress. Like Lady.

Eric leaned closer, his forehead resting on hers. They stood a long time, not speaking. Just embracing each other with their heads bowed as if in silent prayer.

# CHAPTER SEVEN

Eric didn't sleep. Ellie fell asleep quicker than he thought she would probably from sheer exhaustion—physical as well as emotional.

Her head nestled close to his chest in the crook of his arm. He forced his revved up body not to fidget, no matter how his cramped muscles begged him to.

The night, still transitioning from day, was not fully dark yet. How different his life was now. He let his mind go there. Something he rarely allowed now that he'd laid it all aside. January. Just one year ago. The botched Honduras mission. And then the return to Washington three months later to confront the man he suspected to be behind all the leaks. The man who'd sent him on the bogus mission to Africa and almost succeeded in getting him killed—

He jerked awake and reached for his phone. Two minutes before the alarm was set to go off. He must have slept. And slept hard. *Thank You, God.* He'd needed that sleep more than he realized. He clicked the alarm to the off position and tried to disentangle Ellie's leg and arm wrapped around him like tentacles. No need to wake her just yet. His years as an agent served him well. He slid his pillow up against her and waited in stealth mode until she resettled in the middle of the bed.

On a top shelf in the utility room, his tactical bag welcomed him like an old friend. His M-4, extra clips of ammo, his knife, sharpened and sheathed, smoke bombs, and even a few grenades lay inside organized and ready thanks to his long convalescence last summer. And plenty of room to add the extra ammo he'd told Skeet to bring.

He placed the bag by the door then grabbed his Bible and the brown journal he kept by his chair. He clicked on the light over the island counter that separated the kitchen from the living room. Without making a sound, he eased out a bar stool and sat, placing the two books in front of him. He reached in his top pocket for the three-by-five card Dad had given him with a list of Scriptures to read later. The one Dad had read to him earlier topped the list. "Trust in the Lord with all thine heart and lean not unto thine own understanding." Eric read through the list, some familiar and some new to him. The last one on the card helped him the most. "Call upon Me in the day of trouble." With his elbows propped on the counter, he folded his hands and whispered into the silence of the room. "God, I'm calling on You and asking You to be all over this mission. Keep us safe. Tell us how to get Toby out of there—"

He paused, not really finished. He'd promised Ellie he'd come home. But what if he didn't. His hand fingered the journal that had belonged to Nick Templeton, the natural father he'd never gotten to know except through these pages. Eric flipped it open and read the journal entry his dad had made the last day of his life.

Now Eric was going to be a father himself. What would he want to say to his own son, or daughter, if he didn't make it back? Something that would let him know what kind of man he was. And what kind of man he hoped his son would grow to be. And what would he say to Ellie, the one who in less than a year had become his very life?

Adrenaline surged. He flipped to the back of the book and started writing.

*My darling Ellie,*

*It breaks my heart to think of your reading this and what that means. But I couldn't leave this world without giving you something tangible to hold in your hands after I'm gone—to remind you again how much I love you.*

His throat tightened. He dropped the pen on the paper and applied pressure against his eyelids. This was harder than he thought it would be. Married less than three months. It wasn't enough. No amount of time would ever be enough.

He ripped the page from the back of the journal and wadded it up into a tight ball. "God, I can't write it. Just bring me back home." He lobbed it into the can by the door and then pushed it deep under the other trash to hide it.

Then he walked back to the bedroom. The bed was empty with the bedspread flipped back, and a thin shaft of light shone from under the bathroom door. He eased over and tapped. "Mind if I come in?" He asked while turning the knob. Locked.

"Um. Just a minute." She called out in her scared voice, the high-pitched one that made her sound more like a frightened girl.

Seconds went by. The toilet flushed. Water gushed into the sink. Still she didn't unlock the door.

He propped his hand against the doorjamb, and waited. Finally the door opened. His heart stuttered at how shaken she looked even though she seemed to be going out of her way to hide it.

Their eyes met. Then she dropped her gaze. What could he do, or say, to make her feel better?

She scooted under his arm and sat on the edge of the bed. Only then, with the light of the bathroom shining full on her face did he notice how pale she was. He sat beside her, putting his arm around her, pulling her close. She shifted and relaxed against him with her hand splayed against his chest. "I'm trying to be brave."

He could have melted into a puddle at her tremulous words. He smiled. "Me, too, baby."

"You'll let me know how it's going, won't you?"

His chin rubbed against her hair as he nodded. "I'll try. My plan is to get in and out. Hopefully, we'll be back by tomorrow night."

She raised her head and gave him a long look, her

eyelashes spiked with tears she'd already shed.

Eric met her gaze and answered the question in her frightened eyes. "I won't take chances." Unnecessary ones, at least. She needed to hear that. He grazed his fingers against her high cheekbones—perfect skin, like velvet to his touch—and swallowed hard. "I have to go."

Ellie captured his hand and held it tight against her cheek as if she couldn't let go. "I know." Just as quickly, she released her hold and raised her chin. "I can't walk out there with you."

He nodded. Probably better this way. He encased her face with his hands and kissed her. They clung to each other for a long time, as if drawing all the strength the other had to give.

Predictably, Lady showed up and nudged open the door. Eric reluctantly released Ellie and tousled one of the dog's floppy ears. "Okay, girl. Take care of Ellie while I'm gone."

With one more kiss to Ellie's forehead, Eric went from the bedroom, grabbed his bag, and left the house.

Ellie sat still, her hands curled around the side of the mattress in a death grip until the front door clicked closed. Then she lit off the bed and returned to the bathroom.

Lots of women spotted in the early stages of pregnancy. The brownish discharge she'd seen earlier could've been a one-time fluke. No reason to panic. Certainly no reason to tell Eric.

Her hands shook as she checked, hoping the sick thud in her chest was wrong. Bright red. She gasped and stared, willing it to disappear. She checked again and again. Steady but not profuse. Still normal, right?

But the dull ache plaguing her back and radiating to the front was not. A cold chill spread over her. She wrapped her arms around herself and rocked.

"Please, God. Not this, too."

# CHAPTER EIGHT

Eric gripped the side of the Jeep's doorframe as Mac swerved to avoid a deep rut.

"Sorry," Mac shouted over the rev of the engine. "Didn't see that rut 'til I was almost on it."

In good conditions and broad daylight, the ten-mile drive to the airfield could be hazardous. Unthinkable at night after torrential downpours. Mac had been the first to volunteer and being the mechanic and general handy man, was the best choice for the job. Unlike Ellie's dad, Mac never seemed in a hurry to get anywhere and loved to stop and tell lengthy and detailed anecdotes of his adventures at the mission.

But tonight, even Mac was quiet. He downshifted then gunned it. The four-wheel drive skidded over sludge and gravel as it ground its way to the top of a precarious hill.

Eric caught himself leaning forward as if it would somehow help. "Sorry you had to make this trip at night."

The jeep almost went airborne as it crested the hill.

"No problem." The long breath Mac took in and then blew out seemed to indicate otherwise. He shifted back to third. "To tell you the truth, between the two of us," Mac pointed his stubby forefinger to himself and then to Eric, "I'd rather be in my shoes than yours."

"No arguments there." The passenger seat had an uncomfortable slant that made Eric feel as if he was leaning out the door. He bore down on his right leg to compensate for the awkward tilt, and more than once, he had to jerk his leg back to ward off a cramp in his thigh. He shifted and checked the time.

Time. Possibly the one thing in their favor. Toby had been with the terrorist rebels less than twenty-four hours. Best case scenario, they'd get Toby out before he was forced to fly to some unknown destination.

Worst case? Toby would open his mouth and get himself killed.

A fine mist saturated the windshield faster than the flimsy strips of rubber could swipe it away.

Mac sped up at the sight of the Gulfstream 550 already on the runway. One of the pilots opened the door and lowered the steps. The rain picked up. Mac maneuvered so close to the plane, Eric barely had room to get out of the jeep.

Eric turned to Mac. "No need to get out. Thanks for getting me here."

Mac somehow grabbed the tactical bag before Eric could. Despite the rain, he went with Eric to the steps and threw the bag up to the man waiting in the doorway. Mac gripped Eric's shoulder and gave him a direct look. "Come back safe."

"Yes, sir. Thank you again. Be careful going down that hill."

With a wave, Mac turned and jogged back to the jeep.

Eric sprinted up the steps and craned his head to look around the door of the cockpit. "I really appreciate what you guys are doing."

The pilot twisted in his seat and shook Eric's hand. "We're happy to do it. Dr. Whitfield told us what you're up against."

"Yes, sir. If things go as planned, Toby will be the one flying us home." Eric took his bag from the co-pilot. "I'll store this in the baggage pit."

Eric entered the cabin area not knowing what or who to expect. No mistaking Skeet Dawson, Toby's good friend and fellow soldier from their Afghanistan days. Nothing had changed. Same prominent nose with a slight crook in the middle that reminded Eric of a hawk. Same long legs now filling the narrow aisle. Skeet pulled his legs back and sat straighter in a seat too small for his frame. Two men sat behind, making a grand total of four against a possible army of cutthroat rebels.

Eric dropped his bag and extended his hand. "Hey man. Thanks for coming on such short notice."

Skeet gave him a vice-grip handshake. His face, like tanned leather crinkled from too much sun, broke into a wide grin. "Like old times." His voice held the pronounced slow drawl of a man proud of his Texas heritage. "This here is Haskell." He turned and pointed to the man one seat behind. "Thinks he's a better sniper than me. So I brought him along. Told him it's his chance to prove it." Skeet's Adam's apple bobbed as he chuckled. "Told him he could take the shots I missed." He reached a long arm back and slapped Haskell on the thigh. "Ain't that right?"

No wonder Toby and Skeet had hit it off so well. Eric stepped over the pointed toe of Skeet's cowboy boot to shake Haskell's hand. "Good to meet you."

"Yes, sir." Nothing changed in Haskell's granite face. He looked Eric square in the eyes and leaned forward to meet the outstretched hand.

"And this is Gid." Skeet shifted and spoke to the man across the aisle from Haskell. "I reckon you're our demo man."

Eric nodded and shook hands with the man who looked more like a college geek than a seasoned military professional.

"Don't let his baby face fool you," Skeet said. "He's a dad-gum genius when it comes to blowing things up."

A man with demolition skills. Their odds might be improving. Unlike Haskell, Gid returned Eric's smile. Eric heaved his bag over their heads and inched toward the back of the plane. "I'll set this in the baggage pit and then brief you on the plan."

Eric returned and took the seat across the aisle from Skeet. Before he could buckle in, Skeet angled his body to face him. "This ain't your standard regulation military transport. Who's fronting this operation?"

Eric chuckled and clicked the buckle into place. "A man with big pockets and an even bigger heart. A fellow Texan, like yourself. Or rather, used to be."

Skeet's right bicep sported the word NATIVE over the Texas flag. "Any Texan worth his salt is always a Texan."

Skeet's right leg jutted directly in Eric's line of view. Eric looked away and attempted to quash a pang of envy. His first mission with a fake leg. What if he couldn't keep up?

"So, fill us in. What's the plan?"

"Here's what we've got." Eric took out the map and swiveled his chair. "My former boss, arranged for an off-the-record military transport to get us from the airport at Mbandaka to the city of Bolomba. We'll hike due south the rest of the way."

He spread out the satellite image of the rebel compound. "Can't be their main cell. Must be like a relay station for transport. We need to get him out before they move to the main headquarters."

He stopped short of saying he had no plan. Hard for him to admit.

Skeet stared at the map of the compound for a long time, his mouth twisted and puckered. With a deep breath, he leaned back in his chair. "Aw right." He unbuckled and stood, keeping his head ducked low. "Be right back." He returned with combat boots. "Reckon it's time to put these on."

Eric almost laughed. "I wondered if you planned to storm the compound in cowboy boots. So you plan to haul them around in your duffel bag?"

"Nah. Them fellows up yonder assured me they'd still be here when I got ready to go back to the States." He wiggled his toes and pulled up surprisingly white socks before tugging on the regulation combat boots. "They dad-burn better be."

The men said little the rest of the way. They ate protein

bars. Drank water. Lots of it. Filled their canteens to the brim from the bottled water stored on the plane. The grinding drone of the plane changed midair like the shifting of gears on a jeep. Sounds became muffled. Eric worked his jaw until his ears cracked and popped back to life.

They landed and made a seamless transition from the plane to the military cargo truck, thanks to some friends in high places.

The drop-off point outside the city of Bolomba put them within twelve miles of their destination. Hiking over uneven terrain did a number on Eric's leg. By thirteen hundred, they got the first glimpse of the compound's water tower located past a small hill.

The smart thing—and what his own gut told him to do— would be to hole up until dark. But another voice hammered into his subconscious like a lyric from a song stuck in his head. *Move now. Lean not unto thine own understanding.*

They took their last water break. The men spread out and went the rest of the way in crouch position. Eric caught Skeet's attention then held up his hand. Skeet nodded and signaled for the other two to stop. Eric rifled through his bag for field glasses and inched closer to the top of the hill.

Only three ramshackle buildings. Unpainted. Weeks of heavy rains had washed so much dirt from the foundations, the stucco buildings seemed to be at least a foot higher than the courtyard connecting them. Grass and clumps of weeds—in places up to two feet high—earmarked the unused spaces between the buildings. Judging by the stench blowing his way, the large trench to the right of the compound served as the latrine.

Eric ducked closer to the ground as two men left what appeared to be the main building—the one with the curl of smoke coming from a makeshift chimney more like a hole in the tin roof. The men's shirts were sweat stained, and each had an AK rifle slung over his shoulder.

Tiny rocks bit into Eric's underside as he twisted to signal the others to join him.

Skeet slid into place.

Eric handed him the field glasses but continued to scan the area himself. The plane was still there under a tarp. That meant Toby was there, too. But where?

Skeet handed back the glasses. "Nobody's stirring. We can take 'em now."

The sun chose that moment to break through the cloud cover, and within seconds, it was as if they were standing next to an open furnace. Eric tied a handkerchief around his head Rambo style and gave a flick of his fingers for them to follow him. He turned and slid down the hill a few feet. They caught up and huddled close for instructions.

"My guess is Toby's in the small building. The one with the guard outside the door. Gid, I need you to take out that water tower so it hits the big building on the left."

Gid nodded. Eric shifted to face Haskell. "The explosion is your cue. Take care of anybody who comes running out of the building. Skeet, you handle the middle building."

"Copy that." Skeet used the edge of his shirt to wipe sweat from his brow. "Where you gonna be?"

"I'm going for Toby." Something he wouldn't hand off to one of them. He had a debt to pay, and Toby was worth the risk. "Gid, give me ten minutes to get into positon, and then let 'er blow."

"With pleasure."

With a nod, Eric slid the rest of the way down the hill, his mind focused on the target objective. Against all reason, and his own gut cursing him for being a fool, he pushed ahead. *God, make this work.*

The clumps of bushes did little to hide him as he crouched into position on the far side of the makeshift latrine. The stench made him gag, but the cloud of flies surrounding the area kept him from trying to breathe through his mouth. *Come on, Gid.* Maybe he should've told him five minutes instead of ten.

The guard left the small building and turned his way. Eric shifted and moved his M-4 into place, trigger ready. The man moved closer, and only when he reached the latrine did he glance up. His eyes widened as he made eye contact with Eric. The man had no gun. At least not that Eric could see. The man spun around, and with a yell, ran back toward the building, probably to grab his gun. Or warn others. Eric couldn't let that happen, but he couldn't bring himself to shoot the guy in the back either. With a flying leap over the trench, Eric let his left leg field the brunt of impact. He aimed low and clipped the guy in the back of the leg.

The blast he'd been waiting for finally split the air and pulverized two beams supporting the tower. The rebel crawled toward the doorway flailing his arms like a man swimming from a shark.

The staccato of gunfire echoed through the compound. Eric remained focused on the primary objective to secure Toby. His only obstacle the man slithering toward the doorway leaving a trail of blood in the dust. The man reached the door and grabbed for a rifle. Eric kicked it out of the way and used the butt of his own rifle to knock the guy unconscious. With his foot, he rolled the man out of the way. Toby crouched on the dirt floor, one of his hands cuffed to the bed post.

"'Bout time you showed up."

With a quick glance outside the door, Eric rushed over to Toby. "Look away." Eric fired his glock. The first shot chipped the steel cuff. Toby tried to pull his hand free.

"Hold still. You've got to fly us out. I don't want to miss and shoot your hand off." No time to savor Toby's wide-eyed stare. Eric fired again. This time the cuff flew off, ricocheting off the wall.

Toby pushed up, then swayed.

Eric grabbed Toby's arms. "Can you walk?"

"Yeah. I'm fine. Go!"

The gunfire had settled down. Eric scanned the compound. "How many men are here?"

Toby shook his head. "Ten maybe? Good thing you showed up when you did. One of them said a lot more are coming in tonight. And—"

"Tell me in the plane." Eric placed his arm across Toby's shoulder. "Let's go home."

Eric nodded for Toby to go on ahead and get the plane started while he stayed behind to deal with any stragglers.

Outside, water from the tower had flooded the compound. Seven men lay face down, their blood turning the water red. The man he'd knocked unconscious stirred and inched his hand toward the rifle on the ground. Rapid-fire shots pummeled the man's body.

Haskell eased up to the man and kicked him onto his back. Skeet shouted from the other side of the compound. "Nuh-uh. He don't count. He ain't one I missed."

"Anybody left?" Eric shouted and backed away from the compound, his senses heightened to detect any movement.

"Nah. All clear."

"You and Haskell get on the plane. Where's Gid?"

"I'm in here." A muffled voice came from the middle building. "I'm leaving a little welcome home gift in case some more show up."

Skeet cackled. "Figured that's what you was up to."

"Load up." Eric yelled as he jogged toward the plane. "I'm more concerned about our welcome home, not theirs."

# CHAPTER NINE

Eric wedged himself behind Skeet, who rode shotgun—the only place in Toby's Cessna 206 his long legs would fit. Eric scrunched in, leaning on Gid in the middle and reached behind to slam the rear door shut. His leg started to cramp, but he wouldn't remove his prosthesis to make more room. Not for anything. And why weren't they answering? Eric cut the voicemail recording in mid-sentence and shot another text.

"Will she make it up with the extra weight?" Eric had his doubts.

Toby revved the engine. "Yeah. I dumped some fuel while you guys were taking care of business." He taxied to a flat stretch of grassy land. "I just hope I kept enough for us to make it to Mbundaka."

Information Toby could've kept to himself. He waited until they were airborne to take a good look at Toby. Other than the blood matting his short black hair, the trail of dried blood down his right temple, and the caked mud down the left side of his shirt and pants, he seemed to be okay.

"Good thing it's still daylight. I'm flying by the seat of my pants."

Something Toby did well.

Toby leaned forward and scanned the terrain. "Gotta be due west." He aimed the plane directly into the lowering sun and leveled off. "Thank God you guys showed up when you did. I never prayed so hard in all my life. I knew you'd come for me." He grabbed a rag from under the seat and swiped it across his forehead. He winced and dabbed at the wound above his right eye. "But I didn't think it'd be this quick." He glanced at Skeet. "And how on earth did you get here all the way from Texas? I couldn't believe my eyes. Who's your backup?" He gestured behind with a nod. "I still can't believe you found me much less got me out of there. Those were some bad—"

"Tobe." Eric unwedged himself enough to thump Toby's shoulder. "Give it a rest, will you, so we can fill you in."

Toby's face broke into a wide smile that just as quickly changed to a grimace. He fingered the side of his head. "Those guys 'bout cracked my head open."

Skeet nodded. "I figured you'd try to get away."

"Almost made it. When I came to, I was cuffed to a bed post. Okay. I'll shut up. Introduce me. Give me details."

Skeet turned and hooked his arm across the seat. "Gid Ferris and Haskell Jernigan. Some boys from back home. We've been itching for a little action. Ain't that right?"

Toby veered and inched the nose of the plane down. Eric checked the area. Was it time to start the descent or was the plane running out of gas?

"Hang on a minute, guys." Toby grabbed the headset he hadn't bothered to put on and spoke into the transmitter. "This is November one niner four zero Alpha Charlie requesting final approach."

Twenty minutes to retrace what had taken three hours on ground? Not that he was complaining. He chimed in before Toby could fire off more questions. "Dr. Brock arranged the flight. Director McDowall unofficially sanctioned Skeet and his buddies to come over and help out. He arranged ground support, too. I'll fill you in on the rest when we get on the ground. And I'm not buckled, so take it easy."

"Roger that."

The plane glided onto the runway with almost no skips or bumps. For a guy who preferred helicopters, Toby pulled off the landing without a hitch.

When Skeet opened the door behind him, Eric gripped the seat in front to keep from toppling backward. He eased out, back end first. Gid threw Eric the tactical bag and then slid out.

Haskell followed and was the first to offer his hand to Eric as they reached the Gulfstream. "Pleasure working with you." Still no smile. "Anytime you need backup, give me a call."

"Thanks, man. Couldn't have pulled this off without you."

Toby slung his arm across Skeet's shoulder. "I went to a lot of trouble to finally get you over here."

A plane took off, drowning out Skeet's laughter. He leaned in closer and raised his voice. "Next time, come to Texas. Ya'll take care. I've got to see a pilot about some cowboy boots."

Eric followed the men into the plane and grabbed the duffle bag he'd left. He gave a last wave to the pilots and the guys.

The airport had one long runway surrounded by a line of trees. Eric walked toward a tan two-story building, slowing his gait to match Toby's. His friend seemed to be losing some steam. They both stopped as the plane thundered down the long strip and into the horizon. A twinge hit Eric. He'd like to be back in the Cessna, heading home to Ellie. He checked his phone again. A strong signal but still no response to the three texts he'd sent when they'd made it onto the plane.

A white airport van rounded the corner of the building and pulled up alongside.

Mike Cores, field agent and technical support for most of his missions, stuck his head out the open window. "Need a lift?"

Eric grinned and stepped aside as the door swung open. "Mike. Good timing as usual. How've you been?"

"Good." Mike grasped the top part of Eric's arm and shook his hand. "Trying to keep up with the two men it took to replace you. Not the same without you, man."

Eric chuckled and gestured to Toby. "You remember Toby Williams, the guy who created this international crisis?"

Mike shook his head. "But I've heard plenty. Glad you

made it out in one piece." He turned back to Eric. "We have rooms at the best hotel in town."

"Best" meaning only. Fair warning. "Sounds good." Eric opened the back door. "Tobe, take the front."

Toby walked around the van and looked as if he'd be going down any minute.

Mike must have picked up on it, too. "I'm starved. How about you?"

Toby pulled the shoulder strap across his chest. "I could eat, but to tell the truth, I could use a real bed." He glanced over at them, eyebrows raised. "One I ain't handcuffed to."

Eric grinned and gazed out his window. Good to have Toby back. Except for a few abrasions and bruises, relatively unscathed. Almost seamless rescue, thanks to all the prayers. He took out his phone and tried again. Straight to voice mail. He could only hope at least one of his texts went through.

Ahead on the right, one long building of various widths and heights seemed to comprise the entire village of Mbundaka. A sidewalk of large mud bricks lined the wide street made of compacted dirt and gravel. Their van, on loan from the airport, was the only vehicle in the area. Pedestrians, mostly men and boys, stopped to stare as Mike drove to the front of a section of the building with round wooden columns the size of telephone poles supporting the porch overhang.

"Hold it." Eric held up his hand as Mike started to get out. A man pedaled past. "Okay. All clear."

"Thanks. I'd forgotten about your radar." Mike double-checked then opened the door of the van. "Follow me. Your rooms are on the second floor."

The rooms were stuffy cubicles big enough for a chair and a bed that looked more like a cot. No dresser. Not that he cared. He'd slept in much worse. Toby glanced around. "They got any bathrooms?"

Mike gave a one-sided grin and gestured with a nod.

"Community bathroom down the hall. Eric, this is your room. I'll see if I can round us up some food."

Eric rummaged in his bag then stepped across the hall. Toby lay stretched out, his feet hanging off the end of the bed.

"Heads up." Eric tossed a wadded-up bundle.

Toby sat up and caught it with one hand. "What's this?"

"Soap. And clean clothes, compliments of Nicci. After you wash some of that latrine stink off you, I'll share some of this homemade bread she sent." Eric held a towel in one hand and the bread in the other.

Toby snatched the towel. "Just don't eat it all."

"I won't. Don't use all the soap."

"You beat everything, you know that? You hardly break a sweat, and you're off to take a shower."

Eric grinned and bit off a chunk of bread. "It's a gift."

Toby rolled his eyes. "More like a sickness."

Fifteen minutes later, Toby returned looking and smelling a lot better. "Your turn. Good luck."

It didn't take long for Eric to figure out what Toby meant. The cold trickle coming out of the shower hardly knocked off the top layer of dust.

He changed into the shorts and a T-shirt he'd brought along.

Mike returned with two foiled-lined pouches. "End of the day special: Rice and steamed fish from a vender close to the river."

Eric sniffed first before pinching off some of the fish. With only one bathroom, he hoped the fish was still fresh. "Thanks. I'll see if Toby's still awake. We'll bring our chairs and den up in your room."

The men wedged their straight-backed chairs in a tight semicircle around the bedside table in Mike's room. Mike spread out the food and tossed them bottled waters. "We did some snooping. It was a smaller cell of the LRA looking to make a name. The plane was their bargaining chip. Sources say they planned to transport guns to three different bases from Tanzania up to Sudan. As a grand finale, one lucky rebel would go solo with the pilot for a Kamikaze-type mission."

Toby's dark face went pale. "What if they come back?"

Mike took a bite of fish and wiped his mouth. "If I were you, I'd relocate. Closer to Luanda. Almost no terrorist activity in Angola. Odds are they'll close up shop and move to a new base. How many men did you take out?"

Eric pushed back his chair. "Eight."

"Yeah. Insignificant."

"Toby said more were coming in that night. Our demo man booby-trapped one of the buildings. Probably took out some more."

Mike shrugged. "A dose of their own medicine."

"What if they come looking for payback?"

"They won't."

Toby turned to Eric as if to confirm Mike's words. Eric leaned forward and held Toby's gaze. "Think about it. No survivors. Nobody to point back to us."

Toby looked up and released a long breath.

Mike reached over and patted Toby's shoulder. "You're safe now. Get some rest. We'll head to the airport at first light. Your plane will be fueled up and ready to go."

Eric stood. "Are you going back to Langley, Mike?"

"Eventually. Have some unfinished business before I make it back to the States."

Protocol kept Eric from asking what or where. Not something he needed or cared to know.

Eric bolted upright, and reached for his gun, his chest heaving. He blinked a few times, then eased back down and stared at the ceiling, barely visible in the darkened room.

Just another nightmare. But so real. More vivid than the others. Rebel soldiers this time. They stormed the mission hospital, slaughtering everyone in their path.

Except him. It took five of them to bring him down. They pressed his face hard in the gravel of the compound outside the chapel and tied his hands behind his back. Two men dragged Ellie outside and forced her to her knees barely three feet in front of him. She raised her head and cried out his name, her eyes swimming in tears. He'd strained with all his might to break their stranglehold. The man holding her grabbed a fistful of hair and jerked her head back.

He closed his eyes, and tried in vain to shut out the rest.

One of the rebels faced Eric, his putrid breath nauseatingly close. His eyes glinting with hatred, he reached for the knife Eric wore strapped to his belt, and said, "This is for you." He stepped back and nodded to the man holding Ellie's head back. The man laughed and pulled tighter, stretching her neck so taut, she was unable to cry out. With his smug gaze never leaving Eric's face, the rebel punctured the artery in Ellie's neck.

His own fierce yell had awakened him.

He swung his leg over the edge of the cot and ran his hand through sweat-dampened hair. Always the same. Sometimes people. Sometimes animals. But always Ellie in some kind of danger and he powerless to help. He reached for his prosthetic leg and clicked it into place. No more sleep. If he closed his eyes, he'd see the blood gush from her neck again.

He drank what was left of his bottled water and reached for his phone. No rings. Just Ellie's lyrical voice saying, "Leave a message" and ending with "Hope you have a blessed day." His hand tightened around the phone. Why wasn't she answering?

He slid the chair closer to the window and cracked it open. Cool air hit him, and he sucked in some deep draughts before scrolling to the Bible app on his phone.

# CHAPTER TEN

The text Eric had been waiting for finally came while they were midair.

PRAISE GOD! HURRY HOME!

But from her dad. Not Ellie. He read the words twice. *HURRY HOME.* Because we miss you? Or because something was wrong? His gut tightened, and a thousand scenarios flooded his mind. None good.

Toby glanced at him. "You sure are quiet."

"Yeah. I'm glad we're on the way home."

"Me, too, brother. You know what I've been thinking?"

Eric shook his head and relaxed. With a little encouragement, Tobe would talk the rest of the way.

"I'm going to ask Nicci to marry me. It's like my whole life flashed before me that night I was cuffed to the bed. I told God if He'd get me home, I'd settle down. I'd get married, raise a family. Should've asked her already. Just couldn't figure out how to take her away from Dr. Brock. But I've decided to relocate, like Mike said. Makes so much sense now. I'll build a bigger hangar at the airstrip we're flying to. After what happened, I don't think I'll have any trouble convincing Terrance to make the move too. What do you think about that?"

Eric sat up straighter and scrambled to remember Toby's last few words. "I think it's about time. You can build a house in the field behind ours."

"Yeah. That's what I think. Life's too short. You know what I mean? I'm gonna see if she'll marry me quick, like you did with Ellie."

Eric smiled, even though his stomach was churning. No guarantees even when you're married. Something unexpected could happen, and she could be snatched—"Good plan. Step on it. I've got to see my wife."

By noon, they landed on the bumpy airstrip. Toby taxied under the aluminum awning and cut the engine. "Looks like they left the Land Rover for us."

Eric threw his bag in the back of the vehicle and fingered under the rim for the hidden key. "Hop in. I'll drive." He hit Ellie's number one more time and cut off the automated voice mid-syllable. He shot out a group text: ON THE GROUND. COMING HOME.

The ten-mile trip passed in a blur. The Land Rover went airborne a couple of times and fishtailed over loose gravel. Eric braked and jerked the vehicle around a washed-out gully in the road. Toby gripped the dash with both hands. "You're driving like the rebels are hot on our trail."

"Sorry." Eric eased up on the gas. "Guess my fake foot's a little heavy."

"Still no response?"

Eric shook his head.

"They probably have a big surprise party waiting for us."

He responded with a half-hearted grin. Toby was no fool. Neither was he.

The compound finally came into view. A crowd of people, all happy, smiling, stood in the courtyard outside the day clinic. They stepped back as he drove up then swooped in, Nicci leading the way.

But no Ellie.

Miriam bypassed the group surrounding Toby and came straight toward him.

"Where is she?"

Miriam took his hand. "In surgery. Come with me."

"What happened?" Not waiting for an answer, he sprinted ahead, up steps and through curtained-off cots in the clinic.

"Eric. Wait." Miriam caught up in the hall. "Don't go in

there."

He mustered all his strength to stop and not blast through the double doors separating him from Ellie.

She reached him and spoke, her words coming in short breaths. "Please. Sit." She nudged him toward the cushioned bench. "Ellie lost the baby." She placed her hand on his arm. "I'm so sorry."

His mind reeled. So fast? He'd only been gone a day and a half. He raked his hand through his hair. "What happened?" he asked again, this time waiting for the response.

"Shortly after you left, she alerted her father that she was spotting. He ordered bed rest until nature took its course."

"Is she all right?"

Her slight hesitation turned his insides to ice. "She will be fine."

"What's wrong? Why's she in surgery?"

"She began hemorrhaging about an hour ago. Dr. Brock is trying to control the bleeding."

Adrenaline coursed through him. He pushed off the bench and started to roll up his sleeve. "Does she need blood?"

Miriam rose, too. "I don't think so."

Toby came barreling down the hall toward them with Nicci holding his hand and trying to keep up. "I just heard. How is she?"

Eric faced them and shook his head. "Waiting to hear."

Nicci hugged him. "Thank you. I wanted to let you know, but Ellie made me promise not to."

Eric nodded as she stepped back. He wanted details. How much pain did she have? How upset had she been? Eric systematically twisted each finger until it popped, then moved to the next. He didn't do helpless well.

Ellie's father finally pushed open one of the double doors. Sweat drenched the cap he wore, and traces of blood stained his scrubs. His face, lined with fatigue, brightened the moment he saw them. "Good to have you back home."

"How is she?"

"Stable. Iyegha wheeled her to recovery." He squeezed Eric's hand. "She's going to be just fine."

"Can I see her?"

"Of course. I'll go with you." He paused long enough to give Toby a hug. "Right through there." He pointed to a door at the far end of the surgery room.

The door to recovery had a square window big enough to give Eric a quick glimpse. He pushed through and eased to her side. His heart seemed to stop beating. He'd seen a lot of death, and she looked dead, her face chalky white, her lips thin and colorless. So fragile. And lifeless. He folded her limp hand in both of his and chafed to rub warmth into the icy fingers.

"She'll probably sleep the rest of the day." Dad placed his hand on Eric's shoulder. "Why don't we get some coffee? I'll fill you in."

Coffee and details. Tempting. But not enough to tear him away from Ellie.

"Maybe later."

"I understand. I'll change clothes, and then I'll be in the clinic if you need me."

Eric nodded. "Thank you."

Dad whispered something to Iyegha, and the two men left the room.

Finally alone with Ellie, he took a deep breath and slowly released it. She was going to be all right. *Thank God.* The relief seemed to outweigh the sadness.

But not the regret. She'd lost their baby. Alone. Had gone through this ordeal without him. He held her hand tight against his chest and tried to ease the dull ache in his heart.

She must have known before he left. It seemed so clear now. The stricken look on her face when she'd finally come out of the bathroom to say good-bye. Her refusal to see him off.

How could he have missed it?

She did what she'd had to do, just like he had. He released her hand and leaned closer. Smoothing back wisps of golden hair, he kissed her on the cheek, whispering in her ear. "You're quite a woman, Ellie Templeton."

# FREEING ELLIE

# CHAPTER ELEVEN

Someone called her name. Ellie pried open her eyes. Eric sat on a stool by the bed. Not her bed. A hospital bed. Her slow brain started to catch up. "You're back." She took a deep breath and with its release, one huge weight started to lift from her chest.

"Uh-huh." Eric leaned closer and clasped her hand in both of his.

He hadn't shaved in a while. Or slept. He seemed so tired. And worried. More fog lifted. Had Dad called him home too early? Would he have to go back? She struggled to rise, but her body wouldn't let her. "Did you get Toby out?" Her thick tongue slurred the words.

Eric smiled, his expression a mixture of regret and tenderness. "We did."

"Alive?"

"Yes, alive. He's fine."

She relaxed her head against the pillow.

Eric raised her hand to his lips. "When you're better, and more awake, I'll tell you all about it."

She nodded. Her other hand slid across her lower abdomen, searching in vain for what was no longer there.

"I'm sorry I wasn't here." Eric's voice choked with emotion.

She brushed her fingers across his unshaven face. "You're here now."

"Next time, Toby's on his own." He thumb swiped the tear running down her temple.

"Hmm." Too much effort to keep her eyes open.

The bed dipped. He slid his hand underneath and rolled her into his arms. "Am I hurting you?"

She shook her head and snuggled close to his chest listening for the thud of his heart. "I've wanted you to hold me ever since—"

Big, heaving breaths shook her, made all the more violent by her efforts to hold them back. Tears unleashed like a giant wave thundering over her entire being. She quit fighting and let the torrent carry her away.

Eric held tight, stroking her back, her hair, her face. He kissed the top of her head, now almost buried in the crook of his arm. He said nothing. Just held her and rocked her. And let her cry out the grief.

Ellie eased into the bathroom and dressed in baby blue scrubs. She pulled up her hair in a ponytail and applied more makeup than usual. Today of all days, she couldn't afford to look pale.

Her first hurdle sat on a bar stool at the kitchen island. Eric, still in T-shirt and pajama pants, glanced up from his open Bible.

Ellie took a fortifying breath. "Good morning." Ignoring his wide-eyed stare, she smiled, maybe a little too wide, and breezed past him for the coffeepot.

Eric swiveled to face her, his arms folded across his chest. "Honey—"

"You make the best coffee." Out of the corner of her eye, she saw him stand. Her heart almost thumped out of her chest. "I don't know how you do it. Mine never turns out—"

"Ellie." He came from behind and turned her to face him. "What are you doing?"

"I want to go back to work." She raised her chin and held her ground.

He pressed his lips together in a tight line and studied her face.

"You, of all people, should understand. And you owe me, Mister. I rescued you plenty of times when you were going stir-crazy last summer. Against my better judgment, I might add."

His expression softened. "You have me there." He kissed her forehead and then spoke over his shoulder as he walked down the hall. "Drink your coffee while I get dressed."

"What are you up to, Eric Templeton?"

His muffled voice came from the bedroom. "I need backup."

He returned wearing jeans and a gray T-shirt.

"That was fast."

"I hurried. You looked like you were about to bolt." He opened the door and stood interference when Lady rushed over for her morning greeting.

The walk across the field to the staff dormitory taxed Ellie more than she was willing to admit. She slowed at the sight of her dad. "Did you text Dad and tattle on me?"

Eric held up his hand. "I'm pleading the fifth."

"Good morning." Her father met them at the edge of the terrace. "You just missed a glorious sunrise."

She returned Dad's hug. Eric stepped around and pulled over a chair.

Ellie's rubber legs were ready for a break. She sank into the chair and closed her eyes, letting the morning sun hit her full in the face.

"Eric tells me you want to work today." Dad pulled his chair closer.

She lifted her head and shielded her eyes with her hand. "I do. I'll take it easy, but I need to stay busy."

"I don't know, honey. It's only been two days. Might be rushing it a bit." He tapped his finger against pursed lips and cut a glance at Eric. "What do you think?"

Sandwiched between them, Ellie felt like a juvenile delinquent waiting for judgment to be handed down. A rush of anger reared as it always did whenever she felt backed into a corner with no control over the situation. Maybe she should wave her medical degree and remind them she was, in fact, a grown woman. She decided instead to plead her case. Taking a deep fortifying breath, she uncrossed her arms and leaned forward. "Listen, I know you're both concerned, and I love you for it. But I feel fine, and I promise not to faint during a procedure."

Judge and jury held their silent deliberation. Finally, Eric leaned back in his chair. "Your call, Dad."

Dad dropped his gaze to his folded hands then stood. "All right, but with one condition." He placed his hand on her shoulder. "Stop and rest before you start to keel over."

"Deal." She tipped her head back and smiled.

"You can help Ned and Steve in the clinic. I'll make some post-op rounds and join you later."

The chair beside her scraped back, and Eric extended his hand. "You want something to eat first?"

"Not just yet. I'll take a break in about an hour."

With a tug, he pulled her up. "I'll walk with you."

The soft pressure of Eric's hand against the small of her back comforted her. Just like his care of her these past two days. He seemed to know when to talk and when to leave her alone. Always close but never smothering.

"Time to kill more game for the villagers." Eric announced as they stepped away from the staff dormitory. "Mac and I are going to do a little hunting after we drop Toby off at the airfield."

The ugly ordeal of Toby's kidnapping resurfaced. What if she had lost Eric, too? Gravel crunched under her feet as she pivoted to face him. "Thank you."

He slanted his head to her. "For hunting?"

"For coming back alive."

He nodded, his mouth forming a silent *oh*. "You're

welcome." He fell into step as she resumed walking. "You know, I could tell you all about our daring rescue after lunch."

"Okay. I think I'm ready—Wait a minute. Eric Templeton, is this your sneaky way to keep me from working this afternoon?"

"Busted." Eric grinned and gripped his chest in mock innocence.

She laughed. Her first genuine laugh since—Ellie looped her hand through his arm and leaned against his granite bicep as they continued toward the clinic. She had to give him credit. In his own quiet way, he was trying really hard to help her through her pain.

Eric paused when they reached the clinic steps. "You're sure about this?"

"I'm sure."

To their right, Toby flung open the side door of the staff dormitory. "Bro!" he yelled across the compound. "I've been looking all over for you." He jogged over and gave a quick nod to Ellie.

Eric fished in his pocket. "Tobe, I'll ride shotgun."

Toby's hand swung up and caught the keys. "Sure. Take your time."

Ellie stood on tiptoes to kiss Eric's cheek. "See you at lunch." She waited at the top of the clinic steps to see them off. Eric pulled the safety strap across his chest. He glanced up and smiled when he saw she was still there. He put two fingers to his lips and raised them like a salute.

Ellie grinned and waved. Poor guy was probably dying to get out and do something. The jeep disappeared in a cluster of trees a quarter mile down the road.

The hollow ache followed her into the clinic as she knew it would. It would just take time. *Things happen for a reason. God never makes a mistake.* She repeated the litany like a catechism.

Depression. Something she thought was gone forever had begun sucking her down into the abyss again. Her hands clenched. That's why she had to go back to work. Repeating every platitude she knew hadn't touched the black hole in her heart. Neither had the prayers that bounced off the ceiling and fell flat at her feet. She couldn't tell Dad. Or Eric. So far they hadn't noticed. Maybe with time, and work, the suffocating darkness would just fade away.

As Ellie neared the table in the center of the room, Iyegha did a double-take. "You are well now?"

"I am well." She placed her hand on his arm. "I'll help you sort through the patients that are left."

Ellie grabbed a pen and clipboard. The room adjacent to the clinic had chairs lined up around the walls. Open windows and overhead fans did little to filter the stench of sickness and body odor permeating the room. She fixed a smile on her face and let the professional take over.

The boy in the corner chair drew her attention. His mouth and jaw clenched with what seemed to be extreme pain especially when he erupted into a violent coughing fit.

Ellie walked over, took his hand, and kneeled to speak with him eye to eye. The boy remained tight-lipped, but the man beside him, who she learned was his father, answered her questions. She pieced together bits of information without an interpreter. The boy's name was Kalu. He had eaten fish two days before and had started to gag.

Two days. The bone may have already eroded into the thoracic cavity. Ellie steeled her expression to remain pleasant as she gestured for them to follow. She caught Ned's eye and beckoned him over. After explaining the situation, they led the boy and his father down the corridor to the first surgery room.

Within minutes, they had Kalu on an operating table. Other than his wide eyes, the boy showed no sign of fear. He opened his mouth while she applied the topical anesthesia.

Ellie prayed silently and remained by his side. Remarkably, Kalu did not fight or squirm as Ned positioned the esophagoscope and inched it down the boy's throat.

"There it is." Ned shifted to get a better look. He kept his voice low and controlled. "Halfway down. Large and jagged." He inserted long forceps down the tube. "Can you tell him not to move?"

She couldn't. Not in Umbundu. Kalu's eyes never left her face. Out of desperation, she tried Portuguese. With her most soothing voice, she whispered, *"Imovel."*

He seemed to understand.

Ned grimaced and looked at her. "It's farther down than I thought. If he jerks, it may go even deeper."

Ellie nodded and stroked Kalu's forehead. *God, please help Ned get the bone out.* The next few minutes seemed like an eternity.

"Ellie, reposition the light."

Ellie slid the light closer. "Let me know when to stop."

"Okay. There it is. I'll have to extend the forceps beyond the tube."

She held her breath as Ned went even deeper. Kalu remained frozen, not moving even a finger.

"Got it." Slowly, Ned removed the forceps and esophagoscope together.

Tears welled in the father's eyes and in hers. Ned held up the bone to show Kalu the "big fish" he had caught.

"Very good work, Ned. I'm going to take Kalu and his father to meet Moses and Miriam. They'll give them some food, something soft for Kalu, and share with them about the great fisher of men, I'm sure."

Ned wiped his hands and nodded. "Thank you. I couldn't have done it without your help." He hugged Kalu and walked with them to the door. "That is one brave young man."

Ellie left them in Moses's and Miriam's very capable

hands. She could use a break, too. The window in the hallway gave a perfect view of the mission courtyard. Yafatu, an Angolese national who had almost bled to death, sat on a bench in front of the chapel. Dad stood before him, doing what he did best. Without hearing a word, she could make out exactly what he said through his animated gestures. He was sharing the Gospel, and no one did it better or with more passion. Yafatu looked up as Dad pointed to the sky. Dad transferred the Bible from one hand to the open palm of the other, showing how God placed all our sins onto Christ. Then Dad held out his hands, illustrating Christ's death on the cross. He opened the Bible and pointed, speaking, most likely, in the Umbundu dialect.

He sat and put his arm around Yafatu. The man dropped his head and even from a distance, Ellie could detect the shaking of his shoulders.

Tears streamed down her face, too. Two years ago, Dad had taught her these same truths, and she had prayed just as Yafatu prayed now. She'd never forget the joy that infused her whole being. The shroud of darkness that had enveloped her then had lifted like the mist on a field dissipates under the morning sun.

But the darkness was back. Would the joy she'd felt then ever return?

# CHAPTER TWELVE

Ellie grabbed three bottles of water from the cooler in the dining hall and exited the staff dormitory through the side door.

Dad waved her over, his face beaming. "Perfect timing. Yafatu has just prayed and given his life to Christ."

Yafatu spoke no English but returned her smile and bowed to show his appreciation for the water.

Dad placed his hand on the young native's shoulder and spoke again in Umbundu. Something about God's help. Prayer. Dad gestured to Yafatu's chest and spoke, "New heart."

Yafatu listened with all the attention of a man receiving life-giving instructions from a doctor; only this was life instructions for when he returned home today. Back to the same volatile situation that landed him here, fighting for his life.

She smiled and pointed to her heart. *"Esanju utima.*

His head bobbed, and his shiny black face indeed reflected his joyful heart. He wore the typical dress of the Angolese nationals. Lightweight cotton pants, loose, with a tunic over shirt. A gift from Miriam who had made them to replace the torn and bloody ones he'd worn two weeks earlier.

Mac drove the Range Rover into the compound. Before the vehicle even came to a full stop, Dad shared the good news about Yafatu's conversion with Mac. Dad helped settle Yafatu in the front seat and leaned in for one more embrace. Then he closed the passenger door and thumped the top. He waved, a broad smile creasing his face as the vehicle disappeared around the corner of the chapel.

Ellie studied him. "You're amazing."

Dad glanced at her, finished off his water, and cleared his throat. "Not me, honey. I'm just the vessel." He crushed the plastic bottle in his grip. "No good except for the water inside."

Classic Dad answer, which made Ellie think he was all the more amazing.

"How are you doing, honey?"

"Good so far. I'm taking a little break, like you said."

"Great. Let's go into the chapel and sit a while."

Ellie took her last sip of water and looked around before returning her gaze to Dad. He stood beside her, probably waiting for her to make the first move. How could she tell him she wasn't ready to hear all the things she knew he would say? Things she'd already said to herself with little result. But to refuse would draw even more attention. "Okay." She started toward the building.

Dad raced around her up the three cement steps and pushed open the heavy wooden door and waited for her to enter.

The chapel had a different feel from any other building on the compound. A special place with the earthy smell of wood emanating from benches on either side of the center aisle. She walked to her favorite bench, the third one from the front, with the perfect view of the stained glass behind the podium. Her gaze was drawn to the image of the risen Christ, etched into the glass.

Dad sat beside her but said nothing.

Questions welled up. So many she couldn't decide which to ask first. But her lips remained tightly clenched, like Kalu's as he'd waited patiently beside his dad in the clinic holding area. Why couldn't she open up? Dad was nothing like Mom. He would hear her out without interruption or contradiction.

Ellie leaned forward and placed her hands beside her thighs, wrapping her fingers around the edge of the bench. "I watched you and Yafatu from the hall window," she said, her voice low. "Brought back memories." She chanced a peek but saw nothing but love and sympathy reflected in his kind eyes.

She looked away before he could see the anguish in hers.

Dad poked the bench with his forefinger. "This is the very spot where you trusted Christ a little over two years ago."

She dropped her gaze to her hands, now folded on her lap. "It changed my life."

After a long silence, Dad spoke in a soft voice, almost to himself. "There was a prison guard on Cell Block C."

Ellie's heart raced. She straightened and shifted toward him. Dad rarely spoke of those days, but when he did, he had her full attention.

"He was there the night I was brought in. Hated me from day one and took every opportunity to let me know it. 'So all your millions couldn't buy you out of this one.' The inmates called him Ramrod." He gave her a sideways glance. "You can imagine why. It took years before I learned his real name."

Ellie placed her hand on her father's arm. He covered it with his own.

"He had some nicknames for me, too. Most I can't repeat. All meant to drive the wedge of guilt and shame even deeper, if that were possible. Roughed me up a bit at first. Looked the other way if other prisoners picked a fight."

Dad stopped talking and stared at the floor. Finally, he lifted his head and continued, "Anyway, you know the story. After four years of living hell, I hit rock bottom. Learned the truth about God and forgiveness. Trusted Christ"—he raised his open hand to the ceiling—"just as a ray from the rising sun shone through the tiny window of my cell."

A very familiar part of his story made all the more precious from the many sunrises they had shared.

Dad stood and walked to the stained glass. Ellie barely breathed as his fingers lovingly traced the image of Christ.

He turned to face her. "It changed my life just as it did yours." He walked to the side of the podium and let his arm rest on top. "I devoured the Bible like a starving man." He looked down and chuckled. "I guess I was starving. Starving for God's forgiveness and His unconditional love. And the more I grew in my faith, the more Ramrod resented it. I can still hear his smug taunts. 'This phoney religious show won't help you get paroled. You're nothing but drunken scum. You don't deserve to get out.' He was right, but I prayed anyway. I begged God to let me be released. That I'd do whatever I could to make amends to the Templeton family. To your mother. And to you and your sister Gwyneth. When my parole was denied, it hurt more than I can say. I knew God could've orchestrated my release. But He didn't."

He stared into space. "I started to doubt God's love. That time in my faith was a dark one. A very dark time, made even darker with Ramrod's daily jabs."

Ellie had heard her father's story many times, but still, she hung on his words, sensing there was something for her in them.

"But I clung to God and His word." Dad raised his hands, palms up. "Where else could I turn? I quit asking God 'why?' and started asking 'what?'"

Ellie slanted her head. This part she'd never heard. At least not that she remembered. "I don't understand."

"What?" he repeated. "What are you trying to teach me, God? What can I learn from this? I read every passage about prison. Joseph. Paul and Silas. Peter. Even Jonah in the belly of the whale. But the best passage was about Jesus and how he responded to his captors." His voice grew animated. "I tried an experiment. Every time Ramrod bullied me or hurled insults, I asked God to help me respond the way Christ would, with forgiveness and self-controlled dignity." Dad's face brightened. "Drove Ramrod crazy. Made him up the ante. But I was able, with God's help, to look him square in the face and tell him God loved him and wanted to forgive him, too."

Dad shook his head and chuckled. "Took quite a few hits

for that, but I kept it up, no matter what Ramrod dished out. And I prayed for God to break Ramrod's stubborn pride. Parole was denied three more times. Three years later, I was given my freedom. You see, Ellie, God could've orchestrated my release mere months after I became a Christian, but I would've missed so many blessings. Blessings and lessons I couldn't learn any other way. And I would've missed the biggest blessing of all: Leading my first convert to Christ."

"Ramrod?" Her hand flew to her mouth.

He nodded, his face alight with an inner glow. "We kept in touch until his death about twelve years ago."

Unbelievable. She closed her mouth and remained speechless, unable to form a response.

"So you see, our God is truly amazing and never wastes a tragedy."

His last words opened the faucet. Tears again. How many tears would she have to cry? She covered her face and rocked, her heavy breaths changing into deep sobs.

Dad sat down next to her and wrapped his arms tightly around her, like a life preserver keeping her from going under. "Pray ... for me." Her words came out in stilted breaths. "I—I feel myself ... sinking back."

"I am praying, honey. This isn't like last time. You're not alone." He tightened his hold. "God's arms are around you."

Dad's arms, not God's, held her. Strong and tangible. Her full weight sagged against his support. Would her faith ever be strong enough to trust the arms she couldn't feel?

# CHAPTER THIRTEEN

"Ellie and I will arrive on Wednesday, February 3." Eric looked at the date on the calendar on his desk. "That would be great, but I don't want to put you out. Yes, ma'am. Looking forward to seeing you too."

He ended his call to Joy Stockman, the woman who was watching his father's house in Washington. He drank the rest of his lukewarm coffee and checked the time before sending a text to Dad.

NEED TO RUN SOMETHING BY YOU. GOT A MINUTE?

MY OFFICE IN TEN MINUTES. Dad answered.

Perfect. Eric pocketed his phone. He eased down the hallway and inched the bedroom door open, careful not to make a sound. Ellie had needed no extra encouragement to rest after lunch. She remained huddled in a ball under the afghan he'd spread over her nearly an hour before. He studied her. The troubled crease still furrowed her brow, even in sleep.

Eric jotted a note for Ellie then jogged to the main building, with Lady keeping pace at his heels. This time next week they'd be back in Washington. Early February and most likely to-the-bone cold. Ellie would need some warmer clothes. Clothes shopping with a woman. Something new to add to his list of things he never thought he'd do.

Eric rounded the corner of the staff dormitory and entered through the side door directly across from the dining hall. Nicci was inside, her entire countenance happier than he'd seen her in a while.

Toby couldn't have asked her yet. He would've blabbed every detail this morning including her response.

Nicci continued setting plates and napkins on the table apparently unaware he stood at the doorway.

"You look cheerful. What's for dinner?"

She glanced up and gave a four-star smile. "Hello. I hope that means you plan to join us. Curried rice and beef tips. Ellie's favorite."

"Set two extra plates. We'll be here." With a wave, he walked to where two hallways intersected, the one to the left dimly lit and silent. Apparently, all surgeries had ended for the day. He went right, passing X-ray and pharmacy. Dad's office, the last room on the right of the long dormitory building, was situated to catch the last streaks of the setting sun. Eric checked the time. Barring interruptions, Dad would arrive at his usual brisk pace in exactly two minutes.

Eric wandered to the massive bookcase beside the window and clicked on the lamp. Medical books covering everything from internal surgery to tropical fevers dominated the top three shelves. The bottom shelves proved more to his interest. Bible commentaries, books about prayer, and biographies—mostly of people he'd never heard of. Except for David Livingston, the man whose heart remained buried somewhere here in the jungles of Africa.

Eric scanned the titles, searching for more clues into what made Brock Whitfield the best man he'd ever known. The caliber of man Eric could only hope to be one day.

Steps sounded from the hallway. Muffled from soft-soled shoes, but definitely the brisk step Eric's ear knew well.

"Sorry to keep you waiting." Dad gave Eric the trademark hug, sideways with an extra squeeze upon release. "Please, sit."

Eric took the chair in front of the desk. "I just got here myself. I was admiring your collection of books."

Dad nodded and cut his gaze to the bookcase. "My favorites are actually on a shelf in my bedroom. Feel free to read any you like."

"I appreciate that."

Dad folded his hands on the desk and gave him a direct

look. "How's Ellie doing?"

He hadn't planned to lead with the Ellie topic, but maybe getting it out of the way was best. "Tuckered out. I left her sleeping."

Dad gave a knowing smile. "She lasted longer than I thought she would."

Eric shifted and leaned forward, tapping his fingers together. "That's one thing I wanted to discuss. Ellie hasn't told me anything about losing the baby."

"Maybe I can fill you in. What would you like to know?"

"It's not that. What concerns me is her silence. I've never known her to keep things bottled up inside." Eric rubbed the back of his neck. "Granted, I've only known her for less than a year."

"Hmm." Dad gripped his chin and hooked his finger against his mouth. "I see what you mean."

"Ellie tries to act like everything's okay, but she can't hide the sadness. Her eyes have lost their spark. Today I told her all about Toby's rescue, hoping she would talk about losing the baby. But she didn't. So, bottom line: should I try to get her to open up or just wait it out?"

Dad tapped his mouth with his balled-up fist and gave Eric a long, contemplative stare.

Eric settled back in his chair and stretched out his legs, crossing his feet. Maybe he could speed things up. "My gut is telling me to give her space. That's what I'd want her to do for me. But losing this baby hit her hard. I just don't know how to help."

Dad's eyes narrowed. "You two will be leaving for Washington next week?"

Eric nodded.

"The change will do her good. By the way, she needs to see a good OB-GYN. In fact, it would be good to set up an appointment before you leave."

Eric made a mental note to call Joy again.

"She needs time, love, and understanding. Things you are very well-equipped to give her."

"Yes, sir." Eric zoned in, hoping Dad would throw in something a little more concrete.

"A woman's emotions are often precarious. Hormone imbalances especially connected to a pregnancy send a woman on an emotional roller coaster. I spoke with her a little today. Ellie fears she's slipping back into depression." He dropped his chin and peered over his glasses. "I don't think she actually is, but the fear has her paralyzed. I think that's why she's pushing herself to come back to work."

She'd opened up to her dad but not to him. The realization stung more than he wanted to admit. But how could he blame her? He was doing the same.

"When you get to Washington, try to connect with a good local church. Maybe one with a counseling service."

Eric nodded. "I found a church I liked when I stayed with my dad. Couldn't attend much, but I really liked the pastor."

"Excellent."

Eric switched to a safer subject. An update on Toby. Except the part about asking Nicci to marry him. Unlike Toby, he could be discreet. "Toby's found a buyer for his transport business."

"So soon?"

Eric nodded. "A mining company. He's giving them a good price, one they couldn't walk away from. But Tobe's keeping one helicopter and the Cessna."

Dad leaned back in his chair. "I assume he told you his plans to marry Nicci."

So much for discretion. If the knucklehead wasn't careful, Nicci would find out before he had a chance to pop the question. "Yes. I think this kidnapping episode lit a fire under him."

"I think you're right. He talked it over with me before he left. When everything gets settled, he'll be working for me fulltime. He already flies in most of our supplies. It's about time we made it official."

Eric rubbed the gravelly stubble on his chin and took a deep breath. Now or never. "There's one more thing."

"Sure." Dad nodded his encouragement.

He spit out the words before he lost his courage. "I'm afraid I'm going to lose Ellie."

Dad's eyes widened. "You're afraid she'll leave you?"

"That she'll die. Or be killed. I have nightmares about her being in danger. She always dies before I can reach her." Eric curled his fingers around the armrest. "Just last night, I dreamed we were in the plane flying over the Atlantic. Ellie went to the bathroom and got sucked out of the plane when she flushed the toilet."

Dad nodded, his expression maintaining a wide, innocent stare.

"She screamed. I broke down the door. There was this gaping hole with Ellie free-falling, her hands outstretched to me. Crazy, I know."

"Have you told Ellie about these dreams?"

Eric shook his head. "She knows I have dreams, but I haven't told her what they're about. Figure one person being freaked out is enough. Dad, tell me straight up. Is this God trying to prepare me for her death?"

"No. I don't think so."

The vice around Eric's chest loosened considerably.

"Here's why I say that: God has not given us the spirit of fear. Now, I'm no psychologist, but these dreams may have more to do with your former profession than with a premonition of her death. You lived a violent life. Death was the reality. You're probably processing that you no longer have to be on red alert."

Made sense. Had to give him that. "Got any advice about how to make them stop?"

"Hmm." Another long pause. "Usually what we fear most are the very areas that are not fully surrendered."

Checkmate. A chill settled over him. Words he'd heard before. Last summer, before he lost his leg. The vice returned. And tightened. Eric looked away, unable to meet Dad's penetrating gaze.

Dad's chair creaked as he pushed back from the desk and rose. He dragged another chair closer and sat next to Eric. "Listen to me, son." He placed his hand on Eric's shoulder. "Do you realize what a miracle it was for you to be brought here to this obscure hospital? Only our great God could've orchestrated something that spectacular. You recovered from wounds that should've killed you. And you came to know Jesus, I'm sure because of the far-reaching prayers of your father," his voice faltered, "who died before he could share the truth with you himself."

Eric turned to look at Dad. "Your prayers, too."

"Yes. My prayers. That's what I'm trying to tell you. We have a powerful God who loves us and answers prayer. Nothing is too hard for Him. Don't you see? You can trust God. Yes, I know you're thinking: He allowed your leg to be taken."

Eric sucked in his breath. Dad was a better psychologist than he gave himself credit.

"It broke all of our hearts, but through that tragedy, the man who raised you came to know Christ, too. God is too good to be unkind. You can trust Him to take care of Ellie."

"I know what you're saying is true. I just don't know how to get my heart to accept it."

"Tell God your fears. Ask Him to help strengthen your faith and reveal why you're having these recurring nightmares. He does want to enlighten us, you know."

Eric studied the patterned rug under his feet, his thoughts like the geometric shapes. Cluttered and disjointed.

Dad patted Eric's back. "Don't be too hard on yourself. You remind me of myself in my early days of being a Christian. So hungry to know Him more and understand things that seemed beyond my comprehension. I'm proud of you. I wouldn't be surprised if God called you into some kind of ministry one day."

Eric's head jerked up. How could Dad know he'd been thinking the same thing?

"Maybe one day Nicholas Templeton's son will take up the mantle his father left behind."

Eric leaned forward, his steepled fingers pressed against his lips. "Thanks for talking this out with me. You've given me a lot to think about. I really appreciate your advice. And prayers."

"Don't you worry, son. God has given me great peace about you. And Ellie."

# FREEING ELLIE

# CHAPTER FOURTEEN

Ellie settled into the leather seat of her Dad's Gulfstream, unsure if the butterflies dancing in her stomach were from excitement or fear. Probably both.

Eric stowed their luggage in the back and tweaked her arm as he took the aisle seat beside her. He pulled the strap across his chest and clicked the buckle into place. "Ready, Mrs. Templeton?"

"Ready."

The plane started to move, and Eric leaned forward to wave. Ellie scrunched closer to him and caught the last glimpse of her dad and Mac standing by the Land Rover. The plane revved for takeoff and thundered down the field.

"Actually, I'm excited to get away." Her voice vibrated with the plane.

She pressed her nose against the double-paned window as the plane left the ground. A perfect day with the sun cresting the horizon. "Dad would love this."

The plane leveled.

Ellie sat back in the seat. "What time will we get there?"

"With the five-hour difference, sometime around nineteen hundred."

Ellie gave him a blank look. Nineteen hundred? She tapped her fingers, counting from noon.

"Sorry. Seven o'clock. And we'll have some major jet lag. Joy's cooking dinner for us."

"Tell me more about her."

"She's a female version of your dad. I wouldn't have made it through the last week of my dad's life without Joy Stockman. The minute she entered his bedroom, peace came in with her. My dad always calmed down when she was there."

Ellie reached for Eric's hand. "She sounds amazing."

"One classy lady, for sure. You can't help but love her. She offered to move out while we were there, but I asked her to stay so you could get to know her. She's getting the master bedroom ready for us, which will be extremely weird."

"Weird?"

"To sleep in Bob Templeton's room. I'll probably feel his disapproving glare on me the whole time we're there."

Spoken as a joke, but Eric's lopsided smile couldn't mask the pain in his eyes. Ellie squeezed his hand and bounced it on her thigh for emphasis. "I'm glad you had time with your dad before he died. That you got to know him better."

"He was a hard man to get to know." Eric looked away and stared out the opposite window for a long time. "Those months were like God's boot camp, only in hostile territory. I spent hours reading the Bible. It was my lifeline. Kept me from going under." Eric turned and met her gaze. "I prayed for my dad to accept Christ, but in my heart I knew it was impossible. Not even God could make that happen."

"But it did happen."

"An honest-to-God miracle." Eric paused, his jaw working with emotion. "I'll never forget the day Dad trusted Christ. I thought my heart would burst. I finally understood what you and your dad had been telling me all along about how God really cares about the details in our lives."

It struck Ellie this was the second conversation in less than a week that important people in her life had told her stories she already knew. Why? Was God trying to tell her something she'd missed the first time?

"Another miracle happened the day Dad died."

"What was that?" Ellie remained very still, soaking in everything Eric said.

"I was able to thank God, and mean it, for losing my leg." He paused. "'Cause there was no way I would've spent three months with Dad if that hadn't happened."

Thank God and mean it? Surely God wouldn't expect that of her.

"Ellie, I know you're hurting."

She dropped her gaze. "I guess I'm not hiding it too well."

"Why would you want to hide your pain?"

She shook her head and shrugged, still not meeting his eyes. "Because, it's not just pain. It's my whole rotten attitude."

He shifted to angle his body more toward hers. "I want to help."

"That's the problem. I shouldn't be struggling. God has been so good to me. Literally snatched me from the jaws of death when I overdosed. I wasn't supposed to be here. And every day I get now is just extra. So I shouldn't be sinking back into depression. But I am, no matter how much I pray or try to be thankful."

"Don't beat yourself up, baby. Your heart took a big hit. It'll take some time to recover."

"What if I don't recover? I feel myself slipping back into the hole. What if it swallows me up and I never find my way out?"

Eric smiled and wrapped his hand around her wrist like a cuff. "Then I'll walk through it with you."

"I'm serious, Eric."

"So am I." He lowered his tone, his voice almost a whisper. "Stop worrying about what you should or should not be feeling. It is what it is. But promise me something."

She tensed. Her last promise, to be there when he returned from the mission, ended up with a miscarriage and her almost hemorrhaging to death.

"Promise you won't bottle up your pain. Talk about whatever you're feeling. To me. Or Dad. Anybody. Just don't try to handle it alone."

Some of the tightness left her chest. "I think I can do that." After a little pause, she added, "I want to try again. For a baby."

"Now? Here?" His eyes glinted with amusement.

Ellie squeezed and jolted the hand he still held. "You know what I mean."

He grinned. "I'm just trying to provoke a dimple out of you."

She complied and twisted her lips enough to produce it.

Eric clutched his heart with his free hand. "Slays me every time."

She bypassed his attempt to cheer her up. "I think the sooner I get pregnant again, the sooner this funk will leave."

"Okay, here's what you need to do. Make a list of questions for the doctor. How soon we can try for another baby can top the list."

Finally, he was taking her seriously. "Good plan."

"Feel better?"

She nodded, her smile and dimple genuine this time.

Eric took a deep breath and released it. "So do I."

# CHAPTER FIFTEEN

The night was pitch black and bitterly cold as the taxi slid next to the curb at 1516 Chestnut Lane. Felt more like midnight than seven. "No thanks. I've got them." Eric took their bags from the driver, slipped him two folded bills, and waved him away.

Ellie stood on the walkway chafing her arms to keep warm. "I'm having major déja vu."

So was he. Three months had gone by since the night of his dad's funeral when Ellie and her father had spent the night. Seemed longer. Eric scooped up the luggage and followed her to the front door. The knot he usually got in the pit of his stomach anytime he approached his father's house resurfaced. Considerably smaller, but still there.

Ellie paused at the door. "Should we knock?"

Eric tried the knob. "Unlocked. Let's just go in."

The aroma of something decidedly Italian hit them the moment he pushed open the door. Joy Stockman rounded the corner from the kitchen, her face alight with warmth and welcome. "Hello. Just in time."

Being met by a woman in his childhood home who actually seemed pleased to see him was a new experience, one that caused an unexpected lump to form in his throat. Eric dropped the luggage in the foyer at the foot of the stairs and met Joy halfway through the living room. "It's good to see you again."

She returned his hug, smiling up at him. "Married life seems to agree with you."

"Yes, ma'am." Eric turned and took Ellie's hand. "This beautiful lady is the reason. Joy. Ellie."

Joy opened her arms for a hug. "So happy to meet you.

I've heard some wonderful things about you."

"I've heard great things about you, too. And what is that scrumptious smell coming from the kitchen?"

"Lasagna."

Ellie clapped her hands together and glanced at him, her eyes sparkling. "Oh my goodness. I haven't had lasagna in over two years."

Joy smiled, looking pleased. "My son's favorite. I took a chance you'd like it, too." She waved her hand toward the stairs and turned back to the kitchen. "Go get settled while I put the garlic bread in the oven. We can eat in ten minutes."

"I've got it, baby." Eric took the bag from Ellie's hand and juggled the other two pieces of luggage. He dropped the bags in the doorway of his father's old bedroom. "Unbelievable."

Definitely not the same room his father had occupied for over thirty-six years. The new bed drew his attention. Larger, outfitted with a white down comforter and moved from the center of the room to the left wall facing the master bathroom. Light gray walls replaced dark paneling dated from the seventies. Wood-grained laminate instead of shag carpeting the color of dirt. The dresser, understated but beautiful, matched the bed. And the ragged recliner, the one he'd slept in the last two weeks before his father died, was gone too. In its place, a computer table complete with a laptop, and a gray leather computer chair.

Ellie squeezed past him into the room. "Wow. This looks different from the last time I saw it."

"You can say that again."

She took off her shoes and fell backward on the bed. "Feels like heaven."

Joy came up the stairs and stood beside Eric at the door. He turned to her. "I'm blown away."

"When you told me I could make changes, I took you

seriously. I kept all your father's things, by the way. They're in storage."

Ellie left the bed and joined them. "This is beautiful. I love the colors you used."

"Even looks bigger." Eric shook his head. "I don't know what to say."

"Consider it my wedding present to you and Ellie."

Eric gave her a sideways hug and kissed her cheek.

Ellie hugged her from the other side. "Best present ever. Thank you so much."

"You're very welcome. Are you kids ready to eat?"

"Yes." Ellie grabbed Eric's hand and tugged him down the stairs after Joy. "We're starving."

Eric settled Ellie into bed and slipped back downstairs, still too keyed up to sleep. Joy stood at the kitchen counter raking meaty cat food into a bowl.

"Lucky. There you are, fat and sassy as ever." Eric scratched the fur between the fluffy orange tabby's ears. Lucky responded with an obligatory smear of her face against his hand but quickly returned to rub the legs of the source of her food.

"She's a little miffed with me. I put her outside so we could eat in peace." Joy placed Lucky's food on a mat by the back door.

Eric shook his head. "That cat was a total bag of bones when I found her by a dumpster last year. You'd never know it now."

"No. I'll admit I've spoiled her a little. I felt so sorry for her after your father died. She slept outside his closed bedroom door for days after you left.

"Poor thing. I still can't believe he let her sleep with him." Eric opened the fridge. "Would you like some water?"

"Yes, please. Italian food always makes me thirsty."

Eric handed her a bottle and took another one for himself. "Joy, that dinner was outstanding."

She chuckled and focused her attention on the counter she was wiping. "It was nice to cook for someone other than myself."

Eric sat at the table and scanned the room. Even the kitchen cabinets had been repainted. "This place has needed a woman's touch for a long time. I can't thank you enough."

She sat across from him. "You're very welcome. Truthfully, I'm the one who should be thanking you. Living here has breathed new life into me. I needed to get out of the house my husband and I had shared. Too many memories. I'm starting to get my joy back."

Her words surprised him. She hid her pain well. Like Ellie. Maybe it was something women did naturally. "I'm glad it worked out for both of us."

Lucky finished eating and came over to rub against Joy's chair. She picked Lucky up and smiled. "My husband hated cats."

"So did my dad."

"Really?"

"Oh yeah. I'm surprised Lucky survived the first night with him."

She laughed. "I guess you won him over, didn't you, girl? Oh. Before I forget." Joy pushed Lucky off her lap and rose. "I'll be right back." Joy returned with a business card. "Ellie's appointment is on Friday with Dr. Conley."

Eric took the card. Dr. Travis Conley was the fourth name of ten doctors listed for this particular clinic.

Joy answered his unspoken question. "Before I worked with hospice, I was a surgical nurse at Central Memorial. Trust me. Dr. Conley is the guy you want. Really champions the unborn. Specializes in high-risk pregnancies. I had to pull a few strings to get Ellie in, but he'll be worth it."

"I really appreciate that." Eric tapped the card on the table. "Losing the baby hit Ellie hard."

Joy nodded. "I can imagine. I hope I can spend some time with her. Get to know her."

"That would be great. I think you have some things in common."

"And what about you, Eric? How has life been for you in Africa?" Joy clasped her hands and leaned forward.

Not for the first time, Eric wondered if she had a secondary degree in psychology. Joy Stockman had a way of breaking through his defensive barriers, much like Brock Whitfield had. "I'm happier than I've ever been. Happier than I thought possible for a guy like me."

She gave him a questioning glance. "A guy like you?"

"You know. My former profession."

"Oh. I see. Do you miss your former profession?"

Eric chuckled. "Ellie asks me that all the time."

Joy laughed with him. "I'd probably ask, too, if I'd married someone from the CIA."

"To answer your question. No. I don't miss the profession at all."

"But?"

"I don't know." Eric drummed his fingers on the table. "I guess I miss having a purpose."

The compassion evident in her eyes made it clear she understood. "What do you do there?"

"Help out anywhere I can, even if it's donating blood. There's always something to do. I help Mac, the maintenance man. We do yard work. Make deliveries. But probably my favorite thing to do is hunt."

Her eyes widened. "Big game?"

He shook his head. "Small game. The Angolese nationals don't get enough protein. Some of the maintenance crew and I hunt, kill, process, and deliver anything from wild pig to several variations of antelope."

"Impressive."

"Well, it's better than hunting humans like I used to do. I can't save their lives, but I can help feed them. And the Angolese nationals are some of the most humble and grateful people on the planet. You should come visit sometime."

She took a sip of water and dabbed at her mouth. "I've actually considered it."

"You said you were a surgical nurse?"

She nodded. "For twenty-five years."

Eric smiled. Brock Whitfield didn't stand a chance.

# CHAPTER SIXTEEN

Ellie scooted to the middle of the bed, hoping to scrunch up to Eric's warm back. Her hand slid across cool sheets without encountering anything solid. Hmm. She raised her head and peeked at the clock on the bedside table. After eight. His pillow definitely held the imprint of his head, confirming he had, in fact, come to bed sometime during the night. The guy functioned on very little sleep, unlike her. She needed eight good hours and maybe a nap thrown in for good measure. Bless him. He could move through the room like a ghost, never waking her. She, on the other hand, hadn't quite mastered the trick. Even with full lighting she seemed to bump into every jutting corner of the room.

She lay on her back and yawned, contorting her body in a lazy stretch. Totally relaxed and at peace. She would've stayed in the marvelous bed a while longer, but nature called. Ellie's feet hit the cold smoothness of the laminate flooring. Definitely not in Africa anymore. She clicked on the bathroom light and held her head sideways to read the pink Post-it note stuck on the mirror. *Getting agency stuff out of the way. Joy can take you shopping if you're up for it.*

She was always up for shopping. And what agency stuff? Ellie rummaged in her bag for her robe and slippers. Coffee first. Unpack later. She combed through her hair with her fingers as she bopped down the stairs.

Joy closed the Bible in front of her and smiled as Ellie entered the kitchen. "Good morning. Did you sleep well?"

"Surprisingly well. I don't think I moved all night. Oh, good. Coffee."

Joy started to rise.

"Please don't get up." Ellie went to the counter and

poured from the carafe in the still-lit coffeemaker. She cradled the cup and brought it closer to her face, closing her eyes and deeply inhaling the aromatic steam. "Hmm. Smells wonderful."

"Can't take credit. I told Eric he had coffee duty while you guys are here."

Ellie laughed and sat across from Joy. "He has perfected the art of making coffee."

"I would have to agree with that." Joy fingered the notepad beside her Bible. "I'm making a grocery list. Any requests?"

Ellie took a sip of coffee. "I'm still waking up. Let me think about it."

Joy nodded and left the table, notepad in hand. She opened a narrow door in the corner of the room and scanned the items in a very small pantry.

Ellie used the time to discreetly study the woman who had made such a favorable impression on Eric. Petite. Not pencil thin, like her mother who'd obsessed about the slightest hint of cellulite. But not plump either. The amethyst sweater she wore over dark gray slacks was most likely cashmere. The swirls of teal and vivid purple in the accent scarf produced a stunning effect. Her black leather boots had enough of a heel to offset her shortness. Eric hadn't exaggerated. Classy lady, for sure. And stylish. Beautiful silver hair, layered and shaped to fall naturally just below her ears.

Joy returned to the table and jotted more things on the list. "Have you thought of anything yet?"

Ellie straightened and took a guilty gulp of coffee. "Not yet."

Joy's deep blue eyes seemed to pick up the color of her sweater. "Are you sure I can't make you something to eat?"

Ellie shook her head and leaned back in her chair. "I think I'm still stuffed from that wonderful meal last night. I hope there are some leftovers."

"I'm afraid there's a ton left. I've never been good at making just a little. I usually have to freeze the leftovers."

"Don't freeze anything just yet. I might even eat some for breakfast." Ellie grinned and now felt awake enough to get a good up close look at Joy. The woman's expressive face held warmth and wrinkles, untouched by a surgeon's knife or botox injections. Somehow, Joy seemed more attractive than Ellie's own mother, who had taken advantage of both.

"Eric mentioned you might need some warmer clothes. Big snow storm predicted for tonight."

Ellie almost jumped out of her seat. "Like a blizzard?"

Joy laughed. "Very possibly. I have a ladies' Bible study this morning, and then I'll stop for some groceries. I'll come back around noon to unload them, and then we could go to the mall if you'd like."

"Actually, would you mind if I tag along this morning?"

"I would love it, but I didn't want to wear you out your first day."

"Oh no. Shopping energizes me."

"Girl, you're speaking my language. Think you can be ready in thirty minutes?"

Ellie pushed back her chair. "Absolutely." She scampered out of the room and then backtracked. "Forgot my cup."

Joy waved her away. "I'll take care of it."

"Thank you." Good thing she'd showered the night before. Ellie raced upstairs and dug around for the warmest outfit she could find. Jeans and a sweater. It'd do until she could get a decent coat.

A few minutes later, Joy knocked and spoke, her voice muffled through the closed door. "You might need to borrow this."

Ellie opened to find Joy holding a black wool pea coat. Ellie hesitated. "Are you sure? Don't you need it?"

"I have another one. It might be a little big, though.

You're such a petite thing."

"No. It's perfect. Thank you so much."

"You're welcome. Gloves are in the pocket. Are you ready?"

"Almost. Give me five minutes."

Joy nodded. "Take your time. Would you like a bagel to eat on the road?"

"No, thanks. Too excited."

"Okay. I'll be downstairs."

Ellie returned to the bathroom to brush her teeth and put on a little makeup. After a final glance in the mirror, she pulled on the coat as she breezed down the stairs.

"All set?"

Ellie nodded and followed Joy to the side door leading to the garage. The sleek, dark gray BMW confirmed what Ellie already suspected. Joy Stockman was an independently wealthy woman.

"Beautiful car."

"Thank you. My late husband owned several car dealerships. Always kept me in nice cars. Truth is, I'd much rather have him than the cars."

A passing comment that spoke volumes. Ellie floundered for something to say and settled for a sympathetic nod.

Joy buckled in and pressed a button on the side of her door. "Brrr. Let's get that seat-heat going."

The garage door rattled and creaked its way to the top. An American sound she'd almost forgotten.

Joy angled her body to look behind and backed the car down the driveway. "You'll like the ladies' Bible study."

"I've never been to one. In fact, I've never been to an actual church before. I became a believer after I went to Africa. We have a chapel on the compound where we worship. But I'd like to see how it's done in America."

"How long have you been in Africa?"

"In July, it will be three years. What about you? When did you become a believer?"

"I grew up in church. My dad was a deacon. My mother a Sunday school teacher. So I didn't stand a chance. When I was nine, I finally understood what it meant to accept Christ. I'm very grateful for my Christian heritage."

No wonder Joy seemed so full of love and warmth. Being a Christian must be second nature to someone like her.

"Here we are." Joy pulled into a parking area of a building that looked a lot like a large warehouse. Nothing grand or ornate like some of the churches in the Dallas/Fort Worth area where Ellie had grown up. Cold air blasted her and almost took her breath away as she opened the car door. They hurried up the sidewalk to glass double doors.

Inside, they followed the sound of laughter and voices to a room with padded folding chairs arranged in a large semi-circle. Women of all ages and sizes greeted them in a whirlwind of hugs, smiles, and welcomes.

Joy leaned over and whispered, "The lady closing the door is the assistant pastor's wife."

Ellie turned and gave a discreet glance, catching only the back of a tall woman with sleek, shoulder length hair.

"Karin Holsombeck. Absolutely amazing. You'll love her."

Ellie peeked again, finally comprehending the significance as the woman went to the podium in front of the chairs.

"Hello, everyone. Thank you for coming on this cold February morning." Karin picked up a stack of paper and handed it to the woman sitting nearest her. "Take a study guide and pass the rest down." She grabbed some pens and held them up. "Does anyone need one?"

Ellie waited until two other women raised their hands to admit she needed a pen, too. Karin moved closer, extending her hand. "I didn't get a chance to meet you. I'm Karin

Holsombeck."

Ellie took the pen and smiled, relieved when Joy took over. "This is my friend Ellie Templeton. She and her husband are visiting all the way from Africa."

Karin's eyes widened. "Oh my. You've come a long way. We're so happy you could join us."

Ellie thanked her and blew out a shaky breath as Karin stepped back to the podium. Ellie's stomach rumbled and a new fear seized her. Maybe she should've eaten that bagel after all. *Please, God. Keep my stomach quiet.*

The study guides made it to her. She took one and passed the rest down. The word **"faith"** was written at the top in bold print and underneath, the sub-heading: *How to Trust God When He Doesn't Make Sense.*

The first line had two blanks to fill in and very early into the lesson, Karin supplied the answers: Faith does not eliminate <u>questions</u>, but faith knows where to <u>take</u> them.

Something she struggled with for sure, especially now. For the next hour, Ellie drank in every word, filling in the blanks of her study guide.

Near the end, Karin opened up the floor for comments or questions. After a short pause, a woman spoke up, reciting a list of her physical ailments. Karin nodded and murmured a sympathetic comment before looking to the other side of the semi-circle of chairs. "Anyone else have something to add?"

It seemed Karin was looking directly at her. Ellie cringed and dropped her gaze, refusing to make eye contact. Just entering this room of strangers had used up her quota of courage. No way would she open the deep secrets of her heart to people she didn't know.

Thankfully, she didn't have to. The girl next to her must have felt Karin was looking at her, too. Ellie managed a quick peek, so grateful someone else had the courage to speak up. The girl, probably no more than twenty, spoke in a tremulous voice. "Sometimes when things are going great, it's easy to trust God. But when something bad happens—" The girl paused and twisted her fingers. Ellie held her breath and resisted the urge to raise her own hand to twist a strand of hair.

The girl continued in the tight voice of someone trying hard not to break down, "Most of you know my brother was killed in a car accident two days before Christmas."

Karin nodded, her face full of compassion.

"It was hard. For all of our family. He was planning to ask his girlfriend to marry him on Christmas Eve. And I'm still struggling. Because I know deep down God could've stopped the accident. But He didn't. And I don't know ... It feels like God is a million miles away."

"Thank you so much for your honesty. I bet every one of us could relate to what Janice has been feeling." Karin nodded, her gaze panning the rest of the ladies as if seeking confirmation. "And I'm so sorry. You and I have talked a lot about Danny and how hard his death was on your family. It's never easy, but here's what I've learned when God doesn't seem to make sense."

Ellie held her breath and waited for the magic answer.

"First of all, let me assure you God is not far away. One of my favorite verses is Psalm 46:1. "God is our refuge and strength, a *very present* help in trouble." I call it my Faith B-12. When God feels far away, I quote that verse. Very present. That means He is readily available. Have you ever tried to call somebody, and it went straight to voice mail?"

Everybody nodded.

"Isn't that frustrating? Well, this verse is a promise. God will never send your prayers to voice mail."

Ellie jotted down the reference and Karin's words.

"So what do we do when God doesn't seem to hear or respond? Verse ten gives us the answer. 'Be still and know that I am God.' Sometimes He wants us to wait. To be still. It's the hardest part of faith. Waiting on God, and letting God be God. Even when it feels like the world is crashing down around us.

"You know, sometimes God is so good, you can almost feel His arms around you. But like Janice said, when something really bad happens, it's easy to doubt God's love and His ability to help the situation. You get blindsided. It may be something little. Or it may be something catastrophic, like in verse two when the earth is removed and the mountains are carried into the midst of the sea.

"I don't know if you can relate, but when that happens to me, I kind of get my feelings hurt. I might even get a little mad and quit talking to Him for a while."

She was singing Ellie's song. Everything out of Karin's mouth resonated with her.

"And that only makes me miserable," Karin continued. "Makes everything worse. But here's the good news: God loves us. Did you hear me? God. Loves. Us. He doesn't go away or quit orchestrating things in our lives for good. Sometimes we don't see the good. But God promises He is good."

Karin closed her Bible and stepped in front of the podium, obviously speaking from her heart. "Here's your takeaway, something you military wives can relate to: Always retreat to the truth. Not your feelings. Feelings change just as much as our Washington weather. But God is faithful. He won't change. We can trust Him."

*Retreat to the truth. Not my feelings.* Ellie wrote fast and hoped she'd be able to read her writing later.

And even as she scribbled the words, a tiny ray of light broke through the dark cell of her depression.

# CHAPTER SEVENTEEN

Eric stood on the back patio, the only warmth the coffee mug in his hand. A heavy blanket of snow had already re-sculpted the backyard and cast an iridescent glow in the dark, predawn hours. The first good snow he'd seen in two years. He inhaled deeply, letting cold air fill his lungs. Still coming down at a fairly good clip, an occasional horizontal burst of icy pellets would whip across his face. He backed to a patio chair and swiped the surface clean of snow. A shiver ripped through him as he sat on freezing vinyl. The cold dug deep into his old wounds. He used the heel of his open palm to massage his right shoulder, still stiff and tender from the ambush Reznik orchestrated against him almost a year before.

He should go in soon, but not yet. Snow-muffled air held a holy hush that filled Eric with peace. He placed the empty cup on the patio table and leaned forward with clasped hands. "Thank You, God." His quiet words sent out a frosty cloud. "For changing the entire course of my life." Gratitude welled up as it always did whenever he took the time to go through the list. "You saved me. My life. My soul."

His own thoughts interrupted his prayer. This week's visit to headquarters stirred up old memories. And wounds. Seeing a new secretary at Mildred Ware's old desk hit him harder than the new name placard outside his father's office door. Eric walked the cold, gray hallways with blinders off as he greeted fellow agents. Hollow shells just like he used to be. Good men with honor and courage but lacking true contentment that only came from knowing God. Did they feel the same emptiness he'd always felt after a mission?

"God, You filled the hole that had been in my heart for as long as I can remember. I don't deserve it. But I thank You for this wonderful life. For Ellie."

His mind went there, to the nightmares. To the possibility of facing life without Ellie. "I don't know what You're trying to tell me." He held up his hands, palms up. "About the next step in my life. About Ellie. But I'm listening."

The kitchen light clicked on. Eric grabbed his empty cup and pushed open the back door.

Joy gasped and spun around like a sumo wrestler, wielding the spoon she held like a weapon. "Eric!" Her left hand clutched her chest, crushing the folds of her bathrobe. "You're up early."

"Yes, ma'am." He hid his grin. "I was going to say the same about you. I'm sorry I startled you."

She relaxed from her battle-ready stance and placed her hand on his arm. "Don't apologize. Oh my goodness. You feel like ice. How's it look out there?"

"Like a winter wonderland."

She walked to the door and looked into the backyard. "Beautiful." She turned and spoke, her voice muffled as she took two boxes and cooking oil from the pantry. "I need to visit one of my patients who took a turn for the worse last night. Thought I'd take some muffins. You and Ellie will be on your own today."

"I hate for you to get out in this mess. I'll be glad to drive you."

"No. No. I'm used to it. Once I get on the main road, I'll be fine." Joy bustled around, pulling out a stainless steel mixing bowl from under the counter.

"They're blessed to have someone like you." Eric placed his arm around her shoulder and kissed her cheek. "What time do you plan to leave?"

Joy smiled and returned his hug. "Thank you. Eight o'clock."

"Okay. I'll be right back." He used his phone to light a

path through the still-darkened bedroom. Ellie lay curled in a ball, her golden hair fanned out across the pillow and her face tucked under the cover. After grabbing his boots and overcoat, Eric returned to the kitchen to put them on.

Joy placed two metal muffin pans in the oven. "I'm making a double batch so I can leave you and Ellie some."

"Excellent." Eric trudged past her to the garage door. His breath blew like smoke as he turned sideways to slide between the front of the cars and the wall. His destination, the peg board on the far wall beside his Mustang where various yard tools hung on a hook. He reached for the wide shovel Dad had always used for clearing the driveway. The garage door creaked and groaned. Snow crunched under his feet as he stepped gingerly, testing the traction of his prosthesis. Not much difference, thanks to his boots. He planted his feet and delved into the mound of snow with the shovel. Brought back memories. He'd done this same chore hundreds of times as a kid. Not something he thought he'd ever do again. He powered through the pain every time his stiff shoulder bore down on the hilt of the shovel. No doubt about it, he'd pay for this morning's workout for days to come.

He'd been at it hard for fifteen minutes when the front door opened. Ellie came out wearing a bright pink snow suit, stocking cap, scarf, gloves and heavy duty boots. Her hand swung out to catch the wisps of snow still falling. "Wow. This is so beautiful."

Eric propped the shovel and leaned on the handle. "Look at you in your new play clothes. Let me guess. You've got bright pink long johns on under there?"

"Maybe." She grinned and stepped gingerly onto the driveway with a death grip on her coffee mug. "Want a sip?"

He wiped his face with the back of his sleeve and tried not to make a face when he tasted the sweetened concoction Ellie thought was coffee. "Thanks."

"You're actually breaking a sweat in … what? Zero degree weather?"

"Married life has made me soft."

Ellie placed the cup on the porch and rubbed her gloved hands together. "Got another shovel?"

"Afraid not. Dad was a practical man. Never saw the need for two shovels when he only had one son."

"Hmm. Guess I'll have to build a snowman with the excess snow from your pile."

Eric nodded and scooped the shovel under the next section to be cleared. Ellie stepped over the hedge of snow he'd piled beside the driveway and used her boot to burrow out a space for the snowman. "Gray," she said.

He paused and turned. "Gray?"

"My long underwear. But with tiny pink flowers."

He grinned and nodded. "Good to know."

Ellie got on her knees and spread her arms wide, scooping huge mounds of snow toward the middle of the yard.

He decided to turn away and work facing the street, or he'd never get the job done. After a couple of minutes, he slid the shovel deep into a thick pile of snow and heaved it up, sending powdery pellets like a bomb blast Ellie's way.

"Eric!"

He tried but failed to keep a straight face. Her eyes glinted with amused determination as she packed snow into her gloved hand and with a huffing "Umph," hurled the lopsided ball. The snowball whizzed past without his even having to dodge. She threw another one.

Game on. Eric dove behind a snow-covered bush. He kept his head low and scraped together five rounded balls. He raised his head for a peek and got nailed right between the eyes. He wiped slush from his face in time to see her expression change from triumph to concern.

"Oh, honey." Ellie stood and came toward him. "I'm so

sorry."

He seized the opportunity, rapid-firing his ready-made arsenal, pummeling her chest, shoulders, and forehead.

Ellie squealed and dove behind the wall of shoveled snow. "That's it. No more Mr. Nice Girl."

"Mr. Nice Girl?" He laughed and poked his head out, giving her the perfect target. A mistake he wouldn't make again.

"You know what I mean. Take that." She threw more ammunition his way.

Eric ducked, reloaded, and took off his stocking cap, easing it up with a stick. His decoy strategy paid off and gave him time to tuck snowball ammo into the crook of his arm and take a flying leap into enemy territory.

Ellie screamed as he jumped the snow wall barricade. Instead of launching a counterattack, she stood and turned so he could only hit her backside. Eric moved in and tackled, shielding her by falling first and taking her down with him. He rolled with her, tumbling down the slope of his father's yard.

They landed with Ellie on bottom, laughing up at him. Eric brushed hair and snow away from her face and smiled down at her. He held her gaze for a long moment. "I've missed your laughter." Before she could answer, he lowered his lips to hers. An affectionate kiss that deepened in the exhilaration of the moment. Her lips were cold and tasted of sweet coffee. He raised his head. Ellie smiled and slid her hands behind his head pulling him back to her. He kissed her again, his heart almost bursting with love. He wrapped his arms around her and without breaking contact rolled over, bringing her with him. She tugged her hands free from his back and cupped his face, now kissing him as fervently as he'd kissed her only moments before.

One of those romantic, spontaneous moments he loved, hampered only by the fact they were in his dad's front yard, wearing way too many layers of clothes.

And by the BMW backing out of the garage.

Ellie gave a little gasp and stood too quickly. She slipped and fell on her backside. Eric jumped to a standing position with a sweeping sit-up and extended his hand to Ellie. They stood slightly apart, like guilty teenagers, as Joy stopped on the driveway.

The passenger window went down halfway. Joy smiled but gave no hint she'd seen them making out on the front lawn. "Have fun today. I don't know when I'll be back."

Ellie rushed to the window. "Wait. You're leaving?"

"Yes. One of my patients is in bad shape."

"Oh. I'm so sorry."

Eric joined Ellie and leaned down to speak through the half-lowered window. "You sure you don't want me to drive you?"

"I'm sure, but thank you."

The window raised. Eric and Ellie stepped back and waved as she drove off. Ellie turned to him with a wary look.

Eric held up his hands. "Truce." He grabbed the shovel and propped it against the front porch. "Now let's go finish that snowman."

# CHAPTER EIGHTEEN

The half bagel Ellie forced herself to eat sat heavy in her stomach. Not her favorite kind of appointment, particularly with a doctor she'd never met. Two hours. She just had to make it through the next two hours. Then she could relax.

Until then, there was no escaping the queasy stomach, heart palpitations, and jangled nerves. The new outfit she'd bought on her shopping trip with Joy would help. Dark gray cords, deep red cropped sweater layered over cream cami, crinkled scarf, and black leather boots that gave her the illusion of height.

She brushed her teeth, staring at her reflection. Something she tried not to do, especially since her mother couldn't pass a store window without checking herself out. *Help me today. Please let me hear some good news.* Not her first prayer for this appointment. Just a little reminder to God and an even bigger one to herself that God was in control. The ladies' Bible study had strengthened her faith. Made her want to pray again. Trust again.

She scooped water in her hands to rinse and nearly jumped out of her skin when she looked up to find Eric standing behind her.

He handed her a towel. "You look nice."

She smiled her thanks in the mirror. "This is my favorite outfit of the new clothes I bought. I'm wearing it for courage."

"I think it's my favorite, too, although I did love the pink snow suit." He wrapped his arms around her and pulled her close, smiling at her reflection.

She let herself relax against his chest. "You look handsome yourself. I love, love, love your haircut. Just long enough to run my fingers through. She reached up and demonstrated.

"How's your stomach feeling?"

"Better. Be warned. After the appointment, I'll be starving."

"I'll take you anywhere you want to go. You have your questions ready?"

She nodded.

"Okay." He smoothed her hair back and kissed her temple. "Let's go."

By nine o'clock, the office waiting room was already filled. Not surprising with ten different doctor options. Ellie signed her name on Dr. Conley's sheet and received the clipboard of questions to answer. Probably the longest part of her whole appointment, and one of the hardest. Full disclosure about her previous abortion stirred up buried pain. So did details of her recent miscarriage.

Dr. Conley certainly made the process easier. He listened with compassion and no judgment as she repeated her entire history. Every part of her wanted to explain, tell him how different she was now. But she resisted. As Eric would say, not information the doctor needed to know.

But there were definitely things she needed to know. After the preliminary examination and blood work, Dr. Conley met them in the conference room.

Ellie's hands shook as she took out her list and asked the question that meant the most. "When can we try again?"

"I'd like for you to complete two normal cycles before you try to conceive. Gives your body time to get hormone levels back to normal."

Not quite the answer she hoped for. But she'd take it. She rattled off the others: Why had she miscarried? Would it happen again? Did the abortion somehow affect her ability to have a normal pregnancy?

None of her questions received definitive answers, but Dr.

Conley did leave her with some hope.

"Everything looks good. I think the odds are in your favor to conceive and deliver a healthy baby. You might consider relocating to Washington so we can keep a close eye on you."

Something she'd already thought about. At this point, she'd do anything. She looked at Eric to gauge his reaction. He smiled at her, his face giving nothing away.

They thanked the doctor and shook his hand. Eric helped her with her coat and squeezed her arms. "Feel better?"

"Much."

"Good. I know a place that serves a fantastic brunch. A smorgasbord of everything you could think of. Their smoked salmon is outstanding."

"Sounds perfect."

Ellie stared out the window on the short trip to brunch. The streets, now clear, had piles of dirty snow shoved to the curbs. Eric drove with the confidence of a man very comfortable behind the wheel. This was his world. His city. Moving to Washington wouldn't be so bad. But what about her dad and the mission hospital?

Eric reached over and took her hand. "You're quiet."

"I'm trying to process everything the doctor said. What do you think about relocating?"

"It makes sense." He slowed and turned into a parking deck. "Here we are. We'll talk more later."

They entered a posh foyer that had a New Orleans flair. A live jazz band played in the corner. The hostess directed them to a table for two by a window and told them to help themselves to the buffet. Eric guided her to the food. "Still hungry?"

"I am. What do you recommend?"

"The guy in the back makes a killer made-to-order omelet. The shrimp pasta ragout on the opposite side is something I get almost every time I come here. And their Belgian waffles will make you think you've died and gone to heaven."

"Oh dear. I want it all."

Eric handed her a plate. "Go for it."

She lined up for an omelet. Eric went to the far wall for smoked salmon. They met back at the table, both plates piled high. She eyed his plate. "Oh good. Can I taste your waffle?"

He slid his plate closer. "You bet."

She cut off a chunk and stabbed it with her fork. "Oh, my goodness. Delicious. Want a bite of my omelet?"

He shook his head. "I'm good."

"It has the works. Bacon, cheese, ham, and every vegetable they had." She took her first bite and closed her eyes in appreciation.

"Okay." Eric put down his fork. "Give me a bite."

She laughed. "I knew you'd cave." Ellie sliced off a fourth of the omelet making sure it had plenty of the good stuff and raked it onto his plate. "There."

"You want the rest of my waffle?"

"No, thanks. Well, maybe one more bite."

"Another reason I love being married. We get to share food at a restaurant. So many more choices."

She took a sip of ice water. "Can we talk about it now?"

"About moving back?"

"Uh-huh." She wiped blueberry topping from her lip. "You seemed a little vague before, like maybe you had reservations."

Eric pushed back his plate and folded and refolded his cloth napkin into geometric shapes. "It's not that. I don't like to rush into anything."

"Wrong. You put the ring on my finger and insisted we get married by the end of the week."

"Oh yeah." He chuckled and dropped his gaze to the napkin. "That doesn't count. When I'm sure about something, I don't waste time."

A warning flag went up. Did that mean he wasn't sure about having a baby? Not for the first time, Ellie wondered if they were even on the same page. She leaned forward, ready to move from teasing to serious. "Eric, don't you want a baby?"

"Of course I do. Why would you even ask that?"

"I don't know." His defensive tone meant she'd definitely hit a nerve. "Let's just drop it. I don't want to fight."

They ate the rest of their food in silence.

Their server asked for what must have been the tenth time if they would like more coffee. Eric shook his head. "No, thanks. We're ready for our bill."

He waited until the server left. "We're not fighting. And we're not dropping anything."

The server returned.

Ellie pushed her chair back and managed a tight smile. "I'm going to the ladies' room."

Eric nodded and placed his credit card in the black folder.

Ellie's hands shook as she held them under the stream of warm water. He could call it anything he wanted. It felt like a fight to her. How had it gotten to this point? One minute they were joking over the omelet and the next ...

Eric waited for Ellie in the foyer of the restaurant, wondering when the conversation had gone south. She finally came out of the restroom but seemed to go out of her way to avoid looking at him. Neither spoke on the way to the car. He opened the car door for her. She met his gaze and said thanks. Good sign. He got into the driver's side but didn't buckle.

"Now. What's wrong?"

She looked down and shrugged. "Nothing."

He studied her profile, hoping for some clue. She turned and looked out the window. A tear rolled down her cheek.

"Hey." He wiped the tear away before it reached her chin.

"Talk to me, Ellie. Why are you crying?"

"I don't know." She shook her head. "I don't know," she repeated, her pitch rising. "I want a baby. And I'm scared. What if I don't get pregnant again? What if I miscarry again? And you didn't even seem sad when we lost our baby. You almost seemed happy."

Eric wanted to stop her right there, but he bit back his retort and let her keep talking.

Somehow, Ellie's tone took a one-eighty. "I should be over it by now." She sighed. "I'm trying. I'm really trying. But I'm so sad. And so scared. I pray. I try to trust God. And sometimes I feel better and almost happy again. Like that day I spent with Joy at the Bible study and at the mall. And yesterday when we played in the snow all morning. But the black cloud always comes back." She finally looked up, her eyes desperate. "What if I never feel normal again?"

He took a breath to answer, but she continued talking.

"I just want to feel better, but I can't until I'm pregnant again. Even then, I'll be paranoid that I might lose that one, too." She turned away and stared out the window. "And I'm not even sure you want this baby as much as I do."

Her shoulders shook. He wasn't sure whether from the cold or from crying. He started the car to turn on the heat.

"And I'm so sorry. The last thing you need is a hysterical wife who can't get her act together. I bet you wish you hadn't made me promise to talk about my pain. Be careful what you wish for." She chuckled in a self-deprecating way and dug in her coat pockets. "Where are my tissues?"

He opened the glove compartment and found some old napkins from a fast food place. "Here. Try these."

"Thanks." She wiped her cheeks then blew her nose. "And thanks for letting me rant. I feel better now."

She looked so sweet and pitiful with her swollen eyes and red nose, and droopy mouth that was trying hard to smile.

His heart melted, and for the first time, he regretted driving a Mustang. Holding her with a console in the middle would be awkward. And painful. He couldn't take her home. Joy would understand, but Ellie would be embarrassed. So he stayed put, in the parking deck, with the motor running to keep them warm. His leg started to ache as it always did when he sat in one position too long. He drew his right knee up and angled his body toward hers.

She kept her head down as if she were too embarrassed to look at him.

"You were right, Ellie. I *was* happy when I first saw you."

She turned and gave him a sideways glance.

"The night before we came back, I knew in my gut something was wrong. It ate at me. No response to my texts. No voice mail. It was like total blackout. Nobody was there at the airfield to meet us. All I could think of was that you had died, and nobody had the guts to tell me. I drove like a maniac to get back to the compound." He choked on the words. "You weren't there, and my blood turned to ice. So when I found out you were going to be all right, all I could do was thank God. Over and over. I was like a drowning man coming up for air. Nothing else mattered as long as you were still with me."

He stopped and fought hard to gain control. "But you were wrong, too. I *was* sad to lose our baby. To let go of our hopes and dreams for this little life. It made me sick inside, especially when I thought of you going through it alone."

"Oh, Eric." She placed her hand on his knee. "I didn't know. You seemed so cheerful."

"I knew how bad you were hurting. I wanted to help you, not add to your pain."

She dropped her head again. "I'm so ashamed."

"You have absolutely nothing to be ashamed about." He reached over and lifted her chin. "Almost from day one, you've put on a brave face and tackled each day with courage no matter how bad your heart was breaking." He wrapped his fingers around her wrist. "Remember what I told you? I'm going to walk through this with you. And I'm going to hold on to you. Little by little, we're going to climb out of that black hole. And I can't give you any guarantees, but I think we are going to have children. In God's good time. And when we do, you will be the world's best mother."

She sucked in a deep breath, broken by little shudders, remnants of her crying spell. "I don't deserve you."

He grinned. "Wait 'til you see my surprise."

For the first time since they'd entered the car, her eyes lit up. "Surprise?"

Eric pulled a gold-embossed envelope from his pocket. "I was saving this for after the appointment."

"What is it?"

"Open it."

She slid her fingernail under the flap and pulled out the card. "A spa day." She gasped and shot him a grateful look before examining the card again. "The works. Even a massage. Oh my goodness. I don't know what to say."

"I got one for Joy, too. Kind of a girl's day out. It's scheduled for next Monday since I'll be tied up at the prosthetics place most of that day. But if you're up for it, we could go someplace nice for dinner that evening. Like a date before we go back to Africa."

Ellie lunged across the console and hugged him tight. "You're wonderful. Thank you. Thank you for everything."

He laughed and returned her hug. "You're welcome, baby."

Crisis averted, Eric buckled in and repositioned his leg to reach the gas. Maybe on their date next week, he'd talk about their move back to Washington.

# CHAPTER NINETEEN

Ellie sat cross-legged on the bed, reading the latest text from Dad. "He says Steve and Ned left today."

Eric stood at the bathroom sink, shaving. "That'll leave them short-handed." He pushed his tongue against his cheek and slid the razor over the hump making his words sound a little slurred. "Good thing we're going back to Africa tomorrow."

Ellie flopped to her stomach with her feet in the air. "I think I'll leave some of the things I bought."

Eric came into the bedroom, a towel slung over the back of his neck. "I'll miss that pink snow suit."

She sat up and pulled her knees to her chest so she could watch him as he moved around the room. He placed a duffle bag on the bed and grabbed his shorts and running shoes from the closet. "Our reservations are at seven. You might want to dress up."

Ellie pursed her lips and stared at her flexed toes. Nothing in her stash of clothes could be considered dressy.

"Buy something."

Ellie lifted her head and gasped, "How did you know what I was thinking?"

He stuffed the shoes and shorts into the bag and grinned. "I could tell you, but then I'd have to kill you."

He used his arm to deflect the pillow she hurled at him.

"One of these days, Eric Templeton, I'll …"

With a quick swoop, Eric rounded the end of the bed and body-slammed her back against the mattress. "You'll what?"

She gave a wicked laugh. "I could tell you, but then …"

Eric laughed with her. "I've met my match for sure." He rolled up, pulling her with him. "I have to get going."

"Okay. What time will you be back?"

"I'm shooting for four." He buttoned his shirt and pulled a green sweater over his head. His fingers fumbled to roll the cuff of his shirtsleeve over the edge of the sweater.

"Here. Let me."

Eric held out his arm, like a little boy getting dressed for school. "I might even beat you and Joy home."

She reached for the other arm. "You probably will, especially if I have to buy a fancy dress for tonight." Ellie gave his sleeve one last tuck and stepped back. "Okay. All set."

He examined the results. "Sweet. Thanks."

"Wait." Ellie adjusted his shirt collar under the sweater. "Now, you can go. Have fun."

He gave her the you've-got-to-be-kidding look and grabbed his bag. "Right."

"Wait for me." She kept pace with Eric as they headed to the kitchen, already warm and full of the aroma of fresh-brewed coffee. He'd already been there, grinding and brewing the coffee. Had apparently spent some time with God, too. Notecards lay scattered around his open Bible.

Eric stuck the cards in the brown leather journal that had been his father's and carried the stack of books from the room.

Ellie moved fast, grabbing the travel mug from the dishwasher and the creamer from the fridge. Her new campaign: pay more attention to the needs of her husband. Spoil him, the way he spoiled her. Maybe even cook for him. How hard could it be? She managed to snap the lid on the mug just as Eric returned to the kitchen.

He picked up the mug and cocked his head. "Is this mine?"

She nodded, her pleased grin probably giving her away.

"Thank you."

"You're welcome." Resisting the urge to bask in the look of gratitude on his face, Ellie turned back to the counter as if fixing his coffee was part of her everyday routine.

"Okay, baby. See you tonight." With a quick peck to her cheek, he was out the door.

She smiled and watched him leave, loving how he moved. The casual observer would never know he wore an artificial leg. Ellie sipped her coffee and pulled out a bag of bagels from the fridge. Was Eric dreading his appointment today? He said he was able to thank God and mean it for losing his leg. Did that mean it didn't bother him anymore? The pre-split bagel stubbornly refused to separate. Ellie gritted her teeth and dug her fingers into the slit.

"Good morning." Joy breezed into the kitchen. "Did Eric leave already?"

Ellie glanced up, leaving her fingers still wedged in the bagel. "Yes. He has an early morning appointment to get his new leg."

"Oh, that's right."

Ellie finally managed to split the bagel, leaving one half very jagged. "Would you like one?"

"No, thank you." Joy pulled out a small skillet from a bottom cabinet. "I have to have protein in the morning. Would you like an egg?"

"No, thanks." Ellie remained at the counter waiting for the bagel to toast, secretly watching as Joy broke open an egg into a bowl and then whipped it into a frothy yellow liquid. Not once in her life had Ellie ever seen her mom cook anything. Nor had she visited the kitchen to observe the staff.

Joy put a dollop of butter into the hot skillet. When it sizzled, she poured in the mixture and stirred. "I'm excited about today. Do you know, I've never actually spent a whole day at a spa."

"Me either." Though she'd had many opportunities. Her passive way to be as different from her mother and sister as possible. Ellie swiped the excess cream cheese from the side of her bagel and licked it off her finger. "Would you like some toast?"

"I'd love some."

Toast she could do. Ellie stepped around Joy to grab the loaf of bread from the pantry, loving this new experience of girl time in the kitchen.

"We have a couple of hours until we have to be there. Are you looking forward to getting back to Africa?"

"In a way. These two weeks have flown by. Eric said you've considered visiting."

The toast popped up just as Joy dished the egg onto her plate. "Perfect timing. And yes, if I can work out the details, I'd love to visit."

Ellie brought the toast and the butter to the table. "We would love for you to stay in our guest bedroom. But be warned. Once you visit, you won't want to leave."

Joy laughed. "Eric told me the same thing. You might be sorry. I may show up at your door someday to take you up on the offer."

"We would love that."

Joy reached for Ellie's hand. "Shall we pray?"

Ellie bowed her head as Joy offered a quick blessing over their food and their day.

"So, tell me. Do you feel better now that you've seen the doctor?"

"I do." The right answer but not quite the truth. She probably wouldn't feel totally okay until she held her own baby in her arms. "I was wondering about something."

Joy stopped, her fork in midair.

"Does it ever get easier to trust God? I mean, I still have so much to learn. I loved that Bible study you took me to. About faith. I was wondering if faith is easier for someone who's been a Christian for a long time."

Joy smiled as if she really understood. "Oh, I don't know.

Everyone is different. I think maybe some people find it easy to trust God, but I'm not one of them. I'm actually a little prone to depression."

Ellie choked on the sip of coffee she'd just taken. "You?"

She nodded. "I'm afraid so. Not something I tell many people. I'm not proud of it. But I guess you could say trusting God gets easier the longer you know Him. God has been so good to me. And faithful. Living here has been an answer to prayer. I've decided to sell the house my husband and I shared for forty-two years. Losing him was very hard, even though we knew his death was inevitable."

Life without her husband. Something Ellie hoped she wouldn't have to experience. Ever. She placed her hand on Joy's. "I'm so sorry."

"Thank you. I'm better now. He died last April. They say the first year is the hardest. I still cry, but I cry in secret. You'd think I could handle grief by now. Losing Frank was nothing like losing my daughter."

Eric had never mentioned this piece of information which meant he probably didn't know. Ellie put her coffee cup on the table and pushed it back. "Your daughter?"

Joy nodded, her usual bright eyes now saddened. "Savannah. Everyone called her Vanna. We were so close. It never crossed my mind I might lose her."

Joy fell silent. Ellie waited, not wanting to pry but hoping for more of the story.

"You remind me of her. Not your looks, although she was beautiful, too. She had long dark hair and an olive complexion. Vanna's smile could light up a room. Just like yours. Made you happy just to be in her presence." Joy wiped a tear that had rolled down her cheek. "Oh my. I didn't mean to rattle on so. I haven't spoken of her in years."

"Don't apologize." Ellie leaned closer and placed her hand on top of Joy's. "Please tell me what happened and how you found the strength to go on."

"She was eighteen. Had just graduated from high school. She spent a lot of time at the lake with her friends." Grabbing her cup, Joy pushed her chair back. "Would you like more coffee?"

Ellie shook her head.

Joy walked to the counter and poured herself another cup, as if she needed the pause. She added cream and sugar, talking as she stirred. "They went out in a boat and jumped in the water to cool off. A speed boat veered too close. The driver had been drinking and apparently hadn't seen the people in the water. Plowed into them." Joy paused and then added, her voice choked with tears, "Almost severed my daughter's head from her body."

Ellie's hand flew to her mouth. The image left a sick thud in the pit of her stomach. How could she respond to something so horrific? "I'm sorry." The words fell flat in the quiet kitchen. "How did you get through it?"

Joy leaned against the counter and dropped her gaze to the coffee in her cup. "Not very well, I'm afraid. Losing Vanna took the life right out of my body. But I ran to God. It was the only way I could keep breathing."

"Do you ever ask why?"

"I did at first. All the time. I had some serious talks with God about that. 'Where were You, God? Why didn't You stop that boat?' I was so angry. And then I turned the anger inward. The depression threatened to smother me. I fought it. Mostly on my knees because I was literally too weak to hold my head up. It was a dark time."

The words hung heavy in the air. Ellie managed to say what had been hammering at her from the start. "My pain was nothing compared to yours."

Joy returned to her chair. "You lost a child. That pain is very real."

Ellie could not bring herself to meet Joy's gaze. "How did you get better?"

Joy's hand on Ellie's brought a motherly comfort she had often craved.

"You know that old saying, 'Time heals all wounds'?"

Ellie nodded.

Joy shook her head. "Truth—not time—will heal the wounds, no matter how deep."

Ellie took in a breath as she connected the dots. "Like Karin said last week, 'Retreat to the truth, not your feelings.'"

Joy didn't smile or nod or acknowledge the star pupil's declaration. Instead, her mouth twisted to one side in a slight grimace. "Yes." She dragged the word out as if she were searching for the right response. "Truth is the foundation. But feelings are important, too. Your feelings are part of who you are. They make you rich. Even the bad feelings. The ones that feel like they will suffocate you."

Like the feeling Ellie had right then only more like a geyser threatening to blow. The room seemed hot, and her breaths became shallower.

"Sweet Ellie, you mustn't alienate yourself from your feelings. Don't try to stuff down your grief because you think you should be over it by now."

Tears started to flow. Not a raging torrent but quiet tears that seem to seep out from her core.

Joy continued in a soothing voice, "Your feelings, or emotions, are like a wall you lean on. Or like a bean bag you bounce on. God gave you feelings to enrich your life. We only become depressed when we stifle those feelings and refuse to admit they exist. Make friends with your emotions. Don't run from them. Embrace them."

Ellie reached for a napkin and held it against her eyes, letting the paper soak up the constant flow. Joy's words reached deep into her soul, into that dark place no one else could touch.

"During those dark times after my daughter's death, sometimes all I could pray was 'God, help.' And He always came through. Either with a verse. Or a song on the radio. Or the smile of a stranger. God always sent me what I needed for that day. And on really bad days, I could only offer up my brokenness. One verse I clung to was Isaiah 43:2. 'When thou passest through the waters, I will be with thee; and through the rivers, they shall not overflow thee: when thou walkest through the fire, thou shalt not be burned; neither shall the flame kindle upon thee.' And here's the secret ...''

Ellie lowered the napkin and met Joy's gaze, very much wanting to know the secret.

"Suffering is a gift. Usually a gift we don't want or ask for, but a gift nonetheless."

Not even close to what she expected the secret to be. "A gift?"

"Yes. A gift I take out and open again whenever I need to be reminded of God's sustaining grace. I opened it when Frank died. I held on to the same God who brought me through the grief of Vanna's death." Joy took Ellie's hand. "And sometimes I open it up to offer hope to other hurting sisters. Ellie, through suffering, we get to know God more fully as we experience His grace. His comfort. Suffering helps make us humble. It grinds off the sharp edges. Makes us softer, more compassionate, and equipped to show God's love and compassion to a very broken and hurting world."

Ellie could only imagine what it had cost Joy to open up that gift today. She closed her eyes and let the truth wash over her broken heart. "Would you pray with me?"

"I'd love to. But I'm a little choked up right now. Could you pray first?"

Praying out loud did not come easy, but this time it felt right. Ellie bowed her head and leaned in to Joy's embrace, praying the same prayer she'd whispered so many times over the past days. "Dear God. Help me. I'm bringing all my sadness to You." She choked up more than once, and most of her words were punctuated with sniffs as she poured out her pent-up grief. As a last resort, she pinched the sides of her nose with the damp napkin and breathed through her mouth. Her sentences were short, with stilted words, like her feeble attempts to speak in one of the tribal languages. But she spoke from her heart. "Thank You, God. For letting me know Your truth. For my dad. And especially for Eric." After a brief hesitation, she added, "Thank You. Even though we had our baby a very short time, thank You." The tight vice around her chest loosened. She had just thanked God for her suffering. And meant it.

A sense of joy that she'd thought was gone forever, returned. And how like God that it had been a woman named Joy, who'd helped her find it. "And thank You for my wonderful friend Joy. She helped me more than she'll ever know."

# FREEING ELLIE

# CHAPTER TWENTY

Ellie returned from the spa experience and went upstairs
to check out the results. She leaned closer to their bathroom
mirror and examined her reflection. Her skin had a radiant
glow from the facial. The hair stylist had trimmed her hair and
added razor-cut layers, creating a sleek curtain. Everything
about her radiated life and health. Except her eyes. Still dull
and lifeless.

She'd have to do better. She used her fingers to shove up
the corners of her mouth in a practice smile.

Moments of feeling normal were as rare as the sun
peeking through the clouds during monsoon season. This
morning's talk and prayer with Joy had been one of those
moments that she hoped would linger for a long time. But
somewhere between the facial and the massage, the happy
feeling dissipated, and the gloom had returned. Maybe it was
the hauntingly beautiful music playing softly in the
background. Or maybe it was the tender hands of the masseuse
kneading deep into her back and shoulder muscles. Whatever it
was had triggered tears to drip unbidden and unrestrained on
the satin-covered massage table.

What had Joy said? Let the feelings come? But what if
they never went away?

Ellie had an overwhelming impulse to run and hide. This
trip was supposed to help. Why hadn't it? Why couldn't she
snap out of this depression and get on with her life? What was
wrong with her?

Ellie slipped into the black cocktail dress Joy talked her
into buying before they left the spa, then checked her reflection
one more time.

Eric's familiar step sounded on the stairs. Her heart beat

faster as she stepped into the hall, still trying to push the end of the diamond drop earring into the tiny pierced opening on her earlobe. "I was starting to get worried. Did they give you the latest turbo-charged leg?"

Eric glanced up and stopped mid-stride, his eyes telling her more than the words. "You. Are. Stunning," he uttered.

Ellie smiled a wordless thank you. "It's amazing what a spa day can do."

He closed the distance and hugged her, taking a deep breath and slowly releasing it. "Hmm. Smell good, too."

"How was your day?" Ellie tucked her head into the curve of his neck.

"Long. I'll tell you about it at dinner."

She followed him and stood in the middle of the bedroom as he rummaged in a dresser drawer for boxers. He seemed tired. Or maybe just preoccupied.

She started to chew the tip of her finger then stopped, remembering the beautiful French tipped manicure. Maybe she should tell him she didn't feel like going out into the brutal cold or dining in a posh place with a roomful of strangers.

Eric checked the time and tossed the phone onto the bed. "I'll take a quick shower."

"Okay." She chickened out. After all, she'd been pampered and treated like royalty all day while he'd been poked and prodded and fitted for his new leg. This was her chance to practice what she'd been preaching to herself. Ellie sat on the edge of the bed and took out her black patent shoes with the four-inch heels. By the end of the evening, her feet would need another massage.

The water from the shower stopped. After a couple of minutes, Eric opened the door. The bathroom looked like a sauna with steam escaping into the bedroom. He wore his boxers and had a towel around his neck. His towel-dried hair had a wild wet look. He squeezed toothpaste on his toothbrush and glanced her way. He must have felt her staring at him. "I could've stayed in that shower all night." His words came out garbled as he brushed the back of his teeth. "Hot water. Something I never take for granted." He bent over the sink and cupped water in his hand. "You wouldn't believe how many places in the world don't have that luxury."

She smiled and leaned against the door, watching him spread shaving cream over his face. "The technician said I could shower with my new leg still attached."

Her glance went automatically to the leg. "It looks exactly like your old one."

He laughed. "This *is* my old one. New one's in the bag by the dresser. Couldn't bring myself to get it wet."

"Are you going to wear it tonight?"

"You bet."

Before he could continue, she turned toward the dresser. "I'll get it. I want to check it out." Two rectangular boxes stuck out of the bag. She placed them both on the bed and opened the first. Wrong one. She chuckled and spoke over her shoulder. "I don't suppose you plan to wear the one for running tonight."

Eric joined her at the end of the bed and grinned. "Not if you plan to wear those shoes."

"Little known fact: These stilettos are my secret weapon."

"To make you taller?" He opened the other box and pulled out a leg that seemed an identical match to the real one.

"Oh my goodness." Ellie took it from his hands. "This is amazing." She handed it back. "Try it on."

"I tried it on about one hundred times this afternoon. All I have to do now is click it into place." Eric sat on the bed and unhinged the old leg. "So you were saying?"

"Hmm?" Ellie leaned in for a closer look.

Their faces almost touched as Eric bent to attach the new leg. "Secret weapon?"

"Oh, yeah. If a mugger attacks," Ellie straightened and

placed her hand on Eric's shoulder to steady herself, "I'll discreetly slip it off, like so …" She reached behind to her raised foot and took off the black stiletto. "Then I can stab him."

He laughed and raised his arm to counter her mock attack. "Impressive. Nice to know we'll be perfectly safe tonight." Eric stood, rocking back and forth as if trying out a new pair of shoes. "What do you think?"

"Your leg trumps my heels, for sure. Except for the hinge thing, you almost couldn't tell which one was fake. Does it feel different from the first one?"

He nodded. "Like taking Joy's BMW out on the interstate as opposed to the Land Rover over dirt roads." Eric tested it again, staggering his gait to put all his weight on the artificial limb. "I never thought I'd say this, but I love this thing. Huge step in the right direction, I'd say."

"Was that pun intended?"

"It was." Eric laid out his white shirt and suit on the bed and walked back to the dresser. His arms flexed as he pulled an undershirt over his head.

Ellie took the dress shirt off the hanger and handed it to Eric. "I'll feed Lucky while you finish getting ready."

"Joy's not here?"

Ellie shook her head. "She got an emergency call as we were leaving the spa. She dropped me off and said she'd see us in the morning."

Without Ellie to distract him, Eric finished dressing in less than five minutes. His pulse raced, remembering that first glimpse of her in her black dress. She'd be turning heads tonight, for sure. Made him stand a little taller just thinking about it. He slipped his tie over his neck and looked in the mirror to adjust it. After a quick spritz of cologne, he grabbed his suit coat and clicked off the bedroom light. He paid attention to each step on the stairs, surprised that his new leg could make that much difference. More stable. Less rubbing. Maybe he should take Ellie dancing.

Eric closed the blinds in the living room and walked into the kitchen. Ellie leaned against the counter, drinking bottled water. She glanced his way then sputtered, cupping her hand to catch the water dripping down her chin. "I'd forgotten how wicked handsome you look in that suit."

Something fluttered in his stomach. "I remember when you first said that to me."

She closed the distance and slid her hands around his neck. "Said what?"

"Wicked handsome." His arms encircled her waist. "The first night you stayed here after my dad's funeral. Remember?" His head slanted toward the darkened living room. "In there. We were on the sofa, and you were telling me why you were freaking out at the viewing."

"I do remember. Maybe not those exact words, but I remember the freaking out part. Rooms full of strangers do that to me." She smiled up at him. "Sitting on that sofa that night is one of my most favorite memories."

"Mine, too." He held her close, loving how she molded so perfectly to his body. "You know, we could just order pizza and recreate that memory."

Ellie reared back to look up at him. "Really?"

*Really? As in, I'd be disappointed to miss our date, or Really? I'd love to stay home and skip our date.* Her wide-eyed stare wasn't giving any clues. "Would you rather stay home?" Eric asked, trying hard not to sound too eager.

She dropped her gaze. "Only if you want to."

"I want to make you happy." If only he could read her mind. Eric gripped her chin and nudged her head up. "Tell me what you'd rather do."

"Stay home. But I know you've been looking forward to tonight. And you made reservations. And we're all dressed up."

Eric laughed and put his finger on her mouth. "Let's stay home."

She clutched the lapel of his coat. "You won't be disappointed?"

"I can't think of a better way to spend our last night in Washington." He kissed the tip of her nose. "Let's go change and order pizza."

Eric loosened his tie and reached for his phone to cancel the reservations. They walked back through the living room. Ellie, her shoes now dangling from her hands, preceded him up the stairs. He googled the nearest pizza place and glanced up as she disappeared into the bedroom. "What do you want on the pizza?"

"Anything." She craned her neck around the door. "Except anchovies." After a couple of seconds, her head appeared again. "Order it the way you like it."

His stomach rumbled. He considered ordering two but went with an order of hot wings instead.

A few minutes later, Ellie sat on the sofa watching him coax the fire to life. "Brings back memories."

The fire crackled, filling the room with a cozy light and the comfortable smell of burning wood. He washed his hands and with one more poke at the fire, settled next to Ellie. He slipped off his shoes and propped his feet on the coffee table next to hers. "I'm glad we decided to stay home."

"Me, too." Ellie inhaled and then shifted toward him as if she was about to say something else. After a long pause, she spoke in a trembling voice, "I've thought a lot about what you said after we went to the doctor."

He nodded, his mind scrambling to remember what exactly he'd said.

"Losing our baby must have been hard for you. I didn't

realize it at the time."

He could stop her right there but decided to let her talk it out.

"I've been so selfish. Not once have I tried to make you feel better." Her feet fidgeted, tapping against the air, shaking the coffee table. For the first time since she'd started talking, she looked at him. "You've been wonderful. So patient and loving." She dropped her gaze again. "I'm sorry. I've had nothing to give, and you deserve so much more." Her voice dropped so low, he strained to hear. "But I'll make it up to you. From now on, I'm going to try to spoil you like you spoil me."

He placed his feet on the floor and leaned forward, angling his body toward hers. "Ellie ..."

The loud knock at the door made Ellie jump and clutch her chest. Eric stood and held up his hand. "Hold that thought."

The pizza guy fumbled to extract the two boxes from the insulated warmer. Eric helped and then slipped folded bills into the waiting hands. "No change."

Eric plopped the steaming boxes on the coffee table and sat again, positioning himself farther so she could see his face when he talked. At least, she could if she'd look at him. He reached for one of her hands. "There's something you do for me that you don't even know you're doing."

She slanted her head, her expression questioning.

"Every time you see me ..." he paused, turning her hand palm up, tracing the lines with his finger. Being transparent didn't come easy. He played with her rings. "Your face lights up. Every time you look at me, your eyes sparkle, and your face radiates love. Makes me want to leave the room for five minutes and then return just to see it again." He tightened his grip on her hand. "Listen to me." He chanced a peek. Her eyes were wide and bright with unshed tears. "I know you've been struggling. But nothing about you is selfish." He gave her hand an extra squeeze for emphasis. "Nothing."

Her tears spilled over. She jerked her hand from his grasp and gave a forceful swipe across her cheek. "I wish I could snap out of this funk." She stood and stomped over to the fire, her back toward him. "You've got to be sick of me singing the same old whiny song." She turned and faced him, her eyes pleading. "I want more than anything to make it go away, but I can't."

He'd underestimated her pain. The truth hit him with a sick thud to his chest. She'd been struggling far more than she'd let on or allowed anyone to see. Especially him. Eric held out his hand. "Come here, baby."

She hesitated but came back to the sofa. Before she could sit, he pulled her onto his lap and wrapped his arms around her. "What is it that won't go away?"

"I don't even know. It's a bad feeling I get. Like I'm in a room and somebody clicked off the light. It's all dark. And I feel myself disappearing into a black hole. It's like I'm dead." Her hand rubbed her chest. "I can't feel myself in there anymore." She shifted and grabbed a slice of pizza from the bottom box. "Want one?"

Her complete change of subject threw him off guard. He nodded and took the piece she handed him.

Ellie slid off his lap and onto the sofa, grabbing a piece for herself. Eric chewed in silence, kicking himself for assuming more time or the trip to Washington would fix everything.

"That was good." Ellie wiped her mouth and spoke, her voice back to a cheery normal. "So your leg fits better?"

Eric ignored her question. "This feeling. You have it all the time?"

She nodded and then sighed, probably realizing he wasn't going to let it go. "But it gets better when I'm with you. Or Joy. Or when I'm busy at the clinic."

"But you feel it now?"

"Yes. Well. Not as bad as I felt it today. It's worse when

I'm alone." Her hand crushed the napkin she held as she pounded her fist on her thigh. "I'm so mad at myself." She propelled off the sofa again and returned to the fire. "I thought it was gone for good when I became a Christian. It wasn't supposed to come back. I love God. He's real to me. And then when my faith is tested, *bam!* Back it comes. You want a bottle of water?"

His head jerked back in surprise, but she moved so fast, she probably didn't see him. She returned with two bottles, tossing him one. "That's why I'm trying to stay busy. I can't. I won't let it take over again. And destroy me."

Ellie took a long drink of water. He did, too, mostly to give his mind a chance to catch up and absorb all the new data.

"It's why I've got to get pregnant again." Her hand moved across her lower abdomen. "I want to feel life inside of me. I'd snap out of it then. I know I would."

Game on. Eric leaned forward and rubbed his hands together. "Now would be the perfect time to tell you what I think we need to do."

Her enthusiastic nod followed by a deep exhale showed she was very ready to move to a safer subject. Eric joined her by the fire, poking the dying embers into life. "The doctor said you need to wait two months. So we'll go back to Africa, get things in order and move back. Indefinitely."

Ellie stared, her wide eyes filling again. "I've thought the same thing. But what about Dad? And the clinic? And ..."

"God will work out the details. Director McDowall asked me again to consider training new recruits." Eric chucked his empty water bottle into the fire. It crackled and warped before melting into the flames. He took her hand and kneaded her fingers as he spoke. "We're going to give this thing our best shot."

She nodded and moved into his arms. He pressed her head close to his chest and stroked her hair.

Out of nowhere, Brock's words hammered in his mind. *Let God call the shots.* Words spoken last summer. Before the surgery that took his leg.

What if God said no this time, too?

# CHAPTER TWENTY-ONE

March. They were returning to Africa in the middle of rainy season and would leave two months later just as it was ending. Ellie's forehead bumped against the window as the plane touched down on the grassy field and taxied to the waiting Land Rover. She grabbed the smallest bag, Eric the other two. The co-pilot opened the door and lowered the steps. Her dad must have been waiting for the moment. He appeared almost immediately, shook the pilots' hands, and then shot past them to hug her. "Welcome home, honey." He turned and embraced Eric. "Good trip?"

"Long trip." Eric shook hands with the pilots, too, and waited for her to precede him down the steps. Mac took the bag from her and placed it in the back of the vehicle. Eric came behind and stowed the rest before shaking Mac's hand. "Good to see you. How were the roads?"

"Muddy. As usual." Mac raced around the vehicle to open the door for her. "There you go, little lady."

"Thank you." Ellie smiled as she slid into the seat.

Her dad and Eric paused at their open doors before getting in. "Foundation for the new hangar looks good."

Dad turned toward the rectangular concrete slab at the far end of the runway. "We had one day without rain while you were gone. The guys seized the opportunity."

Dad sat up front and Eric got in back next to her. Ellie settled in for the last leg of their almost seven thousand mile journey. Clouds masked the time, but her phone indicated they'd be arriving shortly before dinner. They'd planned it that way, so they could visit with everyone all at one time and then maybe get in bed at a decent hour. It would still take them a few days to reset their internal clock.

Dad stuck his arm out the window and waved as the Gulfstream thundered down the airfield. "They'll stay overnight in Luanda before heading home." He hooked his arm on the back of his seat and turned to face them. "So glad to have you back. You didn't miss much, other than a lot of rain."

"I got to see my first ever blizzard." Ellie shot Eric a quick look. "Was that actually a blizzard?"

Eric laughed. "Sure felt like one when I shoveled the driveway."

"Built my first snowman, too. With a few interruptions."

Eric grabbed her hand and squeezed. "Your daughter threw snowballs like a pro."

"He's exaggerating, Dad. My first snowball fight, and he showed no mercy." She leaned in to whisper to Eric. "Especially when your tackle rolled us to the bottom of the yard."

Eric grinned. "Strategy. Had to take out the enemy."

Dad chuckled. "Glad you had fun. You were sorely missed. Lady even slept on the rug beside my bed."

Eric leaned forward to chat more with Dad. Ellie slid down so her head could relax against the seat. Her neck was sore from sleeping on the plane. A lazy feeling of contentment settled over her as she stared at the foliage whizzing past her window. A steaming mist hovered over the ground, thanks to the recent rain. In two months, the rain would stop abruptly like a giant faucet being turned off. Her breath caught. Two months before they returned to Washington. Maybe the end of her darkness as well.

She must have dozed. Eric nudged her awake. "Looks like we're in for the Red Gravel Treatment."

Ellie sat up and stared at him. "The what?"

"Red Gravel. Rocco's term for African Red Carpet." Eric put his arm around her and pointed as they drove into the compound. "Looks like everybody came out to greet us."

She leaned forward. "Toby and Nicci are leading the pack." She glanced back. "Five bucks, she made your favorite."

"Coffee? That doesn't count. She always makes coffee."

"Roasted garlic chicken. With glazed carrots."

"Hmm. I hope you're right. But my money's on beef tips and curried rice."

"No. She made that before we left."

"Honey." Eric lowered his chin and gave her a matter-of-fact look. "This is Nicci we're talking about."

The Rover came to a stop. Ellie held out her hand, palm up. "Are we on?"

The crowd swooped in. He slapped the top of her hand and opened the door. "We're on."

Ellie slid across the seat to exit through Eric's open door. Miriam fastened rough, leathery fingers around Ellie's wrist and tugged her away from the fray. Miriam scanned her face for a long moment and then said, "You've found your happy again."

Maybe she had. Maybe it would last this time. Ellie covered Miriam's hands with her own. "Yes. I've found my happy."

Nicci joined them and hugged Ellie from behind. "I hope you've found your hungry."

Ellie whirled around and returned the hug. "Hello, sweet friend. I'm starving." Magic words judging from the pleased expression on Nicci's face. Maybe her bet was safe. Eric stood between Mac and Toby, laughing, probably at something Toby had said. Eric turned and for a brief moment met her gaze, his eyes smiling.

The whole crowd trooped together across the compound to the side door leading to the dining hall. Moses, with his long legs and boundless energy, reached the door and held it open for the rest of the group to enter. Nicci plowed ahead and rushed across the hallway. Ellie's stomach rumbled as the warm but indistinguishable smell of something good welcomed her. The group milled around the counter on the left wall, pouring either water or lemonade from glass pitchers and then took their seats.

Nicci backed through the double doors, balancing a tray containing the entrée. Eric's smug look disappeared as soon as Nicci placed the platter almost directly in front of Toby. Cabbage leaves stuffed with what appeared to be a spicy mixture of ground beef and rice.

Toby leaned forward, breathing deeply, before shoving the food more to the center. "Man, oh man. I've been looking forward to this all day."

Nicci returned from the kitchen with a large bowl of what looked like sweet potato soufflé. Eric cocked his head and shrugged, leaning close to whisper in her ear. "Looks like Toby trumped both of us."

Toby grabbed Nicci's arm and reeled her back as she started toward the kitchen. He stood and cleared his throat. "I thought you two would never get back. You know how hard it is for me to keep a secret. Now, we can finally announce our big news. I've asked this amazing woman to be my wife ... and believe it or not, she has accepted."

Nicci laughed and placed her hands on her face, the humble gesture of someone embarrassed not only by the deep ridges on her cheeks but also by the attention now focused directly on her.

Everyone clapped and cheered. Dad slid back his chair and walked over, standing between them and placing his arms around them both. "Wonderful news! Nicci, maybe now we can convince you to stay and eat with us."

Nicci laughed, this time covering perfect teeth with her hand. Toby pulled out the chair next to him and guided her to the seat. Then Toby sat, his eyes wide as he looked across the table to Eric. "Looks like I'm gonna need a best man."

"Time and place, brother." Under the table, Eric squeezed Ellie's hand. "I'll be there."

# FREEING ELLIE

# CHAPTER TWENTY-TWO

A soft tap on her shoulder jerked her awake. Ellie blinked a couple of times. Eric stood beside the bed, a coffee cup in one hand and her phone in the other.

"Honey, Dad just called. Said he needs you if you feel up to it."

Her fogged brain came slowly back to life. Ellie pushed hair away from her face and propped on her elbow. "What time is it?"

"Almost ten."

"Ten? Like in the morning?" Ellie flipped back the cover like she had a flight to catch. "Can I have a sip?"

"Made it for you." He handed her the cup. "Thought you might need it."

She smiled and cradled the cup in her hands. "You wonderful man. Text him. Let him know I'm on my way." At the bathroom door, she spun back around, but Ninja Eric had already straightened the spread and left the bedroom. Ellie did the bare essentials, brushing her teeth, holding back her hair with one hand as she rinsed. She opened the blinds instead of turning on a light and grabbed the first pair of scrubs in the closet. After tying a double knot in both sneakers, she bounced off the bed.

Eric met her at the door. "I'll walk you over."

Ellie nodded. "I can't believe I slept that late." She took a giant step, leaping off the porch. Lady raced ahead of them both.

Eric caught up and stayed steady with Ellie's quickened pace, not once breathing hard. She, on the other hand, was huffing by the time they reached the clinic doors. "Whew. I'm more out of shape than I thought."

Eric held the door for her, and she leaned in, their lips smacking air, more than connecting. "See you later."

Ten fifteen, and as usual the chairs lining the walls were full. Ellie stepped over children sprawled on the floor and entered the second room lined with curtained-off cots. Iyegha glanced her way and left the patient he was attending. "Your father is in the first examination room."

"Thank you." Ellie pushed through double doors and entered the first door on the left. A girl lay on the table, curled on her side and gasping for air.

Dad held an emesis basin close to her mouth.

Ellie positioned the surgical mask and snapped on rubber gloves. She joined him, taking the basin. "I've got this."

The girl heaved and coughed up pink frothy fluid. Ellie spoke soothing words to the girl, who couldn't be more than eighteen. Dad placed a clip from an oxygen monitor on one of her fingers then placed a band around her forearm. Ellie glanced up and met his gaze. Now wasn't the time to apologize for sleeping so late. "Do you want me to get the IV going?"

He shook his head, pressing for the right place to insert the needle. "I've got it. I need you to keep her calm."

Easier said than done. The girl pulled at the oxygen tubing attached to her nose, her eyes wide and desperate. The vomiting seemed to have subsided for the moment. Ellie eased the girl on her back. Dad tapped the IV tubing and then slid the earpieces from the stethoscope back into place to listen to her chest. "Iyegha's first assessment was a severe asthma attack." Dad's voice held a quiet urgency. "But it's much more. Her lungs are full of fluid, like someone with congestive heart failure."

Ellie nodded but kept her expression neutral. How could someone so young have congestive heart failure? The girl writhed on the table, a pitiful sight, heaving the pink froth again into the basin.

The oxygen monitor beeped, an ominous sound that sent her dad into overdrive. "Hold her head still."

Dad forced a plastic tube into her trachea making it possible to suction out her lungs. The oxygen levels dropped, and the girl lost consciousness.

"Father, give this young girl another chance." Dad's quiet prayer shook with emotion. Then he spoke to Ellie. "Continue to suction out fluid and increase the oxygen." He left the room but returned within seconds with Iyegha and the battery-powered defibrillator.

The girl convulsed and stopped breathing. Dad ripped the thin sheathe and attached electrodes to either side of her chest. "Clear." The body jerked and fell flat. Oxygen levels continued to plummet. Dad kept his hands poised above the frail patient, waiting for the recharge. "Clear." Again, the body arched from the table, but just as quickly collapsed back into an inert heap.

Ellie's fingers probed in vain for a pulse. The set line of Dad's jaw reaffirmed what she already suspected.

With a deep sigh, he lowered his surgical mask and shook his head.

Eric shoved open the heavy wooden door of the chapel. Its damp, musty smell hung heavy in the air. Cloud cover kept sunlight from filtering through the stained glass and seemed to rob the sanctuary of its usual welcome. Eric scanned the darkened room and almost missed the still form of his wife on her knees, hunched over a bench near the front.

She turned and wiped her cheeks. "Sorry. I should have texted to let you know where I was." Ellie pushed herself up and sat on the bench.

Eric eased down beside her. "I spoke with your dad."

Ellie stared at the stained glass, a haunted expression on her face. "Did he tell you we lost the patient?"

"Yes."

"She was pregnant." She spoke softly, almost to herself. "Iyegha talked with the relatives who brought her in. She'd been raped, apparently by more than one terrorist rebel." A lone tear streamed down Ellie's cheek. "She drank poison, desperate to get rid of the baby."

Eric's gut twisted, but he remained silent.

"It was terrible. She was so young. So scared." Ellie's hands shook as she covered her face. "Just like me. But my attempt to end my life failed." Ellie turned to him. "Why did God let me live?"

His jaw clenched as he met her gaze. Her pain-filled eyes pleaded for an answer he couldn't give.

"Why rescue me and not her?" She shook her head. "It doesn't seem fair."

What could he say? Fair or not, at least God had chosen to spare Ellie's life. For him, nothing else mattered. Eric took her hand and kneaded warmth into her icy fingers.

She leaned her head on his shoulder. "I've been thinking about that day your heart stopped. I thought we'd lost you." She shifted and looked up at him. "I wish I knew how to trust God more. It scares me to think it could all change in a heartbeat. I don't think I could handle losing you."

Eric drew in a deep breath, mostly to cover his own reaction. How could he even respond? He couldn't seem to get a grasp on trusting God either. Especially when it involved her. He released her hand and placed his arm around her shoulders, pulling her tight against him. He kissed the top of her head and whispered against her hair. "I couldn't handle losing you either."

# CHAPTER TWENTY-THREE

"You work wonders with your needle." Ellie sat cross-legged on Nicci's half bed.

Miriam smiled, her mouth full of pins, but remained focused on the hem of Nicci's dress. She gestured for Nicci to turn.

Nicci shifted to the right, her body remaining taut and rigid.

Ellie's foot started to cramp. She straightened her legs and leaned against the headboard, pointing and flexing her foot. The toes remained bent in a deformed curve no matter how she willed them to relax. She scooted off the bed and stomped a few times.

Miriam gave her a sideways glance. "You need to drink water."

"Take one of those water bottles." Nicci gestured to a box beside her bed.

"Thank you." Ellie drank almost half in one long gulp. Might be psychological, but the cramp started to ease. She sank into the chair next to the mirror. The room held a companionable silence with Miriam intent on her task and Nicci too afraid to move. Dear friends, much closer to her than her own mother and sister had ever been.

Miriam tucked in the last fold of the hem and rose. "Tell me what you think."

Nicci turned to the mirror and gasped. "It's beautiful."

Miriam reached from behind and tugged Nicci's hands away from the scars on her face. "You *are* beautiful."

Ellie leaned forward and touched Nicci's arm. "I couldn't imagine you without your scars. They make you who you are."

Nicci dropped her gaze and gave a nervous laugh. Tears

flowed down ridges in her cheeks like rainwater follows ruts in the road. "Tobias told me that as well." She raised her hand midway to her face but stopped herself. "I did not think love would ever come to me."

Exactly what she had felt, too. Exactly why she was so happy now. Ellie gave Nicci a sideways hug. "You will be very happy."

Miriam's long arms wrapped around both of them and drew them close. A perfect moment of motherly comfort from the woman who'd never had children of her own. "I pray you will be as happy as Moses and I have been." She released them with a gentle shove. "Now, go find your men while I finish this dress."

Eric jumped and swatted just as Toby extended to his full height and poised to shoot the basketball into the net. Eric wasted no time grabbing the ball as it veered to the left. Toby came down hard, pivoted, and threw out his arms to block Eric.

Eric ducked, shouldered his way clear, and took the shot. He shielded his eyes from the afternoon sun and paused as the ball whooshed through the net. He whirled back to Toby. "Are you seriously going to let the one-legged guy beat you in basketball?"

"Aw, come on. You know my head ain't in the game."

"Looks like the girls are coming." Eric heaved the ball to Toby. "Show 'em what you've got."

With a quick glance their way, Toby licked his lips and dug his sneakers into the red dirt. He palmed the ball and with a flick of the wrist, lobbed it toward the net. It teetered around the rim but never went in.

Eric caught the rebound and shot it back to Toby. "Try again. They weren't even looking."

"Nah. I'm done." Toby cradled the ball under his arm.

"And wipe that 'you're a quitter' look off your face. Just be glad I'm stopping while you're ahead."

Eric grinned. "Fair enough." He wiped the sweat from his face and slung the towel around his neck.

Laughter filtered through the air as the women approached.

Ellie paused, her face scrunched in disappointment. "You can't stop now. We're here to cheer our men on."

Toby took the water Nicci handed him and gave a self-deprecating chuckle. "Where were you when I needed you? Your husband's been killing me."

Eric countered. "Hey. I couldn't waste the opportunity to crush the guy who usually dominates street ball. Tobe's so lovesick, he can't see straight."

Ellie placed her hands on her hips. "So, Eric Templeton, does this mean *you're* not lovesick anymore?"

She had him there. Ellie's eyes sparkled with a wicked playfulness that threatened to turn his insides to mush. Truth be told, he was probably more lovesick than ever. She probably knew it. His sweat-saturated T-shirt kept him from snatching her up in a bear hug. Instead, Eric grabbed one of her hands and tugged her closer.

Toby moved in and gripped Eric's shoulder. "While you two are sparring, I'm gonna get cleaned up and help Nicci get our supper ready. I'm starving."

Roasted pork surrounded by whole red potatoes filled the platter in the center of the table. Dad's prayer of blessing was characteristically long. Ellie cleared her throat in a vain attempt to mask the loud rumble of her stomach. Eric gave her hand a little squeeze, which meant he probably heard. She stole a quick peek. His grin confirmed it.

At the "Amen," Eric reached for the platter and handed it

to Dad. "We heard some news today that might interest you."

Dad cocked his head as he raked two potatoes and a thick slice of pork onto his plate.

Eric positioned the platter between his plate and hers and started serving them both. "Remember the hospice worker who's been staying in Dad's house?"

Dad spliced open the potatoes and salted them. "Joy Stockman, I believe?"

Ellie wished she'd inherited Dad's flawless memory for names. She slid the food down to Mac.

"We Skyped with her today. She's considering a visit to the mission."

Dad nodded as he finished chewing. "Sounds good."

"Wait 'til you hear this. She's a retired nurse. Even worked for a short time in the surgical oncology unit at Johns Hopkins."

Dad's eyes widened. "Impressive."

"I thought so, too. When I heard about her background, I mentioned the possibility of a short-term trip over here."

Ellie leaned forward to speak past Eric. "She's actually planning to come soon while her passport's still valid. And her primary patient passed away, so she'd like to visit before establishing a new client relationship."

"I see. Does she plan to come alone?"

"As far as I know." Eric sipped his water and added, "I could find out for sure, though."

"Let me know the date, and I'll schedule the Gulfstream."

"That'd be great."

The group remained relatively quiet for the rest of the meal. Her dad pushed his plate away with a sigh. "Excellent meal as always, Nicci."

"Amen!" Toby leaned back and patted his stomach. "I might have to start running with you, brother."

"Be at the terrace after sunrise. We'll see if you can keep

up." Eric leaned over and whispered in Ellie's ear. "You want to tell them our other news?"

Ellie glanced at Toby and Nicci then back to Eric. "Sure."

He tweaked her hand and scraped back his chair. "Anybody want a cup of coffee while I'm up?"

Mac raised his hand. "I'll take one."

Nicci started to rise as Eric rounded the end of the table. He placed his hand on her shoulder. "Stay there. I've got this." He moved to the counter by the wall and took two Styrofoam cups from a stack. "Ellie has an announcement."

All eyes turned to her.

She twisted the napkin in her hand and gave her dad a crooked smile. Breaking the news to him a few days earlier had been one of the hardest things she'd ever had to do.

Dad gave her an almost imperceptible nod.

She took a deep breath and blurted out, "Eric and I will be moving back to Washington after the wedding."

"What?" Toby whirled around and looked at Eric, his eyes even wider than usual.

Moses and Miriam didn't seem surprised although she doubted Dad had said anything. Somehow those two had an uncanny ability to sense things that were coming.

Eric placed a coffee cup by Mac's plate and then eased back into his own seat. "The doctor Ellie saw in Washington recommended we relocate." He paused and gave her a tender look. "We want to stack the odds in our favor for Ellie to deliver a healthy baby."

"You're pregnant?" Toby asked.

"No." Ellie chuckled and scraped shredded bits of napkin into a mound by her plate. "The doctor told us to wait a couple of months before we try again."

Eric jumped in. "So we may be gone for about a year."

"Or God may have other plans for them."

Dad's words sent a chill through her. Was it possible her

time in Africa was coming to an end?

Ellie turned back to her dad. He met and held her gaze as if to let her know it was all right. She looked away and spoke to Nicci, her voice tight and high-pitched. "Anyway, we want you and Toby to use our house while we're gone."

Toby and Nicci exchanged a long look, and then Toby shook his head. "I don't know, man. It don't seem right."

"You can still build a house in the field behind ours. This gives you time to get your hangar built first." Eric took Ellie's hand. "And you'd be doing us a favor, keeping up the place."

Nicci covered her cheeks. "We don't know what to say."

Ellie rose and moved to Nicci, hugging her from behind. "You and Toby did so much to make our wedding day special." Ellie leaned in with her cheek next to Nicci's. "Let us do this for you."

Nicci placed a calloused hand on Ellie's face and pressed her close. "Thank you."

"You're welcome." Ellie gave her an extra squeeze and glanced over at Eric.

He must have read her unspoken plea. He joined her and placed his hands on Toby's broad shoulders. "Maybe this way, we can talk you into getting married before we have to return to Washington."

# CHAPTER TWENTY-FOUR

In Brock's mind, a hospice worker would need to be a strong woman. Someone capable of exhibiting compassion but with the proper balance of stoic pragmatism. From what he'd heard from Eric and Ellie, Brock envisioned Joy Stockman to be a middle-aged, no-nonsense woman. Possibly big-boned and muscular, with mousy hair and strong hands.

The attractive woman who exited the Land Rover blew that preconceived image out of the ball park. Petite. Trim, but not pencil thin. Silver hair that fell just below her chin and moved freely in the breeze. Joy Stockman was anything but frumpy.

Brock moved from the clinic porch to greet her. Her face lit with what seemed to be genuine warmth as she made eye contact with him.

Eric took her arm and guided her closer. "Dad, this is Joy Stockman, the guardian angel God sent when my father was at his worst."

"It's a pleasure." Brock extended his hand, which Joy enveloped in both of hers.

"Dr. Whitfield, I'm happy to finally meet you. Eric and Ellie have told me some glowing things about you and your work here."

"Thank you. We're delighted to have you visit. And please, call me Brock."

They moved toward the terrace with Eric carrying her two bags. Joy reached the patio area and gasped. "Oh my. This is beautiful."

Ellie stood beside her, looking out at the field. "Dad and I used to meet out here every morning to watch the sun rise."

Brock moved closer but caught himself before placing his

hand on Joy's shoulder. He might have to exercise more restraint for this particular volunteer. He pointed instead. "Just over that hill. It's quite spectacular." He glanced back to Ellie. "Maybe you could get up some morning and bring Joy."

Joy sighed. "I would love that. I'm actually a morning person."

Brock rubbed his hands together. "All right then. Eric will take your bags to the house. After you get settled, Ellie and I will show you around."

She turned to him and smiled, giving him his first up-close glimpse of her eyes. A darker blue than Ellie's. Vibrant and expressive.

Eric started toward the double doors. "Would Ellie's old room be all right?"

Brock paused, surprised. "She's not staying at your house?"

Ellie slid her hand under his arm as they followed Eric through the door. "We tried to talk her into staying with us."

Joy angled back. "She's right, Brock. And I appreciate the invitation, but I wanted to get the full mission experience and be closer to the clinic."

Eric pushed open the bedroom door. "Here we are."

Joy seemed as happy with the tiny room as if she'd been ushered into a four-star hotel. Eric placed her luggage on the half bed.

Ellie checked the bathroom. "Good. Miriam's been here already. You'll meet her later today. She keeps everything around here clean and well-stocked."

Brock stayed at the door. "Does Joy have your cell number?"

Ellie nodded. "I gave her yours, too." She turned to Joy. "It'd probably be a good idea for Dad to have your number."

Joy grabbed her phone. "Of course." She slid her finger across the screen.

Brock took out his phone and reading glasses and began punching in numbers. "Got it." He pocketed his phone. How long had it been since he'd exchanged numbers with a pretty woman? "Okay. We'll leave you now."

The three left Joy's room and headed down the hall to the dining area. He and Eric went to the coffee counter. Ellie grabbed a bottle of water from the cooler.

There were many other things he could, and most likely, should be doing. But he lingered there with Eric and Ellie taking advantage of what little time they had left. How different this compound would be without them.

Brock took his usual seat, flanked by Eric and Ellie. "She's nice, isn't she, Dad?"

"Yes. A charming lady." Brock went on the offensive. "Eric, have you noticed how Ellie's dimple gets more pronounced when she's up to some kind of mischief?"

Eric took the bait. "Now that you mention it, yes sir. I have."

Ellie sat back and crossed her arms. "I don't know what you're talking about."

Brock grinned but said nothing more. Enough for now that he'd hinted he was on to her matchmaking scheme. He took a sip of coffee, surprised most of all that he didn't even mind.

Brock awoke sometime early in the morning. He reached for the clock on the bedside table and angled it toward him. Three-thirty. He pushed back the covers and slid his feet into worn slippers. Not bothering with a light, he fingered the armrest of the recliner, rifling for his bathrobe. He shrugged into it then felt his way through the pitch-black room. He fumbled for the doorknob of the French door leading to the terrace then clicked it shut behind him. A cool breeze blew from the west. He lifted his head and breathed deeply. A familiar creak of the shed door sounded and within seconds a large calico cat was rubbing against his leg.

"Hello, Lucy." He stooped, stroking the length of her back. The cat whipped around, begging for more. "Come to keep me company, old girl?"

Bitsy scampered over, more out of curiosity than loyalty. The one kitten they'd kept from last summer's litter because Ellie had fallen in love with her. Brock swallowed hard. He'd do anything to make that girl happy, which was exactly why he had to let her go now.

Enough. He forced his mind back to the present and settled in a chair. Lucy claimed her rightful place on his lap. Bitsy scampered off, still a kitten in a grown cat's body. He sat for a long time, staring at the dark field and letting random thoughts mingle with prayers.

He leaned forward, flexing and arching life back into the foot that had fallen asleep. Lucy squirmed and finally jumped off his lap. Both he and the cat turned at the unmistakable sound of one of the double doors opening. Joy padded out, her slippers making a slapping noise on the concrete.

Brock smoothed down his own silver hair that he'd not bothered to comb. "Hello."

"Oh." She whirled and clutched the folds of her robe tighter about her chest.

His eyes, by now well-adjusted to the darkness, had no trouble making out the look of shock on Joy's face.

"I'm so sorry." She took a step back. "I didn't think anyone would be out here this early." She returned to the double doors.

Brock rose and powered through the stabbing pin pricks of his lifeless foot. "Please. Don't go."

Joy turned, still clutching her robe. "I couldn't sleep."

Brock touched her arm and gestured to a chair. "It usually takes a while to adjust to the time change."

Joy sat, and Lucy wasted no time jumping on a fresh lap.

"Sorry. That's our Lucy. Ellie says she's an attention-junkie. Just shoo her down if you don't want her there."

"No, she's okay." Joy had a pleasing laugh. "I love cats. In fact, I hated to board Lucky. She's going to hate being cooped up for two weeks."

Lucy stopped licking her forepaw and gave him a self-satisfied stare that seemed to indicate Joy's lap was far superior to his.

"You have a wonderful place here." Joy looked down and nuzzled the fur on Lucy's head. "I was expecting something a little more primitive."

"God has been very gracious. He's sent us some very good people to help out." The predawn darkness kept him from seeing her response. "Eric mentioned several times how much you helped him through the death of his father."

"I'm glad I could be there. It's never easy to witness the death of a loved one. I became especially close to a hospice worker during my husband's illness. After Frank passed, God led me to join the group. I wanted to offer back some of the help and comfort that was given to me." After a moment's pause, Joy added, "Eric is a special young man. I think God has great plans for him."

Something Brock had thought many times himself. "Yes. I think you are right."

"What about you? What caused you to leave America and start a mission compound in Angola?"

Not surprisingly, Eric had not revealed their unique connection. His son-in-law was as discreet as he was loyal. Brock gave her the standard generic answer he gave to all visitors to the compound. "God radically changed my life when I was in my thirties. I became a believer and wanted more than anything to use my skills as a doctor to make a real difference in people's lives."

All true. Maybe one day he would elaborate. Go deeper and tell her the whole story of how he'd caused the accident that killed Eric's parents. About his time in prison. About his wife who'd left him, taking his daughters away for good.

He'd sensed from the moment he met her that Joy Stockman was a woman of genuine faith. Something he admired, whether in man or woman.

"I'm looking forward to helping out during the next two weeks. But I have to warn you, my surgical skills may be a little rusty."

"We're very happy to have you."

Joy gave a little shove to Lucy, who seemed reluctant to give up her comfortable spot. "I guess I'll go in now."

Brock stood, too, thankful the darkness covered the uncharacteristic awkwardness he felt. He walked with her and opened one of the double doors.

She placed her hand on his arm. "I enjoyed talking to you, Brock." She turned to go.

"Likewise." He responded to the shadowy form moving down the hall. "Come back in about an hour and a half if you'd like to see your first African sunrise."

She paused and turned. "Yes. I think I will."

Brock smiled, then entered his bedroom from the hall at his usual brisk pace. He checked the time. If he hurried, he could shorten his devotions and prayer time so he could shower and dress before watching the sunrise.

Just this once.

# CHAPTER TWENTY-FIVE

Eric slid packing tape across the box, sealed it, and wrote on the side with a sharpie: Ellie's Scrubs.

Packing was his specialty and a chore Ellie seemed glad to relinquish. So while she was in the clinic saving lives, he was packing up and sorting. Deciding what would go and what would stay for Toby and Nicci to use.

Saying good-bye was nothing new. Seemed like most of his life had been one long succession of good-byes.

But this one would be hard. Maybe because his gut was warning him that when they boarded the Gulfstream day after tomorrow, a new chapter would begin. One that might not lead back to Africa.

Ellie's dad seemed to sense it, too, and bore it the same way he met every change life threw at him: With quiet trust in whatever God had planned.

Brock Whitfield. Eric's throat tightened. By far, the best human being he'd ever known. One of the most humble and self-effacing men on the planet but with the intestinal fortitude of a spiritual giant. The man who'd refused to give up on him. Prayed him back to life. Prayed him into faith in Christ. Some people would have been surprised at his thoughts, given the connection between Brock and Eric's parents. But that was what God could do. It amazed him still.

At the sound of Toby's clumping footsteps, Eric turned away from the door, his thumb and forefinger applying pressure to the bridge of his nose.

Lady bounced into the room ahead of Toby, who brought more boxes into the room.

"Sorry, man. She rushed in the door the second I cracked it open."

Eric tousled the fur on Lady's neck. "You know, she comes with the house."

Toby dropped the boxes on the floor at the foot of the bed. "That's all right with me. She won't go lacking for some loving. That's for sure. She's like the compound mascot. Hey, where you want me to put my stuff?"

"That's all you're moving in?"

Toby looked sideways at the boxes. "Mostly. I left a lot in my old room in the staff dorms. Thought I'd make it my flight office or something."

Eric turned back to the closet and sectioned off the clothes he and Ellie would need for the wedding and the flight. He put the rest in the last box.

"Want some help?"

Eric shook his head. Maybe he should go ahead and say something. Get the emotional stuff out of the way ahead of time. "One year today."

Toby shook his head. "Huh?"

"You brought me here."

Toby checked the calendar on his watch. "Son of a gun." He sat on the side of the bed and shook his head. "It's been quite a year."

Eric sat beside him. "I guess you know how I feel about that." Eric slung his arm across Toby's shoulders. "I owe you my life. You're better than a real brother to me."

Toby hung his head, for once not even bothering to respond.

Eric continued before Toby recovered enough to talk. "I know you will, but I'm asking you to watch over things around here. Keep me informed."

Toby nodded. "You can count of it." He raised his head and grinned. "You know, I gotta take Nicci to meet Momma pretty soon. Couldn't get Momma on a plane for nothing. So we'll look you up when we come."

Eric laughed. "I can't wait to see Nicci and your sisters gang up on you."

Toby's eyes widened. "Oh, man. Didn't think of that."

Ellie served as backup that wasn't really needed. Joy handled herself in the clinic like the accomplished pro she evidently was. Dad even let Joy close surgeries, a chore he usually reserved exclusively for himself.

They finished the surgeries for the day. Ellie rubbed the back of her neck and drifted through the clinic. A dull ache had weighed heavy in her chest throughout the day. It wasn't the clinic. The glorious sunrises. The rain beating against the butterfly-shaped leaves of the mopane tree. Although she'd certainly miss them.

She was having trouble leaving Dad. Her vision blurred. A tear dropped on the last report she had to file. She used the edge of her sleeve to wipe it.

How could she leave him? Even if it was only for a year. Who would help him when the clinic was swamped? Who would sit with him on the terrace?

She stood at the window of the day clinic looking out at the compound, now quiet after what had been a slow day. The afternoon sun would be in the optimum position to hit the stained glass in the chapel. She checked her watch. One hour until dinner. Then a practice run-through of Toby and Nicci's wedding.

She moved like a person in a trance, drawn by an irresistible pull toward the chapel sanctuary. She reached the steps and shoved open the door with a hefty push of her hip and shoulder.

Her dad sat on the front pew, a clipboard in his hand. He shifted and gave her a warm smile. "Ellie. Come in. I was just going over some notes for the wedding."

She moved to the front and sat beside him leaning in to give him a nudge with her shoulder. "Hey, Dad."

He put his arm around her and hugged her tight. "I'm glad you came in, sweetheart."

She could only nod. One word and the tide of emotions would break through the dam. And if she started crying, she might never stop.

"One of my favorite things to do is get alone with God and replay all the miracles He's done in my life." Dad took it from there, doing what he did best. "Nothing lifts my spirit more." He gave her a tender look. "And one of the biggest blessings has been you, sweet Ellie. To see how God has worked in your life. How you've embraced this life of faith and poured yourself so selflessly into the lives of these people. Watching you grow and thrive has meant more to me than anything. Working side by side with you. Sharing the triumphs as well as the losses."

Yes. The losses, like the girl they couldn't save. Ellie remained still, taking in his words. It somehow comforted her to know he'd been reminiscing, too. "I don't want to leave you."

He nodded and after a moment, said, "We don't have to figure it all out. We just have to take the next step. Do the next thing. That's all. And the next step is for you to go back to Washington. I spoke with Eric at length." He dropped his head to look her in the eyes. "Did he tell you?"

She shook her head.

"About a week ago, I guess. Prayed with him. He has peace this is the right move for you two."

She straightened and looked up at him. "But who will help you? Some days, both of us are going non-stop."

He smiled. "God will provide."

She dropped her gaze to her hands. "And you'll be lonely." The one thing she feared most about leaving.

He shifted and raised her chin with his finger, his face full of compassion. "No amount of miles will change the closeness we share. I will always be as close as your phone. And if you need me, I will come." He choked on his words. "I lost you once, Ellie. I will never lose you again." He hesitated then said, "But I'd like for you to do something when you get settled in Washington."

She waited, expecting it to be something about staying close to Jesus.

"I'd like you to contact your mother. Reconnect with her."

"Mother?" As in the woman who basically disowned her for choosing to remain in Africa?

"Your mother won't contact you. You'll have to make the first move. Invite her to your house. Tell her you want her to meet Eric. Ellie, you might be the only person who could help point her to God. Her heart has closed. She wants nothing to do with me."

"She certainly doesn't mind spending your money." Ellie waited for the reprimand she figured she had coming. Instead, her dad gave her a sad smile that pierced her heart even more.

"Reach out to her, sweetheart. Sometimes the most difficult people are the ones who need the most love. Now, don't you worry about me. I want you to go. I'd like some grandchildren before I leave this earth."

She laughed. "And I'd love to provide you with lots of them. You'll be the world's best grandfather." They both fell silent. "I'm going to miss our talks," she added, her voice now somber.

"You can call me. Anytime. But God has given you an extraordinary husband. He hasn't quite found the path God wants him to walk, but he's seeking. He's sharp, Ellie. And he's got a heart for God."

"You don't think we'll come back to Africa, do you?

His hesitation answered for him. "I can't say. Listen to

me. God gave you and me almost three wonderful years. I'm so thankful. And it will be my greatest joy to see you and Eric find God's purpose and plan for your lives—whether it be here or Washington or some other place."

"I love you, Dad."

He hugged her close and kissed the side of her face above the temple. "And I love you."

"Oh dear. I think we're late for dinner."

"Go ahead. Tell them to start without me. I'll be along in a bit."

Brock maintained his composure as Ellie left the chapel. He waited until the wooden door clicked shut to release the breath he was holding. The heavy ache that had driven him into the chapel returned with a vengeance.

Unwanted tears filled his eyes as he gazed up at the stained glass image of the risen Christ. "You've never let me down, Jesus. I meant what I said. You are enough." He leaned forward and covered his face with his hands. "Why, God. Why is this hitting me so hard? Help me through the lonely days when Ellie and Eric are gone."

Tears streaming down his face, he held out his hands, palms up. "Here they are, Jesus. All the pieces of my fragmented heart. I'm surrendering them to You … Again."

# CHAPTER TWENTY-SIX

Ellie dressed in the cream-colored sarong she had worn on her wedding day. She'd done her hair in loose-flowing waves, the same as then.

"Almost time." Eric pushed open the bathroom door.

Ellie swiped on pink gloss and smacked her lips together. "Just finished." She stuffed mascara, eyeliner, and lip gloss back into the makeup bag and glanced up.

He smiled at her reflection. "I'm glad you're wearing that dress." He moved behind her and placed his hands on her shoulders. "You're even more radiant today."

She grinned back at his reflection in the mirror. "It's because I'm so happy."

He pushed aside her hair and kissed the inside curve of her neck.

"Hmm." A little shiver rippled through her. He wrapped his arms around her and pulled her back against the rock wall of his chest.

She relaxed into him, resting her hands on top of his. "I'm glad I didn't know six months ago we'd be handing over our house to Toby and Nicci and moving back to Washington."

"Having second thoughts?"

She shook her head. "Just being sentimental. We made some good memories in this house."

His expression softened as if he totally understood. "We're not done making memories in this house. There will be lots more. For us and, hopefully, for our children."

Children. The whole reason they were making this move in the first place. She shot him a grateful look and turned, slipping her hand in his. "We'd better go."

A perfect day. Rare for the end of rainy season. The sky was soft blue like a robin's egg with not one cloud in sight. As if God was shining down on the wedding.

Nothing about this day would be traditional. No fear of seeing the bride before the ceremony. No fanfare of the bride marching down the aisle. Just a cozy ceremony witnessed by a small group of people who loved them both.

Ellie left Eric and rushed ahead, maneuvering through the crowd clustered outside the chapel and aiming for the vibrant-colored dress with bold geometric shapes. She reached Nicci and clutched her ice-cold fingers. "You look amazing."

Nicci covered her smile with one hand and slid the other down her dress as if caressing its folds.

Eric caught up and slapped Toby on the back. "Today's the day."

"'Bout time you showed up. I was getting worried."

Eric patted his shirt pocket, his expression serious. "Took me a while to find the ring."

Toby's eyes grew wide.

Eric slung his arm around Toby's shoulder. "Let's hurry up and get it on her finger before I lose it again."

"That ain't funny."

Eric laughed and reached for Ellie's hand. They followed Toby and Nicci into the chapel. Miriam, Moses, and Joy filed in with everyone else who could be spared from the clinic and congregated at the front, not bothering to sit on the benches. The couple stood before the podium facing each other.

Dad gave Ellie's arm a squeeze as he moved past and took his place on the platform. "Welcome, friends. Today is a very special day." He gave Nicci a warm look and spoke directly to her. "I remember the first time I saw you. About twenty years ago, wasn't it?" He glanced at Moses as if seeking confirmation and then back to Nicci. "You'd traveled for days and collapsed right out there on the steps of this chapel. Exhausted. Covered in mud. Miriam took you in. Cleaned you up."

Nicci nodded, wiping her cheeks.

"You were in such shock, it took days to find out what had happened." Dad spoke to the group. "A rebel faction had ransacked her village. Slaughtered her entire family. Nicci had been stabbed but managed to survive by pretending to be dead."

"Barely fifteen." Dad paused and looked down. After a few seconds, he continued, his voice choked with emotion. "Forgive my sentimental musings."

Dad seemed to regain his composure. "We tried to love you back to wholeness. We told you about Jesus, the great healer of brokenness. And I'll never forget the day you came into the clinic and pulled me out into the hallway. Told me you must have Jesus living in your heart."

Dad turned his attention to Toby. "It seems Nicci is the happiest when she is serving others. She will be a wonderful gift to you."

Toby smiled at Nicci, clearly moved.

"And Toby, I remember when you came with your church youth group. Someone had backed out. The church insisted you come instead. A last-minute trip with all expenses paid. There's no doubt in my mind. God orchestrated that trip."

Dad addressed the group. "Toby was the clown of the group."

Toby laughed and nodded.

"He came to my office the night before he was supposed to leave. Told me he'd been pretending to know God, but inside he was faking it. We talked well into the night. Then he got on his knees in my office. Prayed the first sincere prayer of his life."

Things Ellie didn't know. About Nicci or Toby. Her mind drifted back to her early days in Africa, when Dad had loved her through her depression. Had patiently taught her about God and true faith in Jesus Christ.

Behind Dad, the afternoon sun streamed through the stained glass image of Christ, casting a warm glow on the faces of everyone in the chapel.

Then out of nowhere it hit her. With the exception of Joy, each person standing here would probably never have trusted Christ had it not been for her dad. Tears blurred her view as she looked up at him with even more admiration than she had before.

She focused again on what he was saying, "Toby, it will be your job to protect Nicci. To make her feel secure in your love. To stay close to God and seek to fulfill His plan for your lives.

"Nicci, it will be your job to love Toby. To encourage him and help him."

Dad stepped down from the platform to stand in front of the couple, who still faced each other. He spread out his arms, placing his hands on their shoulders as if cocooning them in his embrace.

"Tobias, before God, do you now accept Nicci as your wife."

"I do."

"Nicci, before God, do you now accept Tobias as your husband."

"I do."

"Marriage is a wonderful blessing from God, to give you companionship and mutual enjoyment in each other. Toby and Nicci, you have had many years of living solitary lives. God is now making you a family to become heirs together of the grace of life. May you have a home centered around and grounded upon your faith in Jesus Christ. Gracious Father, we ask Your blessing…"

It took Ellie a couple of seconds to realize Dad was now praying. She bowed her head and wiped tears that had seeped out when she closed her eyes. She paid close attention, not letting her mind stray to her own thoughts as it sometimes did during his lengthy prayers. Who knew how long it would be before she would hear another one.

Eric wrapped his arm around her. She didn't have to open her eyes to know he had left his spot by Toby to stand beside her. She leaned into his embrace and reached up, placing her hand on top of his.

Dad ended his prayer and nodded to Toby who covered the scars on Nicci's face with his hands and leaned down to kiss her.

Eric handed Toby the last bag to store in the luggage compartment of the helicopter. "I still don't know how you talked Nicci into flying in one of these things with you."

Toby gripped Eric's extended hand and leaned in, swinging his left arm up to give him a last embrace. "What can I say? I got the little woman wrapped around my little finger."

"I'd say it was the other way around." Eric tightened his hold and squeezed Toby's arm. "Take care, brother."

Toby held on a moment longer and nodded. "Take care."

Toby turned toward the helicopter where Nicci was already seated and buckled. "Ready, Mrs. Williams?"

Eric backed up to the group gathered on the grassy field for the sendoff and put his arm around Ellie. Toby gave a thumbs-up and took off.

They waved and watched until the chopper disappeared behind the hills to the west.

Moses stepped closer and placed his hand on Ellie's arm. "Tomorrow we will be saying our good-byes to you."

"And I will be sad to leave."

Miriam walked over and gave Ellie a hug. "We will wait until tomorrow to be sad."

The well-wishers dispersed, with Mac promising to have the Land Rover ready by eight to take them to the airfield.

Eric leaned closer to Ellie. "Want to invite your dad and Joy over?"

She gave him a grateful look. "I would love that."

"Think it's safe to raid Nicci's kitchen?"

She giggled. "Probably not. But we'll be long gone before she gets back."

He nudged her toward her dad. "You do the inviting while I steal some eggs and cheese."

"Deal."

Eric squirted olive oil into the skillet and whipped the eggs into a frothy mixture. Omelets. A relatively easy skill he'd perfected during his stay with his dad last summer. He prayed he could still pull it off. Had been a while.

Ellie put Lady and her food bowl on the back porch. "Now we can eat in peace." Ellie wiped her hands and sat at the table next to her dad. Joy sat on the opposite side.

"Are you sure I can't help?" Joy called out.

"No, ma'am."

Ellie hopped up from her seat and joined him at the stove. "What can I do?"

He checked under the edge of the bubbling mixture then gave her a sideways look. "Trying to give them time alone?"

Ellie punched his arm and with an over bright smile, spoke so everyone could hear. "Let me get the plates for you, honey." She dropped her chin and gave him a smug, wide-eyed stare.

"Okay, little Miss Innocent, I'm ready for those plates."

"Right." She rushed to open the cupboard.

"The other door."

She paused, her hand poised in midair, and gave him a blank look.

"The smaller ones."

She switched sides and dutifully grabbed them.

He guided the omelet onto the plate. "Smaller plates make the entrée look bigger."

She nodded, her mouth forming a silent *O*.

He poured another batch into the pan. "Sprinkle a little cheese on top and hand that one to Joy."

Ellie returned and stood beside him, holding another plate in front of her like a street urchin in line at a soup kitchen. "How do you know when to fold it over?"

"Trial and error." Eric slid the spatula under one edge. "See how runny it still is? You have to cover the pan to let the top set without letting the underside get too brown." He adjusted the heat and offered her the spatula. "Want to try it?"

Ellie backed away and shook her head. "Not if we're feeding guests."

He grinned and checked it again. After a few more seconds, he folded the omelet over.

"Oh my goodness." She gave a little gasp as he raked it onto the plate. "A. Maz. Ing. It's like the perfect blend of lightness and fluffiness."

Her praise made him a total sap. Made him want to do the next one even better just to impress her again. He tried to keep the goofy grin off his face as he poured the last batch.

Ellie started getting water bottles and orange juice out of the fridge and totally missed the opportunity to rave over his last omelet. He divided it onto the last two plates, giving her the slightly larger one. Eric joined them at the table. "Sorry it took so long."

"Don't apologize. Brock was entertaining me with stories."

Ellie gave him a knowing smile. He somehow kept a

straight face and asked her dad to pray.

As they started to eat, Joy said, "Eric, I know you were somehow connected to the CIA. Why did Toby fly you here and not to a regular hospital?"

Eric had just taken a bite, which gave him enough time to formulate an answer. Maybe one day he would tell her the whole story with details almost too miraculous to believe. For now, he told her enough to satisfy her curiosity. "I found out one of my bosses was on the take. He sent me on a bogus mission to Zambia. My gut warned me it was a setup, but I was pretty cocky. Thought I could smoke him out. The one thing I did right was to bring Toby in as backup. I would be dead right now if it wasn't for him."

It had been a long time since he'd hashed it up again. His gut churned at the thought of that night. He could still feel the bullet ripping through his leg as if it were still there. He realized he had stopped talking and all three were looking at him.

Ellie's eyes were large and troubled.

Joy shook her head, with her hand covering her mouth.

Dad spoke, his voice quiet and serious. "Eric shouldn't have survived that attack. Toby risked his life to land in the hot spot and pull Eric into the helicopter. He flew him here, stopping twice to refuel. He knew the CIA would check all the major hospitals. Eric almost bled out but somehow survived the trip. We got him into surgery without much hope of keeping him alive."

Joy took a deep breath and slowly blew it out. "What a story. Eric, you're a miracle."

"Yes, ma'am. Thank God, I am."

"So it was while you were here that you learned about God. And your close call with death helped you become a Christian?"

Eric smiled at Ellie sitting across the table and chose his

words carefully. "There were a lot of factors. I guess you could say God took all the props out from under me, so I had nowhere else to look but up."

"Unbelievable. You should write a book telling your story."

"I've thought about it. More like a journal, maybe for my children to read one day. My dad kept a journal. I'm glad he did."

"How wonderful for you to have it now that he's gone."

The room went silent. Never in his whole career as an agent had he made such a stupid slip of the tongue. Joy clearly thought he was talking about the man she knew to be his father. He didn't bother to correct her. "Yes, ma'am. It's helped me really get to know my father in a way I never had before." One day he would fill her in on the rest. For now, it was too much information, way too soon.

"You have an incredible story. Thank you for sharing it with me."

"You're welcome. It was good to go through it again now that I'm a Christian. Changes the whole way I look at it."

Joy gave him a warm smile. "I was telling Brock that I think God has great plans for you."

"Thank you." Somewhere deep inside his gut, he thought so, too. He just wished God would tell him what those plans were.

Joy wadded up her napkin and put it on her plate. "I guess now would be a good time to tell you what God has been laying on my heart. I'm praying about coming here for an extended stay," she spoke to Ellie's dad, who sat across from her. "That is, if you think I could be of some service to this ministry."

Ellie's dad didn't hesitate. "We would welcome your help and thank God for it."

She seemed relieved. "I'm so glad. I need to return to the

States and take care of some things. And try to convince my son I haven't lost my mind."

Ellie reached for Joy's plate and placed it on top of hers. "Don't let that stop you. My mother thinks my dad is a practicing witch doctor who used his black magic on me."

Eric chuckled and hoped she was kidding. He took his and Dad's plates to the sink. "If we have to lose you, I can't think of a better place for you to go."

"I second that," Ellie said.

"I'm very excited about it." Joy pushed back her chair. "What time will we be leaving in the morning?"

"Eight. Ellie and I thought we'd watch the sunrise with you in the morning, Dad. Then we'll come back and get ready. You're welcome to join us if you don't mind getting up that early."

Joy nodded enthusiastically. "I'd love to see the sunrise again."

Again could mean only one thing. He cut his gaze over to Ellie. Her dimple indicated she thought so, too.

Joy checked her watch. "But I need to get in bed pretty soon."

"I'll walk you back." Ellie's dad stood and slid his chair back into place. "Thank you for the wonderful meal."

"Yes." Joy reached for Ellie's hand. "Thank you. Let me help you wash up those dishes."

In unison, he and Ellie said, "No." They walked with them to the door. Ellie slid her hand through Joy's arm. "You did us a favor. We were feeling a little blue after Toby and Nicci left. Your visit cheered us up."

"It was the perfect ending to a perfect day. Thank you again." Joy hugged them both.

Dad gave his hugs, too.

With a last little wave, Eric closed the door.

Ellie grabbed his arm and squeezed. "I'm so excited."

It didn't take long to find out why. She clicked off the lamp then rushed to the window and peeked through the slats in the blinds. "I think they're starting to like each other."

Eric stood behind with his arms crossed. "Are you seriously spying on your father and Joy?"

"Of course not." Ellie maintained her position at the window. "Just practicing my Sherlock skills. If he takes her hand, my suspicions will be confirmed."

"Hmm." Eric scooted next to her for a quick look. "They're going in. Now we'll never know."

Ellie sighed and stepped away from the window. "Poke all the fun you want, Eric Templeton. But you're not fooling me. You'd like to see them get together as much as I would."

Eric laughed and raised his hands in mock surrender. "Guilty."

Ellie gave him a superior look. "Exactly."

She whirled away, providing him the perfect opportunity to swat her on the bottom. "Where are you going now, Miss Sherlock?"

"If you must know, I'm going to the bathroom and then change so I can clean up your mess."

Eric took a moment to enjoy her sassy exit from the room then went into the kitchen. With luck, he could get most of it done before she made it back. He stuck his hands in the hot soapy water and managed to finish the plates and glasses when he felt Ellie's arms slip around his waist. Her hand found the spot on his side where the bullet that had done so much damage had exited. "Tonight brought back a lot of memories." She leaned against him, pressing her face against his back. "I'm so thankful you didn't die."

He reached for a hand towel, dripping water and leaving a puddle on the counter. He turned in her arms, hoping she'd stay put. She did, and he smiled his gratitude.

She kept her arms around his waist and snuggled against

his chest. "I've wanted you to hold me all day."

He complied, holding her close. Her hair tickled his face. He released his hold long enough to smooth it down and then decided to relocate.

"Come on, baby." He kissed the top of her head. "Let's go make another memory."

# CHAPTER TWENTY-SEVEN

By the first week of June, things had settled into a new normal back in Washington. Ellie paused in the doorway with her hands on her hips, surveying what would be their bedroom for possibly the next year. Clean, uncluttered, with not one thing out of place. Just the way Eric liked it.

She reached behind and massaged her lower back. She couldn't keep blaming her tiredness on jet lag. Eric had snapped back to normal after only one day. A little longer for Joy. But two weeks and still dragging? Ridiculous.

She carried the stack of clean clothes to the dresser and deposited them before closing the drawer with a purposeful shove. Last box unpacked and clothes put away. Not exactly worth bragging about since it had taken two whole weeks to accomplish. But weeding out the outdated, worn-out clothes— even some of her favorites—had taken more time than anticipated.

But now it was done, and Eric would be pleased. It had taken less than a week after they married for Ellie to figure out his near-obsessive need to have everything clean and in its proper place. An obsession she didn't necessarily share. Not that he ever said anything about her less than perfect housekeeping skills. Instead, he quietly cleaned up her little messes without the least hint of annoyance.

What kind of guy did that? And how lucky was she to get him?

She tossed the empty box in the hall to grab on her next trip down the stairs. The white down comforter called to her, and she answered, even though she'd vowed not to take a nap today. But Eric wouldn't be home for at least another hour.

She eyed the bed. If she was going to give in and take a

nap, she was going to do it right. She kicked off her shoes and flipped back the comforter. The silky sheets welcomed her as she lay on her back, scooting to the middle. She took a deep breath and released it slowly, letting herself fully relax. Her hand slid across her lower abdomen. Crampy and bloated, which could mean only one thing. She sighed. What a shame. She'd hoped the memory they'd made their last night in Africa might have made something else too.

*Soon God. Please let it be soon.*

Ellie opened her eyes. The room was dark, and it took several seconds to remember where she was. Even longer to remember what day it was. She lay curled on her side. Eric sat beside her with his hand on her thigh.

She raised up slightly and propped her head on her hand. "What time is it?"

He touched the screen of his phone. "Nineteen…um…seven twenty-one." He smoothed the hair back from her face and laid his hand on her forehead. "Feel all right?"

Seriously? Had she really slept the rest of the afternoon? "Have you been home long?"

"A little while. I went for a run."

The faint scent of his body wash clung to him, and his hair was still damp. "I even slept through your shower? I can't believe it."

"I showered in the hall bathroom."

"You did?"

"You were out. Didn't have the heart to wake you." He shifted so she could get her legs out from under the covers.

She sat up beside him and rubbed her eyes. "You sweet man. I don't deserve you."

"You didn't answer my question."

Question? Her disoriented brain scrambled to recall what

question it was.

"Are you feeling all right?" His voice was quiet. And maybe a little worried.

"Oh." She gave a nervous laugh and leaned against him with a playful nudge. "Yeah. I'm fine. Just lazy. I really meant to be up before you got home. Lesson learned. Next time I'll set the alarm on my phone." She rose and pulled up her socks before sticking her feet into her sneakers.

"Feel like eating dinner?"

Ellie whipped around. "Don't tell me you made dinner, too."

He grinned and took her hand, leading her out the door. "Don't get too excited. I stuck some potatoes in the oven before my run. Grilled some chicken breasts. Nothing to it." He gestured for her to go first and then grabbed the empty packing box, placing it on his shoulder. "But I might mention I singlehandedly averted a national crisis at work today."

Ellie stopped halfway and turned. "And solved world hunger, no doubt." She poked him in the ribs. That ticklish sweet spot just under his armpit, guaranteed to make him double over, grip his side, and beg for mercy. The empty box on his shoulder went flying over the bannister. He laughed and captured her forefinger, holding on tight. "You're going to pay for that one."

She poked him with the other hand, seizing the opportunity to jerk free. The second she reached the floor at the bottom of the stairs, he catapulted over the bannister and body slammed her into the living room sofa. She couldn't quit laughing or catch her breath and tried to milk it to her advantage. "Get up." She begged. "I can't breathe."

He shifted but kept her arms pinned to the sofa. "Uh-uh."

She struggled, not quite ready to admit defeat. "Where's Joy? I need backup."

His amused grin held triumph. "Not home."

"Okay. Okay. I give."

"Show me the dimple."

"Never." She folded in her lips, fighting it for all she was worth.

He leaned closer, inches from her face, his eyes boring into hers. "We have vays of making you comply." His mock German accent was her undoing.

She burst out laughing. "There. You win."

He grinned and kissed the side of her cheek. "That's better." He backed off the sofa and extended his hand, pulling her up.

"Whew." She caught her breath and smoothed her hair. "That was fun. I'm fully awake now."

"Let's eat." He headed to the kitchen. "Grab a couple of plates, will you, babe."

"Big ones or little ones?"

He opened the oven and pulled out a covered platter. "Depends on if you want to be impressed."

"I'm already impressed."

His face crinkled into a smile. "Big ones."

He served the food and brought their plates to the table. The meal looked wonderful, but the first whiff of the grilled chicken almost made her gag. A cruel little psychological joke her body was playing on her. Had to be nerves. Or maybe a bug.

Eric reached for her hand and asked God to bless their food. Much shorter than one of Dad's blessings but just as heartfelt.

She smiled and split open her baked potato. "Where is Joy tonight?"

Eric handed her the salt. "She texted this afternoon. A hospice volunteer asked her to cover one of her patients for a couple of days. She booked a room in a hotel to be closer to the patient's house."

They ate for a while. Then Ellie broke the silence. "I guess now would be a good time to break the news to you."

Eric stopped chewing.

"My mother's coming for a visit. I invited her because Dad specifically asked me to. I never dreamed she'd actually come."

"Is there an ETA?"

Ellie gave him an amused look. "You've been spending way too much time at the agency."

"Point taken. Do you know when she's coming?"

"Well. There's good news and bad news."

Eric pushed his empty plate back and folded his hands on the table. "Lay the bad on me."

"She's flying in next Thursday."

"That's the bad?"

"Well. It doesn't exactly leave much time to prepare."

"Five days. Plenty of time to get the guest bedroom ready."

"I meant prepare, as in mentally. To get psyched up."

"I see." Eric took a sip of water and nodded. "But at least this way you won't have long to dread it either. So, what's the good news?"

Ellie couldn't handle another bite. She pushed her plate away and propped her elbows on the table. Something her mother would probably comment on. Along with about a million other things. "She's squeezing in a visit between two important functions so she'll be leaving on Sunday."

"Only two full days." He gave her an encouraging smile. "Baby, we've got this."

"Don't speak too soon."

Eric stacked their plates and took them to the sink. "If I could survive three months with Bob Templeton, I think I can handle two days with your mother."

# FREEING ELLIE

# CHAPTER TWENTY-EIGHT

It seemed appropriate that the first really stormy day since their return to Washington would be the day her mother was scheduled to arrive. Ellie stared out her bedroom window, her mood as black and turbulent as the weather.

Eric came into the room and joined her at the window. "Your mom's flight has been delayed due to weather. Buys us a little time."

She nodded without much enthusiasm and wrapped her arms around her middle. "I figured out why I stayed in Africa instead of returning to Texas." She turned to look at him. "I was afraid. Of facing Allen again. And mother with all her fake socialite friends. And, I guess, mostly of myself." Tears she'd been holding back all morning started to fall. "So I stayed where I felt safe."

Eric put his arm around her. "There's nothing wrong with wanting to be safe. I think God kept you there to strengthen you."

"Then why do I feel so weak right now?"

"You're not weak. I've seen you in action. But I know exactly how you feel. I felt it, too. when I came back to Washington with my dad. Felt like I was walking blindfolded through a mine field. I wouldn't have made it without my daily calls to you and your dad."

Shame washed over her. Only now did she fully comprehend what those weeks must have been like for him.

"God used that time to help me depend on Him. Maybe that's what He's doing for you now."

Deep inside, she knew Eric was right. She turned and pressed her forehead against his chest. He slipped both arms around her and held her, without saying a word.

Despite never having seen a photograph, Eric had no trouble picking out Ellie's mom in the sea of people barreling down on them. A Scandinavian beauty, Ellie had said, with all the enhancements money could provide to keep her that way.

The woman approaching them was certainly a looker and strutted with all the panache of a movie star well aware of people's admiring looks. Taller than Ellie, probably due to the spiked heels she wore. Her hair fell loose and free to the top of her shoulders and had probably been just as glorious as Ellie's back in the day. She wore a silky button-up blouse over slightly form-fitting slacks. Classy and more understated than he'd expected.

She slowed as she drew near and scanned the crowd until she spotted Ellie. She raised a slender, well-manicured hand in a half-wave, causing a bangled bracelet to slide toward her elbow. Her mouth curved up in what must have been an attempt to smile. Nothing else moved on her otherwise flawless face, which made her seem as plastic and emotionless as the discarded Barbie dolls his older sisters had left behind.

And there was definitely no dimple.

He could almost feel a force field of bundled-up nerves and tension emanating from Ellie as her mom closed the distance between them.

"Ellie, darling." She gripped Ellie's shoulders and gave the illusion of kissing both cheeks with her puckered lips.

Ellie's smile seemed much more genuine. "Hello, Mother. I'm glad you could come." Ellie pivoted toward him. "Mother, this is Eric."

"Eric." She clasped his hand and leaned closer, her breath hinting she might have had a cocktail or two on the plane. "I've been dying to meet the man who finally captured my Ellie's heart."

At that moment, he realized he had no clue what her last name was or what to call her. "Nice to meet you, ma'am."

She gave his arm a playful swat. "None of this ma'am stuff. Call me Roz, darling."

It had taken less than a minute for his gut to size her up. The woman was a player whose saccharin words came laced with cyanide. A woman who had to have control and would use any manipulation to get it. The kind of woman who sickened him. Give him the straight-shooting and brutally honest Bob Templeton any day.

The old Eric would've said yes, ma'am just to spite her and put her in her place. Instead, he steeled his face to show more warmth than he felt. For Ellie's sake ... Ellie, who had steadily inched herself against the wall behind him. He turned and gave her a reassuring smile. "If you'll take your mom to get her luggage, I'll pull the car up to the door."

The slight shake of her head made him switch to plan B. "Or I could go with you."

"Yes. I would like that."

He took her hand and started walking. "Baggage claim is this way."

Roz fell into step beside Ellie. "The flight was dreadful. Some child screamed almost the entire trip. You'd think the airline would have the decency to put children closer to the back."

They reached the revolving conveyor. "I hope they didn't lose my luggage. You remember, Mallory Tidwell, Ellie? Lost every stitch she owned. Of course, it was one of those cheap overseas flights ... Oh. There they are."

Eric grabbed the two bags, surprisingly heavy for a two-day visit. "The car is on the first floor of the parking deck. You feel like walking?"

"As long as it isn't very far."

Eric hesitated. "I can drive around and pick you up."

"Maybe that would be best. These shoes weren't exactly made for walking." She hooked a hand through Ellie's arm. "We'll wait right here for you."

Ellie shot him a desperate look that seemed to say, "Hurry back." Not an easy feat considering the amount of traffic.

Twenty minutes later, he pulled the Mustang up to the curb and hopped out, rushing to open the passenger door. Ellie crawled into the back while he threw the bags into the trunk. Roz took her time getting in. He closed the door as soon as her feet cleared then waved to the driver waiting for his spot.

"What a quaint little car." Roz turned back to Ellie. "Your father had a Mustang when we first married. I hated it. So loud. It was like riding in a cattle car." She placed her hand on Eric's arm. "Of course, yours is much nicer."

He glanced up at the rearview mirror and caught Ellie smiling at him. She sobered the minute her mother turned again. "Tell me again. How did you two meet?"

"Eric was at the mission hospital recuperating from an injury. I helped take care of him, and we fell in love."

"Thank goodness he took you away from that horrible place. What exactly do you do, Eric?"

"I work with Central Intelligence training new recruits." He zipped around an SUV and accelerated onto the interstate. "Was it raining when you left?" Small talk wasn't his strength but steering a conversation away from nosey questions was. No need to mention he'd already checked DFW for their take-off weather.

By the time he pulled into the driveway, the rain had slackened to a drizzle. He pushed the garage door button and eased into his spot next to Joy's Mercedes. He could almost hear the wheels clicking in Roz's mind, wondering why they hadn't driven the nice car to pick her up. With her lack of a filter, it wouldn't surprise him if she asked.

Ellie escorted her mom inside and had already introduced

Joy by the time he made it in with the luggage. The delicious aroma of a roast baking in the oven permeated the kitchen giving it a homey feel.

Joy wiped her hands on a dish towel and shook Roz's hand. "Have you ever been to Washington?"

"Good heavens, no. Although I have sponsored one or two political fundraisers." Her tone became even more condescending. "Helped get a few people elected, I might add."

Ellie placed her hand at the small of her mother's back and nudged her toward the living room. "Eric will take your bags up to your room, won't you, honey?"

"Of course." He hid his grin and followed them up the stairs.

"Here you are." Ellie pushed open the door and let her mom enter first.

Roz scanned the room. "You don't have a room with a bathroom?"

"The bathroom is at the end of the hall," Eric said. He wouldn't give up their room—not even for Ellie's sake. Maybe this would make *Roz* go home early. Or at least go to a hotel.

Ellie grabbed his hand and pulled him toward the door. "Mom probably would like to rest a little before dinner."

He took the cue. "Let us know if you need anything, Roz."

He backed out and closed the door before she could respond. He'd started toward the stairs when a hand grabbed him and pulled him into their bedroom. Ellie shut the door and leaned against it, her eyes closed. He put his hand beside her head, bracing himself on the door. "Baby, you're doing great."

She shook her head. "Not gonna make it."

He smiled and kissed her forehead. "By the way, thank you."

She opened one eye and peeked up at him. "For what?"

"For being nothing like your mother."

"Do me a favor. If I ever become like her, hire a hit man."

He chuckled. "I won't need one. I'll take care of it myself."

Ellie gave a soft knock and held her ear close to the door. Maybe she could tiptoe into the room and leave the towels on the dresser.

"Come in."

Ellie pushed open the door and forced a cheerfulness she didn't feel. "I brought you some towels."

Her mother was sitting in the chair next to the window. She glanced up with the same disdain she had shown since entering their house then turned back toward the window. "Such dismal weather for the middle of June."

Ellie closed the distance between them and looked out the window, too. "Yes, it is. Maybe it will clear up tomorrow." Ellie placed her hand on her mom's thin shoulder. The bony sinew seemed to stiffen beneath her fingers. "How have you been, Mom?" Ellie asked, surprised most of all, that she really wanted to know.

"Me?" Her mother's attempt to laugh came out more like a sneer. "I've been marvelous."

Even with no one else to impress, her mother still couldn't be genuine. Ellie settled on the edge of the bed, gazing at her mother as if for the first time. "That's good, Mom. And Gwyneth? How is she?"

Her mother sat erect and proper, like the queen of England with her hands folded in her lap. "Your sister just celebrated her fortieth birthday. Black tie event at the Carrington's. Simply everyone was there."

Ellie smiled and nodded. "I'm sorry I missed it." Not exactly a lie. She was at least sorry she had lost touch with Gwyneth. Ellie dropped her gaze to her hands and picked at a fingernail.

Her mother gasped. "Ellie, your nails! Positively disgusting. We must go tomorrow and get manicures."

"Mom, I …"

"I won't take no. See this nail." The bony forefinger she extended had chipped polish. "I simply must get it repaired."

Ellie scrutinized her own hands. She hadn't had a manicure since her spa day at the end of February. Once the beautiful French manicure started chipping, she removed the rest. There was no place for perfectly sculpted nails at the hospital clinic. "Okay. I'll try to get us an appointment." Besides, it was a nonthreatening way to spend some time with her mother.

Was a real conversation even possible with this shallow woman? She longed to have the same kind of talk like those she had with her father. Only one way for that to happen. "I wanted to thank you for calling Dad when I was in the hospital."

"Oh, please." Her mother stood and walked to the dresser. She rummaged through her purse and pulled out a cigarette case and silver-plated lighter. "Had I known he was going to whisk you away to that god-forsaken place and brainwash you, I would never have made that call." She returned to the window and strained to crack it open.

Ellie jumped up to help. With a hefty grunt, she was able to loosen and raise it a couple of inches. "There."

Her mother lit the cigarette and relaxed against the seat. She took a deep drag and slowly blew it out. The humid air kept the smoke from dissipating.

"And I got so sick of trying to explain where you were. I don't know how you'll ever be able to show your face in Dallas again."

Anyone that dared to argue with her mother lost. She had learned that lesson very well. But she had an unspoken commitment to fulfill, and this might be her only chance. "Do you believe in God, Mom?"

Her mom leaned forward, shaking the two fingers that held the cigarette at her. "Don't you start preaching at me, young lady."

Ellie didn't respond.

"Of course I believe in God. Everybody in Texas believes in God. And I've given plenty of money to charities. Don't forget that." Her mother thumped the edge of the cigarette, flicking ashes out the window.

There was so much more Ellie wanted to say. About how good God is and how He had changed her life. But handling conflict was definitely not her strength, so she chickened out. She wiped her sweaty palms down the sides of her jeans and stood, trying hard not to fidget. "We should be eating in about an hour. Can I get you anything to drink until then?"

Her mother shook her head and continued her brooding stare out the window."

"All right then. I'll see you then." Ellie turned to go, not waiting for a response.

The hour passed all too quickly. Ellie escorted her mother to the table and pulled out a chair.

Her mother hesitated. "We're going to eat in the kitchen?"

"Yes, Mom. This is where we always eat."

"Oh, of course." She nodded and took her place. "I should've realized you're just staying here until you find something more suitable."

Ellie didn't bother with a reply. "What would you like to drink?"

"Chardonnay will be fine."

Ellie kicked herself for not mentioning options first. "Sorry. There's water, tea, or coffee."

The queen of disappointing looks shot her another one.

"Water, I guess. Do you have Perrier?"

Eric stood at the counter, carving the roast beef. "Check the pantry, babe. Might be one or two in there."

Joy arranged the serving bowls on the counter next to the roast beef and took off her apron. "Okay. Grab one of these plates and serve yourself over here. It'll give us more room at the table." She handed a plate to Ellie's mother and motioned for her to go first.

Ellie sat next to her mom. Joy came to the table last and set her plate beside Eric's. "Let me grab the salt and pepper, and then you can ask the blessing."

With a sharp intake of breath, her mom asked in a whisper clearly meant to be heard. "You allow the help to eat with you?"

Eric's hand on his water glass stilled. He turned and leveled his gaze at her mom.

Ellie held her breath and looked down at the napkin she twisted in her hands. Whatever Eric was about to say, her mother certainly had coming.

His tone, when he finally spoke, was surprisingly kind. Almost pleasant. "Joy isn't the help, Roz. She's our guest. Just like you."

Joy returned to the table and either hadn't heard or was pretending she hadn't. Probably the latter.

Eric reached for Ellie's hand. Ellie took Mom's hand and whispered, "Eric is going to pray and bless the food."

Her mother's hand remained limp and unresponsive, and she made no effort to take Joy's hand. She probably didn't bow her head or close her eyes either. Ellie didn't bother looking.

At least, his prayer was short. At his "Amen," Ellie reached for her glass of water, suddenly feeling very thirsty.

Maybe she drank too much. Or too fast. She swallowed hard and debated if she should excuse herself.

She shouldn't have waited. She started to rise, but her foot got caught on her mother's chair. Holding the liquid back with just her hand proved as futile as trying to cork Old Faithful. Water spewed through her fingers, covering her mother's hair and dripping down to her shoulders.

Her mother gasped and jerked away from the table, which finally freed Ellie's foot. Ellie sank to her knees and continued to gag, only now with dry heaves.

"Ellie, what's the matter with you?" Her mother's hysterical question hung in the air.

Eric knelt beside her and held a wet paper towel to her forehead with one hand and her hair back with the other.

"I'm so sorry," Ellie managed to whisper.

"Shh." Eric took the paper towel and wiped her mouth. "It's okay."

"You don't have some kind of virus like Ebola, do you?" Her mother's lip curled.

Ellie's gagging subsided. Eric wrapped his arm around her and pulled her closer.

She tried to pull away. "No. You'll get it all over you."

"You're not pregnant, are you?" Her mother was even more insistent.

Eric tightened his hold on her.

Joy came to the rescue. "Let me help you get cleaned up, Roz."

He waited until the two women left the room to reposition and pull Ellie against him. He smoothed back her hair. "Feel better?"

She nodded. "Of all people I had to throw up on."

He chuckled. "I wish you could've seen the look on her face. Priceless." He tilted her chin up. "Are you?"

"Pregnant?"

He nodded.

"I don't know. I've been queasy lately, but I think it's too early for morning sickness. I figured it was just nerves."

He gripped her shoulders and stood, pulling her up with him. "Let's go upstairs and get you cleaned up."

Ellie reached for the glass of water on the table and took a sip. "Not until I clean up the mess I made."

"Leave it. I'll take care of it after I take care of you."

"You are so sweet, but no." Ellie wadded several paper towels and held them in the stream of water from the kitchen faucet. "I'm totally mortified. This is my penance for ruining Joy's wonderful dinner."

She dropped to her knees and started dabbing. "There's not as much on the floor as I thought. I think most of it landed on Mother." Ellie glanced up and caught Eric's barely concealed grin. She lowered her gaze so he wouldn't see hers. "Um. Why don't you check on Mother and Joy while I finish here?"

"No, thanks." Eric grabbed more paper towels and joined her on the floor. "I think I'll let our resident professional deal with your mother."

# FREEING ELLIE

# CHAPTER TWENTY-NINE

Ellie stood next to Eric and waved as the taxi backed out of their driveway and disappeared down the street. "Well, Mom's visit was an epic fail."

"Oh, I wouldn't call it epic."

"I spewed vomit all down her hair the first night. She announces that she's leaving the next morning and insists on calling a taxi instead of having us drive her."

"Yeah … you're right. Epic."

Ellie elbowed his ribs.

Eric gripped his side and laughed. "But she did mention she was leaving so you could recover from your virus. That shows a huge degree of motherly concern, wouldn't you say?"

"I don't have a virus."

"I know. Which is why you and I are going to spend the day together."

Her eyes lit up. "The whole day?"

"The whole day. That is, if you're feeling up to it."

She turned and stood on her tiptoes to bring her more to his level. "I'm feeling on top of the world."

He kissed the tip of her nose. "Good. 'Cause I'm going to show you my town."

Ellie squealed and threw her arms around his shoulders. "You mean it? Like the Lincoln Memorial and the Washington Monument and—"

He chuckled and picked her up, making her feet dangle over the porch. "And the Tomb of the Unknown Soldier and anything else you want to see."

"Put me down. I've got to get ready."

"Me, too. Right behind you."

Ellie sat beside Eric on a grassy hill overlooking the National Mall, methodically peeling strips off the twig in her hand. "This has been a perfect day."

He lay back and placed his hands beneath his head. "I know something that would make it even better."

She tossed the twig and lay back beside him. "What?"

"We could stop and get a pregnancy test."

Ellie raised up on one arm. "But what if I'm not?"

He closed his eyes and spoke in a casual tone. "Then we try again tonight." He opened one eye and squinted, looking up at her. "Which would really make this a perfect day."

"Oh you." She lay back, feeling very lazy and perfectly content. Eric wanted a baby, too. Why should that surprise her? Maybe not surprise her. It just pleased her to know he was excited, too.

A feeling of overwhelming happiness swept over her. A tear trickled out but she had no idea why. It slid down her temple and into her hair, soon followed by another one. Before she knew it, the trickle became a flash flood.

It might have gone unnoticed if she hadn't sniffed a couple of times.

Eric turned and looked at her. "Are you crying?"

She covered her mouth with her hand and nodded.

He brushed away a tear with the back of his hand. "Why?"

"Because." She moved her hand up to cover her eyes and took a couple of jerky breaths. "I'm so happy." The last word brought a fresh torrent of tears.

"Come here."

She shook her head and kept her hand over her eyes. His hand slid underneath her neck, and he rolled her into his arms. She burrowed against his chest and released a long shaky sigh. "There. I feel better."

Eric held her a while longer, stroking her hair, massaging her back. "Hey, baby?"

"Um?"

"I don't think we'll be needing that pregnancy test. I think your spontaneous meltdowns are confirmation enough."

# FREEING ELLIE

# CHAPTER THIRTY

Eric did the math. According to his calculations, it was entirely possible their child could be born on his birthday. He pushed the end of his tie through the loop and tightened it. Of course, their visit to Dr. Conley next week would be more specific.

Eric stepped into the bathroom to double check his tie in the mirror. Ellie slid over to give him more room.

"You look handsome." She smiled, her mascara wand poised over her eye.

He tugged his tie into place and cringed as she applied the mascara, coming dangerously close to her eye. "Do you ever poke yourself with that thing?"

"Sometimes." She moved the wand to the other eye and spoke without blinking. "I try really hard not to. It hurts like the dickens."

An involuntary shudder ripped through him. "I can imagine."

He lingered a while, completely fascinated as always, that she could go from freshly scrubbed innocence to diva gorgeous in a matter of minutes.

She finished the ritual, and he instinctively stepped back, knowing what would come next. Ellie bent over, throwing her hair forward. She splayed her fingers and rifled through her hair. Then she straightened, tossing her hair back with a couple of shakes of her head.

She squeezed pink gel-like stuff onto the tip of her ring finger. Then she smeared it across her lips and pressed them together.

And seemed completely unaware what she was doing to him.

"I used to have this little voice inside of me. Kind of like my conscience, I guess. Called him Simon."

Ellie glanced at his reflection in the mirror and nodded. "Seems vaguely familiar. Has Simon been talking to you again?"

Eric shook his head. "Swapped him out. I try to listen to God now."

"That's good. I like a man who listens to God. And what exactly has God been telling you?"

He moved behind and slid his hands to the front of her waist, smiling at her in the mirror. "He's telling me the next time you're getting ready for church, I need to be downstairs, drinking coffee and reading my Bible."

She chuckled and leaned back against him. "Good plan. Especially if we want to get to church on time."

A feeling of gratitude washed over him. He splayed his hand across the slight rise of her lower abdomen and gave her a serious look. "I'm really happy, Ellie. Happier than I have a right to be. About our baby. About our life together. I'm a blessed man."

Ellie turned and hugged him, holding him tight. "Don't make me cry and mess up my makeup. Not on the day we're supposed to join the church."

Ellie usually had no trouble following Pastor Tim's sermon. But today, all she could think about was having to go forward to join the church. Her mouth went dry. If she hurried, she could go get a sip of water. A long sip. But then she'd probably have to pee. Just thinking about it made her have to go. And what if, out of the blue, she threw up, right in front of God and everybody? She pushed away memories of the night she'd thrown up on her mother.

Eric reached over and took her hand. He must have read

her mind. Or maybe she was fidgeting so much that he took her hand to keep her still.

And if walking to the front of the church was freaking her out, what would she do next week when they both were baptized?

Music began to play, and as the congregation rose, Eric looked at her as if waiting for her to give him the go-ahead. Ellie met his gaze and took a deep breath. Feeling more like Joan of Arc marching to the stake, she nodded and took his hand, following him down the aisle.

Surprisingly, the worst part was taking that first step. After that, a feeling of peace enveloped her like nothing she'd ever felt before. Like taking that leap of faith and having Jesus catch her.

Pastor Tim greeted them and shook their hands. After the invitation had concluded, he announced their news to the congregation.

"We're so happy to have Eric and Ellie Templeton come forward to join our church. I've had the privilege to get to know this sweet couple over the last couple of weeks. They have a wonderful testimony of salvation, and they'll both be following the Lord in believers' baptism next Sunday. Stick around and shake their hands and welcome them into our church family. Eric. Ellie. God bless you. We're excited to see what God is going to do in your lives in the days ahead."

The pastor prayed, and afterward, throngs of people came to the front to shake their hands or hug them. Joy was one of the first, and she stayed beside Ellie the rest of the time.

Pastor Tim and his wife, Heather, also hung around until the last person had congratulated them. "Well, Miss Joy. Next week will be your last Sunday with us, is that right?"

"That's right. I pushed back my departure one more week so I could see Eric and Ellie get baptized."

"Heather and I would like for you three to eat Sunday

dinner with us next week."

Eric looked at Ellie first before accepting. "Thank you. We'd like that very much."

Joy placed her hand on Heather's arm. "Let me bring something."

"Oh, no. Just bring yourselves. Consider it our little sendoff."

# CHAPTER THIRTY-ONE

Ellie pulled the white maternity tee over her head and turned sideways. It hugged her baby bump enough to make her actually look pregnant.

Mid-July. She'd made it to eleven weeks. Maybe after today's ultrasound, she could start to relax.

She stepped out of the bathroom. "What do you think?"

"One second." Eric finished typing something on his laptop and then swiveled around. "I like it."

"You've liked them all. You need to commit."

Eric pulled his lower lip and nodded. "Definitely this one."

Ellie studied his face. "Is that what you really think? Or are you caving so I'll leave you alone and let you get your PowerPoint done?"

"Want to know what I really think?" Eric left his chair and joined her at the mirror.

Her hands slid around his neck. "Um-hum."

"I think you're adorable, especially in these denim shorts. The white top looks great. So, I commit."

"Good. 'Cause it's my favorite." She stepped back and pulled the material taut over her abdomen. "Look."

Eric grinned and placed his hand against the tiny bump. "Feels like a little walnut."

"I know. I can't wait to see our little walnut today."

He kissed the tip of her nose. "Me either."

Ellie settled in a chair against the wall in the waiting room. She and Eric seemed to be the oldest couple there. A girl across the room looked to be no more than fifteen. Just a child herself, profoundly pregnant, unsmiling, and staring at the floor. The woman next to her kept her head down, her focus on a book.

*God, I know how scared that girl must be. Send her some help.*

The girl left her seat and went to the restroom.

Ellie's heart started racing. Was she the help God planned to send? She ripped a page from the back of her notebook and hastily wrote her name, phone number and the name of their church. Then wadded it up and tore out another sheet. She started over, printing the information instead. Not great but at least legible this time.

She entered the bathroom. The girl was washing her hands. Ellie pulled out a couple of paper towels and handed them to her. "Hi. My name's Ellie."

The girl's expression had the beat-down look of someone who had lost hope.

Ellie dug her fingernails into the palms of her hand and jumped in. "Listen, I just want to say I think you're a very brave young lady."

The girl looked up, tears flooding her eyes.

Ellie touched her hand. "I don't know you or your circumstance, but you look very young. And scared."

The girl dropped her gaze and wiped the tears now dripping off her cheeks.

"What's your name, honey?"

The girl hesitated and then spoke in a muffled voice. "Heather."

"Heather, I've made some really bad decisions in my life. I wish I'd had the courage to have my first baby instead of caving in to the pressure to abort." She placed the crinkled notebook paper in Heather's hand. "This is my name, phone number, and the name of my church. I am kind of a new Christian. Learning about God and His forgiveness has totally changed my life. God loves you. He wants to help you go through this. Call me. Or text me. Or come visit our church. You'd like it. In fact, the pastor's wife is named Heather, too."

Heather stared at the paper. "I can't believe this. I asked God last night that if He was real, would He do something to let me know it."

Ellie put her arms around Heather and hugged her tight. "God is very real, and He loves you. Do you happen to have a Bible at home?"

Heather nodded.

"Let me see that paper I gave you." Ellie took it and wrote "the Book of St. John" at the bottom of the page. "Find a Bible and start reading. This is a good place to start. And text me. I'm serious. I will help you any way I can."

Heather took the paper. "Thank you so much."

Ellie took Heather's hand. "We need to get back out there, but before we do, would you mind if I pray with you?"

Heather shook her head, and Ellie didn't hesitate. "Dear Father, Thank You for letting us talk without interruption. Thank You for Heather's courage to have her baby. Send her help. Open her heart to Your love and truth. Fight for her, Jesus, the way You fought for me. Amen."

With another hug, Heather slipped out of the bathroom.

Ellie stayed behind and placed her hand over her chest. Definitely not her comfort zone.

She returned to the waiting room, but Eric's seat was empty. Surely he wouldn't have gone back without her, would he? Maybe he went to the men's restroom. She glanced around the room and found him, seated next to Heather's mother. The woman responded to something Eric said, and then she smiled. Eric stood and nodded to the woman and to Heather when she reached her chair.

What a guy. He gave her arm a little tweak as he sat beside her.

Ellie turned to him. "Were you doing what I think you were doing?"

"What do you think I was doing?"

"Running interference."

"You were both gone for a long time. The mother started fidgeting and glancing at the bathroom door, so I tried to buy you more time."

Ellie's mouth fell open. "You are amazing. How on earth did you know?"

"Not many people rip out, not one, but two pieces of notebook paper. Write something, very fast, I might add, and then rush off to the bathroom." He grinned and hooked his hand under her arm. "It also confirms what I've always suspected."

"And what's that?"

"You're an angel."

Ellie shivered as she lay on the ultrasound table.

The technician smiled. "I'm Sandra, everybody's favorite person in this office. I'm going to give you a sneak peek of your baby." Sandra took a tube off the tray. "Sorry. This gel feels like it's been in the freezer."

Sandra squirted a generous glob on Ellie's belly, which sent another shudder rippling through her. Eric stood beside her, holding her hand.

The pressure on her bladder made Ellie squirm. She craned toward the indistinguishable gray mass on the screen.

"Right there." The words came out slowly. The technician drew with a stylus, making a white circle on the screen. "There's the fetus." She took a measurement and made a notation on the screen. "Approximately 1.5 inches. Everything looks good.

Ellie gasped and wiped her eyes to clear her blurred

vision. Eric leaned in for a closer look.

"Wait a minute." Sandra moved the wand to another spot.

"What's wrong?" Ellie's gaze left the screen and flew to Sandra.

Sandra held up her hand, her focus on the screen. "Nothing's wrong."

Her soothing tone wasn't enough to calm Ellie's racing heart.

"Okay. Look at this." Sandra made an arrow on the screen. "Another fetus." She whirled around and held her hand up for a high five. "Woo hoo. You're having twins!"

Ellie's hand flew to her mouth instead. Could this possibly be true? "Show me." Her tears fell freely down her cheeks.

Sandra highlighted the two fetuses with an arrow pointing to each.

Ellie took her eyes off the screen long enough to look at Eric. He was staring at the screen, his jaw working with emotion. He squeezed her hand and leaned down to kiss her.

Sandra took a few freeze shots before wiping the excess gel off Ellie's stomach. She pulled out a Doppler stethoscope and turned up the volume. After a few tries, sounds of the heartbeat echoed through the tiny room.

"Okay. That's one..." She repositioned the stethoscope. "And here's the other one."

Ellie's shoulders convulsed with unrestrained emotion. She took some deep breaths to suppress the sobs that wanted to come. "Thank you. Thank you so much." She was so grateful. To Sandra, to Eric, and mostly to God. She wanted to thank the entire universe. How could she contain this much happiness?

# CHAPTER THIRTY-TWO

Eric fumbled with the key, hardly able to unlock the door fast enough. He pushed it closed with the back of his foot and pulled Ellie into his embrace.

She wrapped her arms around his waist and clung to him.

He settled his chin on top of her head. "I texted your dad."

Her head jerked back. "You didn't …"

"No. I told him we'd Skype around six his time."

Ellie nestled back against his chest. "Good. That gives me two hours to catch a nap."

"Come on. I'll tuck you in." Eric followed her upstairs. He closed the blinds, pulled back the comforter, and waited while she made a pit stop in the bathroom.

She backed up to the bed and kicked off her sandals. They landed nowhere near each other. She lay on the bed and burrowed toward the middle. "Thank you." Her hand reached toward him. "Stay with me a little while."

One of his shoes landed on top of her sandal. He aimed the next for her other one but missed by half a foot.

He settled next to her. Ellie lay facing him, her nose no longer red, but her eyes still puffy.

Eric smiled at her. "I could tell you were happy today. You cry when you're happy. You cried a lot when you heard those heartbeats."

"I got a little loud, didn't I?" Her hand caressed his face. "I noticed you shed a tear or two."

He nodded. "You must be rubbing off on me. Twins. That was nowhere on my radar screen."

"January 14. You know what that means?"

"Let me see." He rubbed his chin. "If they come a little early, they'll be born on my birthday?"

"Something even better. That's the week I lost our baby. And now we're having two. It's like God's sending us a double blessing during that same time. Like the rainbow after a storm. Gives me hope. Makes me feel like God really does love me. I'm so happy."

"Does that mean you're about to cry again?"

"Probably. You'll have to get used to the floodgates. I'm going to be happy for a very long time.

"Just the way I like you." He leaned over and kissed her. "Now, get some rest. I have a couple of errands to run. What can I bring you for lunch?"

"Um. Some kind of salad. A Caesar maybe, with grilled chicken on top."

"Yes, ma'am. Anything else? Dessert?"

"Better not. I have a feeling this walnut-sized baby bump is going to morph into a basketball before we know it."

Ellie slept hard and woke to Eric's soft touch on her shoulder. She turned on her back with a long, lazy stretch.

"You know, when you do that, you look like Lucky."

She grinned. "Is that why you're stroking my belly?"

"I'm still in shock. Touching them makes it more real." He moved to the computer desk and pulled out the chair. "Time to Skype."

That energized her. She settled in the chair with Eric on his knees beside her.

With a few clicks, her dad was smiling back at them. "Hello, kids. I've been counting the hours until we could talk. Tell me the news. Do we have a due date?"

"They'll be here sometime around January 14."

"They?"

Ellie laughed. "Twins, Dad! We're having twins."

His eyes dominated the screen. "Honey. I'm thrilled. How

are you feeling?"

"I'm on cloud nine. Eric is spoiling me rotten."

"Good for you, Eric. What do you think about all this?"

"It's almost too good to be true. It's crazy. I wanted to stand on the street corner and pass out cigars to perfect strangers."

Dad chuckled. "I know what you mean. I think I'll call a staff meeting after we say good-bye. Can't wait to see their faces when I tell them."

Ellie leaned closer to the screen. "How's Joy doing?"

"She hasn't stopped working since she arrived. She and Miriam have become quite close. I think God sent her at just the right time. She's even convinced Nicci to let her help out in the kitchen."

"Be sure to give her our love."

"Will do. I'm sure you'll hear from her after I tell her the news. She'll want details, I know."

He looked down at his folded hands, a gesture that sent a pang of homesickness through her. "You will come when the babies are born, won't you, Dad?"

"Absolutely. God willing, I'll be there."

"And pray hard that nothing goes wrong."

"Let's pray now."

Eric placed his arm around her. Ellie touched her dad's hand on the screen.

"Gracious Father, thank You for the good news today. Children are a blessing and a heritage from You. Bless Ellie and Eric during this time. Protect Ellie from harm. Strengthen her and the babies. Grant peace to Ellie and Eric. Once again, You've done exceedingly, abundantly above all we could ask or think. We commit Ellie and the health of these precious babies into Your loving hands. In Jesus' name, Amen."

"Thank you, Dad."

Eric leaned closer to the screen. "Thanks."

"You're welcome. I'm going to sign off now and share the news here."

"'Bye, Dad. Love you."

Dad touched his mouth and then waved back to her.

Eric closed the Skype app then turned her chair to him. "I got you something."

"My salad?"

"And something else."

"Oh, fun. What is it?"

Eric grabbed her pinky and tugged her toward the bedroom door. "It's on the table."

"Do I have to wait 'til after we eat?"

He brought her hand to his lips and grinned. Not exactly a definitive answer, but she'd take it. Two wrapped gifts were on the center of the table set with salad plates. Eric sat and pulled one of the salads to him. She picked the smaller box first.

Eric squirted Caesar dressing on his salad. "Not that one. Open the other first."

The other one was rectangular. About eight inches long and a lot heavier than the first. Ellie had never been able to open a present slowly. She plucked the ribbon off and ripped the paper. The cardboard box gave no clues.

Eric took out his Swiss army knife and slit the tape holding the top secure.

She pulled out a carved figurine wrapped in white tissue paper. A faceless couple. The man had his arm around the woman. Each holding a baby. Ellie stared at it until tears blurred her vision and then pressed it to her chest. She gave him her best appreciative look. "Oh, honey. How perfect."

He nodded, still chewing. "I went to a novelty store, not really knowing what I was looking for. Then I saw that."

She went behind his chair and threw her arms around his neck. "I love it. I'm going to put it on my bedside table so I can see it first thing every morning."

He put his fork down and clutched her hands still clasped around his neck. "Open the other one."

Once again, she mutilated the paper. It had to be some kind of jewelry. Her breath caught as she flipped open the box. A necklace. Two sterling silver hearts entwined and studded with two diamonds that lay couched on a sheath of white velvet.

"Oh, Eric." She took it out and dangled it from her fingers.

He stood and took it from her, surprisingly deft at opening the clasp and securing it around her neck.

She turned, fingering it. "I'm going to cry again."

"Because you're happy?"

"Because I love you so much." She threw her arms around him. "With every ounce of my being."

At that moment, she was happier than she thought she would ever be again.

*Please, God. Don't let anything happen this time.*

# CHAPTER THIRTY-THREE

Eric did his best work after Ellie went to bed. He moved the computer out of the bedroom so he could work well into the night. Not only to finish the recruit training manual. The less he slept, the less he'd dream.

The nightmares had returned with a vengeance, always of Ellie in trouble and he powerless to help. Often in these dreams, Eric again became the killing machine he had once been, plowing down the men who harmed Ellie. Then, he'd jerk awake, drenched in sweat and his chest heaving.

Full-on exhaustion seemed to be the only cure.

Reading the Bible helped. Pastor Tim had given him a read-the-Bible-in-a-year schedule. Just the thing his OCD regimented personality had been looking for.

But he also found time to read about David. His mighty men. His sin with Bathsheba. A complex man to whom Eric felt a deep connection. A man who loved God. And a man who was capable of killing, sometimes ruthlessly. One time, even for the woman he loved.

His father's journal helped, too, and became his go-to manual. Eric greedily read every detail about the days when his mother was pregnant or when his father had learned something new about God. Most of all, Eric hungered for more insight into the man himself. The man who'd been willing to sacrifice himself if it meant his brother would come to Christ.

Eric started journaling a little every day, hoping to chronicle their pregnancy journey.

Life with a pregnant woman was never dull. He could use a survival guide for new fathers-to-be. Maybe by the end of this process, he'd write one himself, at least, to help other guys thrown into this experience with no prior training.

It seemed pregnant women were loose cannons, capable of changing moods quicker than thunderstorms could pop up in the summer heat.

Their shopping trips were usually good, with Ellie riding the high as they went from store to store picking out duplicate sets of baby furniture.

Keeping her fed was key. A dip in her blood sugar could spell disaster to what might otherwise be a perfect day.

Finding creative ways to make her believe she wasn't fat often proved problematic.

And the things that could make her cry could fill up a volume.

But hands down, her food aversions and preferences had become the most difficult challenge to manage. Apparently, his babies hated coffee. Hated to smell it brewing. Hated to smell it on his breath. For a man who had coffee running through his veins, giving it up for the duration was not an option.

So he set up shop outside, moving coffee grinder and coffeepot to the back porch. Lucky didn't seem to mind the company now that she was officially banished to the outside as well.

And he kept mints, gum, and mouthwash handy. There. Babies and Daddy happy. Problem solved.

But the pickled beets …

He could almost set his watch to the frequency of her nightly bathroom visits. One night, she was taking way too long. He dragged himself out of bed for a quick check. No light under the bathroom. No way she'd pee in the dark. His search ended in the kitchen.

There she was, leaning over the counter with a fork and a jar of pickled beets. She stabbed one and put the whole thing in her mouth and then turned, giving him a somewhat guilty smile that made her cheek poke out even more. Some of the red juice escaped and ran down her chin.

He shuddered and swallowed hard, trying to keep his voice normal. "So, our babies have developed a fondness for pickled beets, have they?"

Her face lit up as she nodded. "Want some before I finish the jar off?

He leaned against the doorframe and held up his hand. "I'm good. Wouldn't want to deprive the babies."

"Mock all you want." She raised her chin with haughty disdain and shook her finger at him. "Pickled beets are delicious. The perfect blend of sweet and sour."

Her hair hung in tousled disarray around her shoulders. Her baby blue tee was pulled tight across her belly with the waist of her pajama pants pulled underneath the mound. In that moment, she'd never looked more beautiful to him. She dropped the fork in the empty jar and turned the adorable grin on him. And with it the Kryptonite dimple.

The little vixen knew full well what she was doing.

He marched over to her, being careful to breathe through his mouth to escape the slightest whiff of the disgusting concoction. He took the jar and set it on the counter with deliberate purpose then reached for her hand. "Ready to go back to bed?"

She nodded.

"Okay. After one quick stop."

"Good. I always have to pee."

"Not just pee. We're going to brush our teeth."

She slowed and tilted her head, giving him a confused look.

"Baby, I can't handle kissing pickled beets."

# FREEING ELLIE

# CHAPTER THIRTY-FOUR

Granted, there had to be room for two babies in the limited condo of her womb but surely not this much room. Ellie's favorite white tee could no longer stretch over her watermelon-sized belly. She opted for a white maternity tank, the coolest thing she could find.

She pulled her hair into a ponytail, as she had every day for the past five weeks. Anything to get it off her neck in the brutal August heat and humidity

At least, the freezing air of the doctor's office would be a blessed relief.

Half an hour later, Ellie waddled down the hall of the doctor's office with Eric right behind her. She knew the drill by now. Bloodwork. Urine sample. And finally, the long-awaited ultrasound. The big reveal.

Eric helped her get positioned. The frigid table felt glorious to her overheated skin, as did the ice-cold gel on her belly.

Sandra slid the wand over the tight mound. "Ready to see what you're having?"

Ellie reached for Eric's hand. "I thought this day would never get here."

"Okay. Here goes."

The babies tightened into a ball. Sandra did some prodding. "Come on, little babies. Help me out." She applied pressure to the right side of her abdomen. "There. Now she's cooperating."

"A girl?"

Sandra nodded. "Look at this little sweetie. That's her hand. Oh, look. She's sucking her fist." She moved the wand to the other side. "Okay, girlie, let's see if you have a brother or a sister."

Ellie blinked only when she had to.

"Whoa. Did you feel that kick?"

Boy, did she.

"Looks like you've got a little soccer player in there."

"A boy player or a girl player?"

"Boy." She pressed some more. "Yep. Definitely a boy." Sandra laughed. "How adorable. Look at that cute nose. He's a little bigger than his sister."

"Does everything look okay?"

"Looks great. I'm getting their measurements now."

It was like she knew them already and had been waiting for them all her life. Ellie squeezed Eric's hand but couldn't tear her gaze away from the screen. "Aren't they beautiful?"

Eric leaned down and kissed her cheek. "Yeah. They look like a combination of you and pickled beets."

# CHAPTER THIRTY-FIVE

Eric stole out of bed. Ellie automatically shifted to the middle of the mattress without waking. He clicked the bedroom door closed and dressed in the hallway. Then he switched to his Flex-fit prosthesis. The one Ellie said made him look like Inspector Gadget.

Cold October air hit him as soon as he opened the door. Out in the yard, he stretched his calf and thigh muscles before his run, crunching dead leaves under his feet and stirring up their musky smell. A smell he loved even if it stirred up memories of high school and football practices and a father he couldn't please no matter how he busted his butt.

He started with a slow jog down the driveway. Still dark. One bright light shone just above the horizon in the east. His breath blew like smoke as he picked up the pace. No cars out. Just a stray cat. One of Lucky's gentleman callers, no doubt. Good thing his dad had her spayed.

His dad. Coming up on one year since he'd died. What would his dad be doing right now? Would he have reconnected with Nicholas? And could they see him and Ellie? Or know about the twins?

*God, I want to thank You again for what You did in my life. For letting me find out about You. For letting Dad find You, too.*

*Help me be a good father. Not like he was. Help me be like Nicholas. God, don't let me mess up my babies' lives.*

Sweat dripped down his face, in spite of the cold. Eric paused at an intersection then shot across the street at the first lull.

*Help me find what I'm supposed to do with the rest of my life. Africa? CIA? God, I'm walking blind. Give me some light.*

---

*And take care of Ellie ...*

Pink streaks brightened the sky as he finished his run. He bypassed the front door and went around to the back porch to start his coffee. Something to look forward to after his shower.

Maybe he should knock the wall out between his old bedroom and the guest room. Make a bigger nursery. He could start it this afternoon after the doctor appointment.

That wouldn't work. Ellie took her nap then.

Plenty of time before the babies got here. Maybe Toby could help knock the wall out when he came in November.

In stealth mode, Eric got his clothes from the bedroom. Ellie lay, burrowed under the cover, dead center of the bed. It was cold in the house. Maybe he should bump up the heat. Take the chill off before she got up.

The October doctor appointment. Ellie would probably skip breakfast as she always did on "Doctor Day."

He checked his phone for the time. Just enough time to shower and drink some coffee before she had to get up and get dressed.

Eric adjusted his steps to Ellie's slower ones as they followed the nurse down the hall.

"Here you go. Dr. Conley will be right in."

Eric nodded to the nurse as Ellie plopped down in the chair. She seemed a little out of sorts. "I'm starving."

Eric leaned against the wall. "We'll go somewhere and eat after the appointment."

"Good. I know just what I want."

*Please. Not pickled beets.*

Dr. Conley opened the door with his usual vigorous push and extended his hand to Eric first. "Good to see you." He turned to Ellie. "How are you doing?"

"Hungry."

He gave her a fatherly smile. "The babies have grown a little."

Ellie ran her hand over her stomach. "They're not the only ones who have grown."

He chuckled. "You're a little past twenty-five weeks. We want those babies growing." He sat on the stool and opened Ellie's chart.

An awkward silence followed as he took several minutes to read, occasionally flipping back to a previous page. Finally, he lowered the chart. "So, Ellie, how have you been feeling?"

"I've had some headaches. I get tired. Probably normal stuff."

Dr. Conley nodded. "How about this swelling?" He placed his hand around her swollen ankle, his fingers leaving an indentation. "Significant increase from last month."

"Probably those pickled beets." Eric said, mostly to himself.

"Pickled beets?" The doctor made a face. "That's a new one. Not as bad as the woman who spread peanut butter on sardines like they were crackers."

"Don't give her any ideas."

Ellie crossed her arms. "You two are ganging up on me."

Dr. Conley took her hand and examined her fingers. "Seriously. You might want to check the sodium level of the beets. We need to get this swelling down. Your blood pressure's elevated, too. I'd like to do a couple more tests to rule out anything more serious."

Ellie gasped.

"Just a precautionary measure," the doctor added. "We do it all the time. I'm going to give you something to help with the fluid. We'll get those tests set up for tomorrow at the hospital. Stay off your feet as much as possible. Go home. Prop your feet up. Get Eric to wait on you."

The doctor gave him a wink and with a quick handshake,

he was gone.

Eric maneuvered around the sharp spiraling turns of the parking deck and tried to shake the sick feeling in his gut. What was Dr. Conley not telling them?

Ellie's voice brought him back to earth, but he needed her to repeat. "What, babe?" he asked.

"Pancakes."

"Okay. That's what our munchkins want today?"

She nodded. "From that place on the corner of the strip mall by our house."

"Sounds good. We can drop off your prescription and go back for it after we eat."

Ellie sat with her hands folded on the ready-made shelf of her stomach. "I can drive Joy's car to the hospital in the morning."

Eric stopped at the light and looked at her. "I'll take you."

"That's sweet of you, honey, but it's just a routine test. I don't want you to have to miss another day of work."

"That's not a problem. I want to take you."

"Good. I hate parking at the hospital. And I have a hard time reaching the gas pedal 'cause I can't fit my stomach behind the wheel without pushing the seat all the way back."

He smiled and reached for her hand. "It's settled then."

Eric opened his eyes. He was accustomed to Ellie flailing around, trying to get comfortable. But whatever she was doing now was shaking the entire bed. Either she was cold. Or crying. Or both.

He turned over to take a peek.

Her eyes had rolled back, and her entire body shook with violent spasms.

He jerked up and grasped her face in his hands. "Oh, God, no." He grabbed his phone and with shaking fingers, dialed 9-1-1. "My wife's having a seizure."

"What is your name?"

"Eric Templeton." Eric spouted off all the necessary information and begged them to hurry.

Then he called the doctor. The answering service called back and told Eric Dr. Conley would meet them at the hospital. He pulled Ellie into his arms. The jerking had subsided. She was breathing, though her breaths were shallow. She lay limp and unresponsive.

Paramedics arrived and started an IV. Eric threw on his clothes and rode with her to the hospital. The doctor was waiting for them as they wheeled her in.

"Eric, wait out here until we get her stabilized. We'll get you back as soon as we can."

Eric watched them take her away then stared at the double doors, repeating the only coherent prayer he could think of. "God, please don't take her."

He probably should've waited until he knew more, but he made the call anyway. "Dad. Ellie's had a seizure. We're at the hospital. They're trying to get her stable. That's all I know, but—"

"I'll arrange a flight. I'll get there as soon as I can."

"Thanks, Dad. Dr. Conley just came out. I'll call you later."

He met the doctor halfway. The doctor placed his hand on Eric's shoulder. "Let's go down the hall to the conference room. I'll fill you in on what's going on."

Conference room. All the blood seemed to drain from Eric's face. Was she dead? Was the doctor waiting to get him to a private place to break the news? The doctor's grim face gave away nothing.

Eric followed the doctor down the hall. Dr. Conley opened

the door, and Eric went in and sat at the oval table almost identical to the one at the agency.

Dr. Conley sat and folded his hands in front of him. "Ellie has developed a condition called eclampsia. It's very serious. Can cause damage to the kidneys, the liver. It's what caused the seizure she had tonight. We've got her on magnesium sulfate to keep her from having another seizure."

Eric nodded, letting the doctor finish before bombarding him with questions.

"The only cure is to get the fetuses out. But I'd like to buy them more time. We're also giving her steroids through the IV to speed up the babies' lung development just in case we have to get them out."

"What if she has another seizure? Could she die?

"Unlikely. We've got her in a high risk unit. We're hoping the medication and the bedrest will keep her blood pressure down and eliminate the potential for more seizures."

"Could the babies survive if you got them out right now?"

"At almost twenty-six weeks, odds wouldn't be in their favor. The longer they're allowed to develop, the better. But eclampsia can put them at risk in the womb, too. We've got them hooked up to a monitor to determine whether they're in distress."

"Worst case?"

"We lose all three." Cut and dried, with no hesitation.

Eric held his breath.

The doctor put his hand on Eric's arm. "But she's stable right now. We're monitoring all three very closely. It's a waiting game. We'll know more in the morning."

Eric nodded. "Can I stay with her?"

"Of course."

The doctor led Eric back to Ellie's room. A nurse was beside the bed, reading the monitors. Ellie was asleep, her mass of golden hair framing her face. She looked like an angel. He pulled a chair closer to her bed and sat, holding the hand that wasn't connected to a tangle of tubes. He stayed in that position the rest of the night, his eyes never leaving her face.

Sometime the next morning she awoke with a jerk and gave him a blank stare. "Where am I?"

Eric forced himself to appear calm. "The hospital. You got sick last night. The doctor has you here as a precaution."

"What do you mean, sick?" She pulled her hand from his grasp and felt her stomach. "Eric, what happened? Are the babies okay?"

"The babies are fine. They're being monitored, too. Right now, everything's all right."

"Eric, stop patronizing me. What's going on?"

He sighed. "You have eclampsia. You had a seizure last night."

Her eyes closed. "Oh, no." Her mouth formed a tight line as she shook her head.

She opened her eyes with a start and grabbed his hand. "You've got to promise me you won't let them take the babies."

"Honey, they're not talking about taking the babies. Not yet."

She continued as if she hadn't heard. "They're too small. Eric, I can't handle losing them."

A nurse entered the room and looked at her monitors. "Your blood pressure's rising. We're going to give you this sedative to relax you a little bit." The nurse injected something into the IV.

The nurse left, and Ellie grabbed his hand again. "I know what eclampsia is. Promish me you …"

Her words slurred as she drifted off to sleep.

He leaned forward on the chair and placed his head in his hands. *God, do something."*

Eric dozed off and on but jerked awake every time the door opened. At seven, Dr. Conley came in. Eric stood and studied the man's face, searching for any sign of alarm.

"Good morning." The doctor shook Eric's hand while gripping his upper arm in much the same way Ellie's dad often did. "Looks like that sedative calmed her down."

Eric followed his gaze to Ellie. "Yes. I don't think she moved the rest of the night."

The doctor backed away from the bed and spoke in hushed tones. "We'll let her rest. I'll come back later and give you both an update."

Eric nodded and followed him to the door.

"Doctor?"

They both stopped at the sound of Ellie's weak voice. Dr. Conley smiled and returned to the bed. "Good morning." He took her hand and leaned over the bedrail. "You gave us quite a scare last night."

"I don't want you to take the babies."

He patted her hand and gave a reassuring smile. "We don't want to take the babies either. Here's what we're up against. The preeclampsia you showed signs of yesterday developed into full-blown eclampsia sometime during the night. That's what threw you into a seizure."

"Why? Did I do something to bring this on?"

The doctor shook his head. "There are lots of factors. Probably heredity played a big role. What happened last night is rare. We're having trouble getting your blood pressure stabilized. You have too much protein in your urine which puts you at risk of kidney failure. It's not good for the babies either."

Eric stood at the foot of the bed. Ellie's eyes were huge, frightened, and her face as stark white as the sheets.

Dr. Conley angled his stance to address them both. "The fact that she's had one seizure isn't a good sign. Another one like that could give her a stroke. Emergency C-section would be the only option at that point."

Ellie struggled to sit up, her face frantic. "I don't want you to take the babies this early."

"I understand." The doctor said patiently. "But if you die, the babies would die with you."

"Couldn't you keep me going artificially until they're old enough to survive?"

Was she seriously offering to sacrifice her life to insure the babies made it? Eric's hands tightened into fists. Not something he'd let happen. Dr. Conley paused and sent him a look that seemed to indicate they at least were on the same page.

Dr. Conley gave Ellie a reassuring smile. "Let's hope it doesn't come to that. We're pumping steroids into you to speed the babies' lung development."

The words the doctor probably meant to bring comfort seemed to have the opposite effect on Ellie.

Dr. Conley took her hand again and placed his other hand on top. "Try not to worry. You're in good hands. I'll be back this afternoon."

Eric followed the doctor out of the room, his need for more information outweighing his need to stay near Ellie. He spoke as soon as they closed the door. "Level with me. How much danger is Ellie in?"

The doctor moved farther away from the door and leaned closer, his tone hushed. "It's likely we'll have to take the babies. She's not responding well to the medications. Another seizure is likely as long as those babies are in there. We're going to get her semi-sedated. As you can see, she's a little hysterical. Understandable given the circumstances."

Give him an international crisis any day over an irrational

pregnant woman. Eric's respect for Dr. Conley went up a notch.

Once again the doctor gripped his upper arm. "Stay calm. Reassure her as much as possible. We'll take this one day at a time."

# CHAPTER THIRTY-SIX

Brock left the taxi and approached the sliding doors of the entrance, moving so fast he almost ran into the still-opening door. He hoped the hospital staff wouldn't give him grief about arriving in the middle of the night.

The information desk sat unoccupied in a darkened corner. Brock moved down the hall looking for anyone he could ask. Finally, he found a nurses' station and explained his situation. They directed him to the right floor at least. First hurdle down.

He made it to fifth floor and approached the central hub where a nurse sat in front of a computer screen. "I'm Dr. Whitfield. My daughter—"

"We've been expecting you. I'll take you to her room."

"Thank you." Brock released the breath he'd been holding. Either Eric or God had paved the way. Or both.

He nodded to the nurse and pushed open the door. The semi-darkened room was silent except for the hum and intermittent clicking of the machines around the bed.

Eric roused and glanced up, his face haggard and unshaven. He stood and moved closer, giving Brock a quick embrace. "I'm glad you're here."

"Any change since we last talked?"

Eric shook his head and motioned for him to follow to the hall. "Her body's not responding well to the medications. Dr. Conley's not sure how much longer they can let the babies stay. Every time he mentions a C-section, Ellie goes ballistic. They're keeping her pretty sedated."

"I see. You don't look like you've slept much. Why don't you go home. Get cleaned up. I'll be here."

"I'm all right. Maybe after she wakes up and sees that you're here ..." Eric wrapped an arm around him as they walked back to the room. "I'm really glad you came," he said again.

"Nothing would've kept me away, son."

They entered the room. Eric motioned for him to take the chair he'd just left. Brock shook his head and went to the other side of the bed. His throat tightened as he took Ellie's limp hand. Out of habit, his fingers probed her wrist. Elevated pulse.

He glanced at the monitor, scanning the numbers. Thank God she was here. He shuddered to think what might have happened had they not gotten back to the States when they did. Location alone, tipped the odds in her favor.

Ellie became restless and stirred, opening her eyes. She stared a few seconds as he smiled down at her. "Dad. You're here."

"Hello, sweetheart." He leaned closer, smoothing back her hair. "How are you feeling?"

Her hand tightened on his with a death grip. "Don't let them take the babies. They're too small to survive, Dad."

"Honey, God's in—"

Ellie jerked her hand from his grasp. "God's punishing me. Don't you see?" Her voice rose. "Twenty-five weeks. Just like the last time. Only then I chose to cut short my baby's life. I'm begging God to just take me and let my babies live." Ellie covered her face, her shoulders shaking with quiet sobs.

Brock rubbed his chin and glanced at Eric. No wonder the poor boy looked so wiped out. Brock placed his hand on Ellie's and silently prayed for wisdom.

Of this he was certain: God loved Ellie and would do whatever was necessary to free her, once and for all, of this deep-rooted guilt. Guilt that kept her defeated and that distorted her view of God.

Across from him, Eric lowered the bedrail and slid onto the bed, slipping his arm under Ellie's shaking shoulders. She relaxed against Eric, and her breathing slowed with occasional sniffs. It wasn't long before she drifted back into a drugged sleep.

Eric smoothed Ellie's hair down and met her dad's gaze over the top of her head. Thank God, he was finally here. Ellie needed help. Help neither he nor Dr. Conley had the skills to provide. *God, help her.*

Her dad leaned over and kissed her forehead before turning to Eric and whispering, "Walk me out, will you, son?"

Eric slid his dead arm out from underneath Ellie and waited until Dad cleared the door to massage away the stiffness. He turned to his father-in-law, willing his voice not to break. "You are the wisest man I've ever known."

The man before him brushed off the praise and gave him a direct look. "How are you holding up, Eric?"

"To be honest, I'm struggling. I'd like to talk something over with you." Things he'd hinted at before. It was time to nail this thing down. "There's a prayer room. Maybe we could go there."

The tiny room at the end of the hall had a loveseat and an upholstered chair. A small table with a lamp gave the room a homey feel. Eric sat on the loveseat. His mouth went dry, and he fumbled for where to start. He leaned forward, looking at his folded hands. "Ever since we married, I've had this fear that I might lose Ellie. It haunts me. Gives me nightmares." His voice broke. "I'm terrified."

"Fear is not from God, Eric. God doesn't want you to live in paralyzing fear. God stresses over and over that we are to 'fear not.'"

"But what if He takes her?"

Brock gave him an understanding smile. "He has that right, son. He doesn't need our permission. He is God Almighty. Life and death are in His hands."

Eric shook his head, finding it hard to breathe. "How could I go on living without her?"

"God would help you."

Eric raked his hand through his hair. "I wish I had your faith."

Brock leaned back in his chair and looked past Eric. "It's not easy trusting God. But not trusting is even harder. I've learned to trust because God has proven trustworthy. And you have more faith than you think.

Brock opened the drawer of the table. "Ah. I was hoping there'd be a Bible in here." He opened it and flipped through some pages. "There. One of my favorite verses." He held the Bible in the palm of his hand and pointed as he read. "God is able to do exceedingly, abundantly above all that we ask or think." He closed the Bible and placed it back in the drawer. "Your coming to Christ was nothing short of a miracle. Then God did something abundantly above. He used you to lead Bob Templeton to Christ."

Eric nodded, unable to deny it.

"It'd be a slap in God's face to doubt now. People get God's miracles all wrong. They assume that since nothing is impossible to God, that He will prevent tragedy from ever happening. And He could. But the real miracle—the real impossible thing—may be just to help you go on. Even if Ellie died."

The words hit a chord. Was that what God was preparing him to face? Eric felt all the blood drain from his face.

"Give her to God, son. Like Abraham was willing to offer up Isaac. Give her up, and let God's peace fill your heart."

Eric teetered on the brink. The moment of truth. He stared at his hand still clenched before him.

Brock spoke again, giving him the nudge that tipped him in the right direction. "Ellie's struggling. She's not ready. Hormones are playing havoc with her emotions, even her sanity. She needs you to be the rational one. You can't be rational if you're struggling, too. You've got to step up. You need to have faith for both of you."

Eric lifted his head, his decision already made. "Pray with me."

Brock moved to the couch and put his arm around Eric. "Dear Father, I bring my children to You. They need Your help. Your grace. The peace that only You can give." He paused and then continued, his voice breaking. "I ask that You spare Ellie and the babies. But more than that, help Eric and Ellie to learn to trust You and grow closer to You, no matter what Your will might ask of them."

Eric wiped his eyes and looked up. "I can't pray as well as you."

"Just tell Him what's in your heart."

Eric nodded and bowed his head. "God, I'm afraid to ask for Your will to be done. I'm afraid Your will might be to take Ellie from me. I'm asking. I'm begging You to let Ellie and the babies live." His voice broke and he dropped to his knees, his head dropping almost to the floor. "But I'm done fighting." He opened his hand. "Do whatever You have to do. She's yours." Eric experienced an almost palpable sensation like a vice grip being loosened from his chest. He jerked his gaze upward.

Brock laughed and embraced him. "You're wrong. Your prayers are perfect."

A nurse came to the door. "Eric, Ellie just had another seizure."

Eric lit out the door. The nurse caught up. "It was less severe than the other one. The doctor's on his way up."

They entered the room with Brock not far behind. Eric moved to the bed. Ellie opened her eyes and gave him a tremulous smile. "I had another one, didn't I?"

He nodded. The peace he'd experienced when he prayed was still there. A real miracle. He took her hand and kneaded her fingers. "The doctor's on his way up."

"I know what he's going to say. Don't let him. Promise me."

The doctor came in and walked with purpose to the other side of her bed. "Okay, Ellie. I don't think we can put it off any longer.

Her hand tightened around Eric's. "One more week."

The doctor's eyes softened as he shook his head. "They're almost twenty-six weeks. The babies have a good chance. You don't. We don't want to risk losing you."

Ellie turned toward Eric, her eyes pleading. "Please. Make him wait. Just a little longer."

"Honey, I trust the doctor to make the best call."

"No, Eric. Not this time." She pulled her hand away from his. "Dad. Tell them."

The doctor met Eric's gaze. "I'll be at the nurses' station."

Ellie turned back to Eric. "Please, Eric. Don't let them do a C-section. I've got a bad feeling about it. They won't make it. I know they won't."

*God, take my other leg. My arms, but please don't make me hurt Ellie. God help me not to make a mistake.*

"Baby, it has to be this way. It's going to be okay."

"How do you know that? You can't stand there and tell me you are one hundred percent certain our babies will not die."

Eric remained silent.

"I didn't think so."

He was done arguing. Eric took a fortifying breath. "I love you, Ellie. But I will not stand by and do nothing." He turned to leave.

"Eric, wait. I'm begging you."

He'd lose his nerve if he turned around. He powered through the door and only after it closed did he let himself lean against the wall.

The doctor glanced up and came over. "It's the right call."

Eric nodded. "I know."

The doctor squeezed his hand. "The nurses will prep her. It won't take long. I'll meet with you after it's over."

"Thank you."

Eric followed the nurse back into the room. Brock stood beside the bed. Ellie refused to look at either one.

Two attendants came in to wheel her down to surgery. As they rolled her bed from the room, she leveled her gaze at Eric. "If anything happens to my babies, I will never, ever forgive you."

# FREEING ELLIE

# CHAPTER THIRTY-SEVEN

Eric watched at the window, not taking his eyes off the tiny bundles with tubes protruding out of their little bodies. *God, help them to live.*

In less than an hour, the two babies—weighing a little less than two pounds each—had been delivered and immediately placed in the neonatal intensive care unit.

Dr. Conley came out. "Everything went well. Ellie's numbers are much better, and I think they'll continue to improve. You can sit with her in recovery."

"Thank you. Are the babies doing all right?"

"They stand a good chance. Dr. Owens will be their doctor. He'll give you and Ellie a briefing later today."

"Sounds good." He followed the doctor back to recovery. The room felt like a meat locker. Ellie lay with her eyes closed, looking more dead than alive. He swallowed hard and searched for her hand underneath the sheet grasping it, more for his sake than hers.

The attending nurse came in and spoke in a loud voice. "Mrs. Templeton." The nurse took Ellie's other hand. "Mrs. Templeton. Ellie? Wake up."

Ellie's eyes fluttered open. She pulled her hand from his and reached to feel her stomach. "Are they all right?" Her voice was weak and barely above a whisper.

"They're in the neonatal unit. They're both okay. They have their own doctor. Dr. Owens. He'll come by later and give us an update."

She looked at him with a lifeless expression. "Where's Dad?"

"In the waiting room."

She nodded. "Eric?"

He leaned closer and took her hand, but she immediately jerked it away. "I'm not trying to hurt you, but I think it'd be better for you to go home for a while."

He met her gaze without flinching. "You want me to go?"

"I need to be by myself for a little while. I need to sort through some things."

He stared at her for a long time and finally sighed. "Okay. I'll go home and get cleaned up. I'll be back in a couple of hours. Anything you want me to bring you?"

She shook her head. "You don't have to come back tonight."

His jaw clenched. He spoke in a low voice. "I'm coming back, Ellie, whether you want me to or not. I'll stay away from you if I have to, but I'm coming back."

Ellie closed her eyes and turned her face away.

He turned and walked out.

Brock met him at the door of recovery. "How is she?"

"Not totally out of the woods but improving. Still groggy. I'm going to check on the babies and then head home for a little while. Will you stick around and call me if anything changes?"

"Of course."

Eric started to go but turned back. "Stay with her, Dad. Don't leave her alone."

Brock nodded. "She just needs time, son."

"I know." He left, barely keeping it together.

Eric left the hospital and realized he had no car. Or money.

Ten miles, give or take. Wrong leg for an extended workout. But he'd hop home on one leg before he'd go back inside that hospital.

He tried to remember the last time he'd eaten. Or slept.

Deep down, at his very core, he knew it was all going to be all right. But by the time he limped into his backyard, broke into the house through the back door, and practically crawled up the stairs, he was past feeling or caring.

With the water as hot as he could stand, he undressed and stepped into the shower. He sucked air through his teeth as the water hit his raw leg and formed a pink liquid swirling at his foot. Only then, with the scalding water pouring over his head, did he give vent to his pent-up emotions. "God ..." He balanced on one leg and splayed his hand against the side of the shower. His breaths came in short gasps as he gave in to the crushing anguish in his chest. "God, help me. Ellie didn't die, but I feel like I've lost her. Help me hold on enough for both of us. Help our babies get stronger. But most of all, help Ellie. Bring her out of this dark place."

Getting cleaned up made him feel human again. He applied Neosporin to his stump and wrapped gauze around the raw and swollen area. His stomach reminded him it was empty. But sleep won out.

All done in, he collapsed on the bed, still unmade from that night when his whole world changed, maybe forever.

"God, take the watch." He was asleep almost as soon as he closed his eyes.

# FREEING ELLIE

# CHAPTER THIRTY-EIGHT

Ellie regretted the words the minute they'd left her mouth, but she'd stubbornly kept her eyes closed and her head turned away until the door closed behind Eric. What was wrong with her? This wasn't his fault.

Her hand rubbed lightly over her now empty and very sore stomach. She felt cheated. Angry. And so tired. Like all of the blood had been sucked out of her body.

She couldn't even cry.

The nurse came back in. Ellie forced herself to open her eyes so the woman wouldn't try to wake her up again. She just wanted to be left alone.

She wanted Eric.

A tear she didn't think she could produce escaped and slid down her temple into her hair.

"We're about to take you back to your room."

Ellie asked, "Are the babies still all right?"

"They're doing well. Dr. Owens will come around to your room a little later and give you an update."

They wheeled Ellie back into her room. Her dad was sitting in the chair where Eric had spent so many hours. Dad stood as they got her settled and then came closer to the bed.

"Hello, honey."

When he took her hand, she unexpectedly burst into tears, wishing more than anything she'd never sent Eric away.

He handed her a tissue but thankfully didn't ask why. "The doctor said your levels were going down but weren't back to normal yet."

Ellie nodded, her crying spell winding down.

A soft knock preceded the door opening. A man walked in carrying a clipboard. He extended his hand to her dad. "I'm Dr.

Owens."

"Brock Whitfield. I'm the grandfather."

"Congratulations." The doctor turned to her and smiled. "And you must be the proud mother. Hello, Mrs. Templeton."

Ellie left the crumbled tissue under the sheet and shook his hand. She fumbled with the control on the bedrail and raised her head. "How are they doing?"

"Good. Your little boy was delivered first. One pound, fifteen ounces. Twelve inches. Little sister, one pound, thirteen ounces. Eleven inches. Preliminary tests came back good. No bleeding on the brain. Apgar scores surprisingly good for extreme preemies. They're both on oxygen, but with time, they should progress and develop normally. All things considered, they're in good shape."

She released the breath she'd been holding and glanced at her dad.

He returned her smile, and the unshed tears glistening in his eyes started a fresh torrent of her own. She rummaged under the sheet for her tissue. "When can I see them?"

"As soon as you feel up to it. Let a nurse know. She'll bring you down to the unit and help you put on the stylish sterile outfit you have to wear."

After he left, her dad pulled a chair closer.

"The babies are going to make it, aren't they, Dad?" Somehow it seemed important to hear it from Dad, too.

He reached for her hand through the bedrail. "Yes, honey. I feel confident they will."

The door swung open. Ellie's pulse raced and then slowed as if doused with cold water. Where was Eric? He'd promised to come back. The stat technician placed the blood pressure cuff around her arm. The electronic cuff tightened until she thought her eyeballs would pop out of her head. As the cuff loosened, Ellie asked, "Could you help me see my babies?"

The technician typed something into the computer and met

her gaze. "As soon as Dr. Conley gives us the go-ahead, we'll get you down to see them."

Ellie swallowed her disappointment. Maybe Eric would be back by then. Her head hurt. Her heart hurt even more. "Would you ask the nurse if I can have something for pain?"

The tech finished typing updates in the laptop on her cart. "I'll get it for you."

She left but soon returned. "You'll be sore for a couple of days." She injected medication into Ellie's IV. "This stuff is good. It'll help you rest tonight."

The tech left the room, and within minutes, the pain meds kicked in.

"Dad?"

"Yes, honey."

"You remember when Eric called his pain medication good stuff?"

"I do." Her dad took her hand and massaged it.

"That was a good summer, wasn't it?"

"In many ways. But it was also hard, especially for Eric."

"He's a wonderful man, isn't he, Dad?"

"Yes. He is."

"He's like you. You're a wonderful man, too."

"Thank you, honey."

"I want to see my babies."

"Get some sleep. You'll see them tomorrow."

"Okay. I'll just rest my eyes a little bit."

"Good idea."

"Dad?"

"Umm?"

"I think I'm turning into my mom."

"What? Why do you think that?"

"'Cause I told Eric to leave. And not to bother coming back."

"I'm sure he understands, honey."

"But he didn't … come … back."
"Eric loves you. He's fighting for you."
"He's … fighting … for …"

Brock stayed by Ellie's bed for a long time, half expecting her to rouse again and talk some more pain-induced gibberish.

"God, if you love Ellie more than I do at this moment, You love her very much. So I'm asking you again to complete the healing You've begun to do in her heart. Free her from guilt. Teach her to trust Your love for her. Help her to know how deeply she is loved."

# CHAPTER THIRTY-NINE

Ellie woke with a start with a nurse placing yet another blood pressure cuff around her arm. "Did the doctor say I could get up?"

The nurse shook her head and gave a sympathetic smile. "You're wanting to see your babies, aren't you? Dr. Conley should be here soon."

Her dad, not Eric, occupied the chair beside her bed.

The nurse left the room.

Her dad stood and stretched. "Good morning, honey."

"Did Eric come last night?"

He shook his head. "He was probably exhausted."

Ellie bit her lip and looked away. Her fingers twisted into a knot. How could Eric stay away even if she'd told him to?

Her dad eased beside her onto the bed. "It grieves me to see you go through this. You've lost your sparkle. This whole thing has put a strain between you and Eric."

"I know." Ellie shrugged. "Believe me. I don't like being this way. I feel stuck inside. I've got all these mixed up thoughts and feelings." She raised pleading eyes to him. "Talk to me. Help me work through them."

He looked down at the floor and rubbed his chin. She knew her father well enough to know that meant he was either praying or working out a strategy. Or both.

With a deep inhale, he lifted his chin and directed his gaze to her. "Tell me what's bothering you the most. If you had to narrow it down to one thing, what would it be?"

Bothering her the most? Ellie shook her head. "I don't know. It's hard to put into words." She dropped her gaze and shrugged. "I was terrified when I woke up and realized I was in the hospital. I didn't remember anything about how I had gotten here. And then it was like the doctor and Eric ganged up on me. Yes …" She nodded slowly. "That was it. They ganged up on me. And nothing I said changed their minds. I felt so helpless and frustrated and, I don't know, like I was backed into a corner." She glanced up and finally met his gaze. His nod encouraged her to continue. "But I guess the worst part was the feeling I had inside. It was a smothering feeling. Like something really bad was going to happen. I just knew in my heart that if they took my babies, they wouldn't survive." Tears fell now in rapid succession. Ellie didn't bother wiping them away. "And the one who was supposed to be protecting us actually signed the consent form even when I pleaded with him not to. I felt betrayed. I still do."

"Like the decision was taken out of your hands?"

Relief washed over her. Finally someone got it. "That's exactly how I felt. Still feel."

"Does it help to know the babies most likely will make it?"

"It makes all the difference in the world. But Eric didn't know things would turn out all right. He gambled with something I wasn't willing for him to gamble with. But I wish he'd show up. I'm ready to put this mess behind us and focus on our babies."

"What about God, Ellie? Were you able to cry out to God for help?"

"I did cry out to God, but it was like He wasn't listening either. I felt like I was in a black hole."

"Like you felt when you terminated your first pregnancy?"

Ellie flinched. "Dad. Don't you see? I messed up the first time and an innocent beautiful little baby was the victim of my selfishness. This was my chance to make it right. But nobody would let me." She flung out her hands in a downward sweep. "Not the doctor. Not Eric. Not even you."

"God wants to bring you out of that black hole, but He can

only do it with truth. Honey, it is truth that will set you free. You have clouded judgment, and you're telling yourself lies. You have yourself convinced."

"How can you say that? It's pretty clear to me my plan would've worked, but nobody would listen to me. And I was forced. *Forced.* Into something that all you men decided was the right thing for me and my babies. Now, I realized that Eric can decide all kinds of things and do them without listening to anything I had to say." She raised her hand in frustration. "He can even decide to be an agent again and just disappear. And nothing I do will stop him."

"Eric is still learning to trust God, too. This hasn't been easy for him. As frantic as you were to protect your babies, he was just as frantic or even more so to protect you. The night before surgery, he prayed and surrendered you to God. When he signed the consent form, he was not doing it to save your life at the expense of the babies. Honey, he felt in his heart that it was the right thing to do. He signed it, knowing that if something went wrong, he might lose you forever. It took a real man to do that. Ellie, you can trust him. He's not another Allen, who coerced you into an abortion you didn't want to have."

He leaned closer, taking both her hands. "Honey, I'm going to tell you the truth, and I want you to hear me."

She nodded. "Okay, Dad. Tell me the truth. I'm listening."

"The real issue here is not about the babies. Or about the decision that was made."

Her breath caught, his words hitting a sensitive spot in her heart.

"The real issue, Ellie, is that you are afraid to trust. Sweetheart, you learned from a very early age that you can't count on men to be there for you. To protect you."

Ellie dropped her gaze feeling very much like her dad had shined a spotlight into her heart.

"Your own father walked out of your life when you were

just three. Honey, don't you see? There was not one male in your life who proved trustworthy. And you spent a lot of time looking for that missing piece of your life, always with disappointment. All the boys and men you had relationships with used you and then walked away. You were an innocent victim."

Ellie crumbled. "Not so innocent. I knew what I was doing." Her shoulders shook with the sobs that seemed to come from her very core. From the depths of that black pit. She cried with a violence that pulled every stitch and cut off her breath, making her heave to get enough air.

Her dad moved closer and pulled her against him. She collapsed against his strength and made his shirt wet with her tears. Her heaving coughs ripped through the muscles of her unhealed gut. She cried until she had no more tears, and no strength left in her body. Totally spent, Ellie sagged against her dad and let him be her sole support. "What you said makes so much sense." Her voice was hoarse from the force of her sobs. "All my life I had this black hole inside of me. I thought it was gone, especially after I became a Christian. Even then, I always struggled with trusting God, but I never knew why. How could you know?"

"Because I had a black hole, too. Before the accident that killed Eric's parents, I tried to fill that emptiness. I drank. A lot. I was unfaithful to your mother. After the accident, my life was completely turned upside down. I lost everything. Especially my self-respect. Only when God took out all the props did I finally turn to Him."

Her dad settled her back against the pillow and reached for the box of tissues on the table by her bed. "Hear me now, and believe that I am telling you the truth."

She nodded and took a couple of tissues to blow her nose.

"God is the only one who can fill that emptiness inside you. Not Eric. Not your babies. Not me. God wants you to trust

Him. But you're holding back."

Of course she was holding back. What else could she do? "I can't help it. How can I trust when God could snatch away everything I love most?"

"Because God is good. And He loves you. Honey, your earthly father let you down. But your heavenly Father will never let you down. He wants to prove that to you. Believe it or not, God allowed this crisis in your pregnancy to prove His great love for you."

"I don't understand."

"Honey, He knows the deep fears inside of you. He created the perfect storm of circumstances to reveal things to you that you didn't even know. Things that needed to be dealt with. Things like the guilt you still carry around. Ellie, God has forgiven you. It's time to forgive yourself."

How was that even possible?

"And God is helping you learn to trust Him by putting you in situations where He can show Himself strong for you."

"But what if the babies die?"

"He would carry you through the grief. He still wants you to trust Him."

"I can't, Dad. I just can't."

"Listen to me. You have a son in there that you were willing to die for. Think about it. God willingly gave up His Son so that you could live forever. He didn't spare His own Son. He gave Him up for you. Now that's a love you can trust."

"I know. And I believe everything you're saying. So, why am I so stuck?"

"Because you trusted Him to forgive you, but you haven't trusted Him yet with your life. There is a part of you that is holding back out of your need to protect yourself. Honey, we can't control what happens. Eric could die today in an accident. Your babies could die. Life is precious and fragile. God wants all of you. Give your fears, your longings to God. Trust His promises. They're true. All true. His truth will set you free."

Ellie looked at him a long time, a silent war raging inside.

He handed her a Bible and wrote down a Scripture reference for her. "Give your babies to God, sweetheart. They are His anyway. Take that one little leap of faith. He'll be there to catch you."

He kissed her cheek then turned.

He was almost to the door when she realized he was leaving. "Dad?"

He paused and turned, his face radiating love. "I'll be back a little later. You need some time to talk to the One Who loves you more than I can."

Ellie stared as the door clicked closed behind him. Alone for the first time, a crazy panic came over her. She took the Bible from her lap and held it close to her chest, as if it might magically fuse into the hollow space in her heart. If she were back in Africa, she'd go to the chapel and talk to the image of Christ in the stained glass. Could she find the same sense of peace here by praying in this stark and empty hospital room?

Words didn't come. Ellie opened the Bible and found the verse her dad had written down. Romans 8:32: *He that spared not His own Son, but delivered Him up for us all, how shall He not with Him also freely give us all things?*

Ellie read the verse more than once. *Spared not His own Son.* Its truth sank deep into her soul. She flipped back to the beginning and read the entire chapter. *No condemnation. No judgment. All things work together for good. Nothing can separate from the love of God.* Nothing?

Did this mean she could finally let go of the guilt that had plagued her every day since she'd had the abortion? Her pulse quickened as she closed the Bible and spoke into the stillness of the room. "God, I'm ready. I'm ready to let go and trust You with my life and with my babies."

She poured her heart out to God just as if she were talking

to her dad. Things she'd prayed before, but this time, it felt like God was opening up the deep dark recesses of her soul and shining His light into them. The longer she prayed, the lighter she felt.

Finally, for the first time since she could remember, Ellie was free.

# FREEING ELLIE

# CHAPTER FORTY

The grinding noise of the garbage truck woke Eric. The moment he opened his eyes and saw sunlight streaming through the slats of the blinds, he knew he'd blown his promise to return to the hospital last night. He grabbed his phone from the bedside table and stared at the time. Somehow the quick power nap he'd meant to grab had become eight hours of dead-to-the-world sleep. He threw his leg over the side of the bed. His jaw clenched as he gingerly removed bloody gauze from the stump, then with gritted teeth, attached the prosthesis to his leg.

He shaved and dressed in a rush. Without Ellie, the house seemed like a cold, lifeless shell. Like his life had been before she'd entered it.

He'd have to find a way back into her good graces. He prayed as he brushed his teeth. For Ellie and the twins. And for wisdom for the next step in their lives.

After a quick call to the hospital for an update, Eric packed up clothes and all the toiletries he and Ellie might need for the next few days. He dumped a can of cat food in Lucky's bowl and set it outside. His own hunger and craving for coffee could wait. Nothing mattered but getting back to the hospital. He grabbed his keys and wallet and headed to the garage. Each step he took brought a new sensation of pain. He'd probably have to break down and have his leg checked out. But not today.

He took the time to stop by the florist shop in the lobby of the hospital. He scanned the display case, then turned and spoke to a woman wearing a blue smock coat. "I was looking for something a little more spectacular. Is it possible to custom order an arrangement?"

"Of course. We do it all the time." The lady smiled and reached under the counter. She used both hands to lift the binder and set it before him. "These pictures might give you some ideas."

"Thank you." Eric flipped through some laminated pages. "We had twins yesterday."

"Twins? How wonderful." The news seemed to energize her. She wedged herself between him and the book and eased a short stubby finger under some of the pages. "May I?"

Eric nodded and let her flip to the back of the book. Her enthusiastic response made him feel less of a sap for telling her. He'd already told the stranger at pump nine at the gas station. Would probably tell the captive audience in the elevator on his way up to fifth floor.

"You might find something spectacular back here." She slid the book back in front of him.

She was right. "This one." He placed his forefinger on the first one he saw maybe because he was ready to be on fifth floor. Definitely spectacular. A large arrangement with flowers of every imaginable color interspersed with wisps of baby's breath.

She turned the binder around. "Absolutely gorgeous. But I've never actually made it before. Might take a while. Would this afternoon be all right?"

"Perfect." He handed her his credit card. "Room 512."

After the transaction, she handed him the receipt and a white card. "Would you like to write a personal note?"

He took it, his mind as blank as the white square in his hand. He tapped it on the counter a couple of times and stared into the distance trying to come up with the right words. With a sigh, he decided to quit wasting precious time. The generic "I love you." would have to do.

He rode solo and nonstop to the fifth floor and paused at the window of the neonatal unit. His heart almost stopped when he only saw one incubator with the Templeton name. The nurse inside waved and gestured to another incubator next to the back wall. He smiled his thanks and placed his hand on his chest, while his breathing returned to normal. They were so tiny and seemed so fragile with tubes connected to their bodies. Baby Girl Templeton was closer and gave him a better view. They had put some kind of stocking cap on her little head. He could only see a portion of Baby Boy Templeton.

The touch on his shoulder, though familiar, made him jump and turn. "Dad!"

"Sorry. I didn't mean to startle you." He gave Eric a sideways hug. "I just left the cafeteria. I wanted to check on Ellie, but now that you're here, I think I'll go back to the hotel and freshen up."

Eric sighed and raked a hand through his hair. "I had every intention of coming back to the hospital last night. I conked out and didn't wake up 'til this morning."

"No problem. I told Ellie that's probably what had happened. In fact, I think it worked out for the best."

Eric nodded, not sure exactly what "the best" meant. Probably that she still didn't want to see him. "How is she?"

The slight hesitation was not a good sign.

"She's working through some things, but we had a good talk." He gave Eric a fatherly pat. "Don't you worry, son. It's going to be all right. Go talk to her. Maybe they'll let you both see your babies."

"Okay. Thank you for staying with her last night."

"I was happy to. Let Ellie know I'll come back this afternoon."

After a quick look at the babies, Ellie's dad squeezed his arm and walked toward the elevators. Eric waved and turned down the hall to Ellie's room.

*God, please help us find our way back to what we had before.*

Ellie winced as she stood for the first time since her C-section and tried to convince herself her insides weren't really ripping apart. This experience would at least give her a whole new appreciation for post-op patients back in Africa.

The nurse helped her to the bathroom. By the time she had sponged off, brushed her teeth and changed hospital gowns, she felt like a new woman.

"You're doing great, but I think I'll wheel you down to the unit so you can save your energy for your babies." The nurse held the bathroom door for Ellie to walk through.

"Good idea." Ellie forced herself to stand erect and not walk bent over like an old woman.

"Stay here. I'll get a wheelchair."

Ellie stayed at the foot of the bed not willing to go through the agony of sitting and standing again more that she had to. She glanced at the clock on the wall. If only Eric were here so they could meet their babies together.

The door opened and there he was. Her heart felt like it would explode. "Eric!" Suddenly all was right in her world, and only the gut-wrenching stitches kept her from running to him and jumping into his arms.

He closed the distance and wrapped his arms very gently around her. "Baby, I'm so sorry I didn't make it last night."

She nestled against his chest and let out a deep sigh. "You got here just in time. I finally got clearance to go see our babies."

He tightened his hold, and they stood that way for a moment longer as if they were fusing together and drawing strength from the other.

The nurse pushed the door and wheeled in the wheelchair. "Here you go." She glanced at Eric and smiled. "Hello."

Eric released his hold and turned.

Ellie took a step toward the chair. "This is my husband, Eric. Could we both go in and see the babies?"

"Of course. In fact, he can take you there."

The nurse helped get her settled in the chair then Eric took over. He pushed her down the hall and hit the buzzer at the door of the neonatal unit. The door opened, and they were greeted by a nurse in a foyer. After a quick briefing and an update on the twins' condition, they scrubbed and put on sterile garb much like preparing for surgery.

At long last, they entered the unit to meet their babies. The nurse directed them to the incubator that held their son. "I'll push your daughter closer so you can visit them both at once."

Ellie nodded, already sliding her hand into the hole to touch their son. He lay on his back with a breathing tube in his nose and an IV in his tiny foot. So perfect. Eric stood on the other side and nudged the little hand with his finger. The nurse pushed the other incubator so that the two were side by side. Ellie gasped as she got her first glimpse of their daughter. Dainty hands with perfect little fingernails.

Eric slid his finger down the curve of her porcelain cheek. "Is there a dimple, little princess?"

She turned her face slightly to his hand, her lower lip jutting out as if she were puckering up to cry.

Ellie's heart melted. She tore her gaze away long enough to catch Eric's reaction. His eyes, glistening with unshed tears, seemed to smile back at her.

All the pain and doubt and fear she'd experienced was worth it for this one perfect moment.

"What about you, little prince?" Ellie caressed the cheek of their son. He responded like his sister, and Ellie wondered if her heart would burst with love.

She had wanted to talk it over first, but maybe now was the right time. "I have an idea for their names."

Eric stood with one hand on their son and the other one

touching their daughter. "Good, 'cause I've got nothing."

"I was thinking Nicholas Brock and Rebekah Joy."

With only his eyes showing, it was hard to gauge his reaction so she gave him an out. "I know we haven't talked about the names yet, so—"

"They're perfect."

"Really? You like them?"

"Love them."

They stayed for double the allotted time, but it still tore her heart out to have to leave her babies. Even though it was only a token kiss, she placed her gloved fingers against her surgical mask and then touched the top of each cap on their tiny heads. She could feel the pull in her gut causing her to stoop and only when she sat again in the wheelchair did she realize how totally spent she was. The nurse held the door of the foyer open for Eric to push her into the hallway.

Ellie shifted in the seat and looked up at him. "Why are you limping?"

Eric shrugged it off. "Overstressed my leg yesterday."

"Are you okay?"

"I'm fine." Eric leaned down and cupped her face with his hand as if he knew she wasn't just referring to his leg. "It's you I'm worried about."

"Can we talk? Some place we won't be interrupted?"

He nodded. "There's a prayer room down the hall." He wheeled her to the door and gave an apologetic look. "I don't think your wheelchair will fit."

"No problem." She forced herself not to wince as she stood. She went for the upholstered chair near the door and gingerly sat.

Eric sat on the loveseat and leaned forward, his hands folded. He gave her an expectant look as if to let her know the ball was in her court.

Her body craved water, and she needed to lie down. But

she couldn't go one more minute without making things right. "I regretted telling you to leave the minute I said it, but I was too stubborn to take it back." Not sure where to start, she jumped in, saying the first thing that came to mind. "I paid for it. I missed you so much last night."

Eric looked as if the weight of the world lifted from his shoulders. He reached for her hand. "I really intended to come back, but I fell into a deep sleep." He raised her hand to his lips. "I'm sorry, baby."

"No. It was a good thing. It gave Dad and me the opportunity to have a long talk this morning. He told me some things I've needed to hear for a long time but wasn't ready to accept until now. I finally got it today. I gave it all to God." She dropped her gaze to her lap. "I'll probably have to do it many more times." She raised her head and met his gaze again. "But I want you to know I'm back now. And I'm okay. I can't believe I'm saying this, but even if the twins don't make it, I'll be okay."

His brown eyes softened. "Come sit here next to me."

She didn't have to be asked twice. She moved to the loveseat. He shifted and drew her in to the crook of his arm. She splayed her hand against his chest. "I'm sorry I was a little nuts. I didn't even consider how hard this was on you."

"You were hurting so much yourself. And I've got a lot to learn about trusting God, too. Thank God for your dad. We had a little talk ourselves. In fact, it was right before your last seizure." He kissed the top of her head. "I've replayed the last two days a hundred times. When I think of all that could've gone wrong …"

"Thank God, so far nothing has gone wrong." Ellie tightened her hold on his chest. "You did the right thing. I'm glad you didn't give up on me."

"That will never happen."

His quiet tone, reserved for the times when he meant

business, reassured her as much as his words. She released her pent-up breath and smiled against the comfort of his embrace, feeling they'd somehow passed a milestone. "So you really like the names? You're not just saying that?"

"I'm blown away. They're perfect. But are you sure? You never knew my parents."

"Neither did you. Yes, I'm positive. I played around with other options but kept coming back to Nicholas and Rebekah. Just felt right. The Brock and Joy came later."

He chuckled. "As long as it isn't Roz and Bob, I think we're good."

Eric settled Ellie back in her room and left her to rest until the next opportunity to see the babies. His plan was to go to the hotel where Brock was staying and convince him to stay at their house.

Maybe because he, too, was now a father, Eric took a slight detour and drove through the gates of Arlington to pay his respects to the only father he'd ever known. He edged the Mustang to the side of the road and walked down the row of well-manicured graves to the marker that read Robert Earl Templeton. He shifted his stance and tried to alleviate the pressure on his swollen stump. Even though his dad had been in the grave for almost a year, Eric still had an unconscious compulsion to hide any sign of weakness from the man who demanded perfection. He took a deep breath, slowly released it then spoke to the headstone marker. "I meant what I said, Dad. I'm grateful for the values you instilled in me. And with God's help, I want to pass those same values to my children. I wish they could've known you."

He left Arlington and drove across town to a smaller cemetery. Brown leaves strewn on the ground crunched as he maneuvered around the graves, searching for the names that would also be on his son's and daughter's birth certificates. He found the two graves, the discolored headstones showing weather-beaten wear. A strange longing welled up in his chest, and he struggled to find just one memory of his life with them, but there was nothing. Had his parents experienced the same overwhelming love he had the moment he laid eyes on his babies? Had his dad loved his mother with the same all-consuming love he had for Ellie? "Mom. Dad. I wish I could've known you." He closed his eyes and envisioned the couple he had seen the night he had hallucinated. "If Jesus lets you get a glimpse of what is happening on Earth, look in on your grandchildren. I need you in their corner."

Eric glanced around to make sure no one could see him talking to the graves. "I lived most of my life never knowing you even existed. But I know you now. Thank you, Dad, for honoring God even when your brother made it difficult for you. I want to make you proud. We named our son and daughter after you and Mom. One day, I want to introduce your grandchildren to you."

# CHAPTER FORTY-ONE

January 4. The day Ellie thought would never come was finally here. After three months, Nicky and Bek were coming home. Best of all, they were coming home on Eric's birthday. How perfect.

Unlike the birthday cake she'd attempted to bake. No matter how Ellie tilted her head, the cake was still horribly lopsided. She plopped more frosting on the low side, hoping to offset the difference. "Oh well, Lucky. It's the thought that counts, right?"

Lucky, now grateful to be elevated back to housecat status, rubbed against Ellie's legs. Ellie counted out thirty-seven candles and spoke to Lucky as she arranged them on the cake. "We're bringing our babies home today, and you're going to have to be on your best behavior." She surveyed her handiwork then bent to pet the cat. "'Cause if you don't, you'll be an outside cat again."

Lucky responded with a pathetic mew.

Ellie ruffled the fur and scooted upstairs to change. Going to the gym every day with Eric after visiting the babies in the hospital had helped her get a couple of pounds below her pre-pregnancy weight. She slipped on her favorite jeans and the gray-striped sweater that was Eric's favorite.

Keeping an eye out for the Mustang, Ellie spread gift wrap on the bed and placed his gift in the center. Wrapping presents wasn't one of her strengths.

The garage door rattled and creaked up as she stuck the last piece of tape. She bopped down the stairs and stood in the kitchen with the present behind her back.

Eric entered through the kitchen door that led to the garage. Cold air from the garage blew in with him. His face lit up as soon as he saw her. "Hey, babe. You look pretty."

Ellie maintained her stance while Eric turned and hung his coat on a peg. When he came close to kiss her hello, he finally caught on. "So that's why you're standing there grinning at me. What's behind your back?"

Ellie swung the present to the front. "Ta-Da!"

Eric grinned and took it from her then methodically slid his finger along the edge to save the paper.

Ellie resisted the urge to help him rip off the paper. His birthday. His present. His OCD obsession to maintain order. But just wait 'til her birthday.

Eric gasped. "Ellie, I don't know what to say."

He liked it. She could tell by the way he held it and looked at it. He might even love it. An exact replica of the journal his father Nicholas had used after he got married. She'd spent hours googling journals to find this particular one. She'd had one of his favorite Bible verses engraved on the front. "And having done all, to stand."

To stand. Even if one of his legs was artificial. To stand no matter what life threw his way.

His fingers slid over the engraved verse on the front. "I love it. Thank you."

"You're welcome. Thought you might need it since we're finally bringing the twins home today. And I took the liberty to write the first entry. Kind of like staking my territory."

He sat at the table and opened to the first page then handed it back to her. "Read it to me."

"You're just making me read it because you can't read my writing."

"Come here." He pulled her onto his lap. "I'm not making you read it. I want you to read it. Your words. Your voice."

"Okay." She grinned, secretly glad he wanted her to read it. "Since it's your birthday, I guess I'll humor you."

January 4

Little did I know on that April morning a man would literally drop out of the sky and into my heart. I was working with my father Brock Whitfield on a secluded mission compound in Angola, Africa. Life and love had been less than kind and with nothing to lose, this broken girl embraced the faith of her father and chose to live out her days celibate and serving Jesus.

And then came Eric Templeton. From the start, I knew this man was something special. At least, after we cleaned all the blood off his wounded body. I was drawn to this quiet man with the brown eyes that seemed to see into my soul.

It may have been love at first sight. I don't know. I do know I found excuses to check on him. Spending time with him became the highlight of my day.

I really did try to fight it. I mean, after all, we were from different worlds. And having recently survived (emphasis on survived) a love affair gone wrong, I wasn't eager to put myself at risk again.

And there was the little problem of our difference in faiths, or should I say, my faith and his lack thereof. So my dad and I began a covert mission of our own called Operation Eric Templeton. We prayed for him. And found ways to sneak in some Jesus love as well as some Jesus truth.

It didn't happen overnight, but little by little, Eric began to hunger for what he saw in my dad and maybe in me as well. He accepted Christ into his life one early morning in July.

Our times together were laced with friendly banter and lots of laughter. And mutual respect. I admired the way he handled the extreme suffering he endured through the extent of his injuries. With no complaints, Eric endured more physical agony than most people experience in a lifetime. You gotta love a guy like that.

And I witnessed firsthand the cunning trap he laid for the apprehension of an agency leak. Then to see him forgive the man who had brought him so much pain, pretty much made me a goner.

The love and care he gave to the harsh man who raised him sealed the deal for me.

So I fell in love. Utterly, completely, hopelessly in love with the most handsome wonderful man in the world. And I thank God for giving me love and happiness again. As my darling father would say, our God has done exceedingly, abundantly, above all that we could ask or think and has made Eric and me to be "heirs together of the grace of life."

And what a wonderful life this is! God has given us not one, but two wonderful blessings and today, on your thirty-seventh birthday, we get to bring our children home!

I love you, Eric Templeton. Your unconditional love has freed me to be all that God has intended me to be, and I can't wait to see what God has planned for the rest of our lives.

Ellie Templeton

# THE REDEEMED SIDE OF BROKEN
## Thoughts from the author

*Freeing Ellie* continues the story of Ellie Templeton and takes her into a deeper knowledge of living a life of faith. Ellie has some deep-seated guilt and trust issues that subconsciously control her whole belief system.

In many ways, Ellie's journey mirrors my own walk with Christ. As I shared in *Saving Eric,* I accepted Christ as a teenager, and it was the defining moment of my life.

All true. But I entered this wonderful life of faith bound by much baggage from my turbulent childhood. Having grown up with a mentally ill father, I developed a coping system that involved looking good on the outside while crumbling on the inside.

Getting saved was a real game-changer for me. But when challenges or tragedy came into my life, my fragile soul wondered why God didn't intervene. Why did God let that terrible thing happen?

Little by little, God brought the perfect storm of challenges into my life designed to teach me that He loves me and is a God Who can be trusted. He sent some challenges only He could fix. I learned through these events that "God is my refuge and strength; a very present help in trouble." I wish I could say I learned this lesson quickly. But I didn't. It took a long time, but God freed me of my fears, my phobias, and my self-doubt.

That's what I tried to show in Ellie's life, and I wove into the story the things I myself have learned. About His sovereignty. His goodness. His faithfulness. His love.

Sometimes, those life lessons from God don't make sense, and it's easy to doubt His love at such times. You know, faith wouldn't really be faith if we had it all figured out.

I love this quotation from Hudson Taylor, a great

missionary to China during the nineteenth century: *We were to prove, however, that no unforeseen mischance had happened, but that these circumstances which seemed so trying were necessary links in the chain of a divinely ordered providence, guiding to other and wider spheres. He was leading us by a way that we knew not, but it was nevertheless, His way.*

Is God leading you right now in some dark places that you "know not"? May this book help strengthen your faith. God knows exactly what we fear and what we need, and that seems to be the very thing He goes after. Our God will do whatever it takes to free us from our fears and teach us to trust Him. He loves us that much!

I'd love to hear from you. Feel free to share your own stories of growth and faith as God has freed you to love Him and trust Him. No. Matter. What.

God bless.

www.joandeneve.com

# ABOUT THE AUTHOR

Joan Deneve teaches English in a Christian school and has a passion to help young people fall in love with Jesus and equip them to become all God wants them to be. Joan began her walk as a Christian when she accepted Christ as her savior two weeks before her sixteenth birthday. She graduated from Tennessee Temple Bible College in 1975.

Joan and Rene', her husband of forty-plus years, reside in Prattville, Alabama, a charming city in the Heart of Dixie. They count their son and daughter-in-law, daughter and son-in-law, and their seven phenomenal grandchildren to be their greatest blessings on earth.

Joan enjoys time well-spent with family and friends, but finds equal joy in quiet moments of solitude on her back porch. There, surrounded by bluebirds and yellow butterflies, she began writing her debut novel, *Saving Eric.*

An active member of her church, Joan enjoys singing in the choir. She is a member of American Christian Fiction Writers and is currently working on the third book in the Redeemed Side of Broken Series. She enjoys chatting with fellow writers and readers.

**Visit Joan on the Web:**
www.JoanDeneve.com

# OTHER BOOKS BY THE AUTHOR

**Saving Eric**
**Book One of The Redeemed**
**Side of Broken Series**

Templetons don't break
down. Even when their world
is falling apart.

Eric Templeton's well-
ordered life as a top CIA agent
is shattered when a traitor
within the agency plots to
have him eliminated. Sent on a
bogus mission to Africa, Eric
is ambushed and critically
wounded. A helicopter pilot
flies him to a remote mission hospital where Dr. Brock
Whitfield and his daughter, Ellie, work to save his life.

If Eric survives, his life may never be the same, and he
still has to deal with the traitor who wants him dead. Eric wants
justice, but Brock and Ellie know that Eric's survival is the
least of his worries. What he needs most is mercy and truth.

**Available on Kindle and in paperback**
**from Amazon and most booksellers by request.**

**The Heart Seekers Series**

**Three books in one, plus added bonuses!**

**Available in Paperback and on Kindle**

*A Dozen Apologies*:

Mara Adkins, a promising fashion designer, has fallen off the ladder of success, and she can't seem to get up. In college, Mara and her sorority sisters played an ugly game, and Mara was usually the winner. She'd date men she considered geeks, win their confidence, and then she'd dump them publicly. Now, Mara stumbles, bumbles, and humbles her way toward employment and toward possible reconciliation with the twelve men she humiliated.

*The Love Boat Bachelor*:

What's a sworn bachelor to do on a Caribbean cruise full of romance and love? Brent will either have to jump ship or embrace the unforgettable romantic comedy headed his way.

*Unlikely Merger*:

If her best friend has her way, Mercy will simply marry one of the single, available men she meets, but they overwhelm her. So handsome and kind. And so many. Even if she felt obliged, how could she ever choose?
BONUS MATERIAL!

**The Heart Seekers Series** also includes:
>Updates on many of your favorite characters!
>Videos from two of our authors!

AND:

*The Christmas Tree Treasure Hunt*:

Grace takes delivery of a package and her life is turned upside down by nine sealed mystery envelopes from her late grandmother. Grammie's instructions require Grace to take the journey of her lifetime, not only to far off places, but also into the deepest parts of her heart. As she follows the trail laid out for her and uncovers her family's darkest secrets, Grace is forced to confront the loss and betrayal that has scarred her past and seek the greatest Christmas Treasure of all.

For the first time, all four stories are offered in this "boxed" digital set. And for the first time, they're all offered in a single print volume.

## The Love Boat Bachelor

Jerusha Agen
Theresa Anderson
Julie Arduini
Joan Deneve

Marji Laine
Fay Lamb
Elizabeth Noyes
Betty Owens

Romance is a joke.

After the love of Brent Teague's life came back into his world only to marry someone else, Brent is through with women. He might be through with being a pastor, too.

Brent was so sure that God brought Mara Adkins home to him so they could marry and live happily ever after. Six months after her wedding to another man, that theory is obviously a dud. If Brent could be so wrong about that, who's to say he's not mistaken about God calling him to pastoral ministry?

Tired of watching Brent flounder for direction, Brent's feisty older sister boots him out of Spartanburg and onto a cruise ship. Brent's old college buddy manages the ship's staff, and he's thrilled to finagle Brent into the role of chaplain for the two-week cruise.

As the ship sets sail, Brent starts to relax. Maybe a cruise wasn't such a bad idea after all. But there's just one little thing no one told him. He's not on any ordinary cruise. He's on The Love Boat.

What's a sworn bachelor to do on a Caribbean cruise full of romance and love? He'll either have to jump ship or embrace the unforgettable romantic comedy headed his way.

*Available on Kindle.*

**Look for other books**

**published by**

**Pix-N-Pens Publishing**

**www.PixNPens.com**

and

www.WriteIntegrity.com